Her Triumph is the final novel in the Laura's Dash Series and takes Laura through the lowest moments of her life to her final triumph as a wife and a single mother during the Depression era. The novel begins where the previous one left off, finding Laura in the most precarious position for a single mother during any period in history—providing for one's children when there is no work to be had. Complicating the matter is the time in which Laura finds herself living, a time that believed every woman had a man providing for her—a cruel hoax that was never true.

In a stark contrast between wealthy and poor, Laura seeks help from the worst sort of hypocrite, the one who believes she is doing right, but does more harm than good. Realizing she's been gulled, Laura tries desperately to right the wrong. The consequences are as raw and agonizing as they are real.

Darrow has a particular strength in writing pathos that makes you feel it in your soul because we've all been Laura at some point in our lives—making choices out of desperation that have resounding consequences, but the true life stakes are what make Laura's determination and grit all the more satisfying.

Taken together, these four novels are a tour de force chronicling the plight of one woman, while holding up a magnifying glass for us to evaluate our history and our societal ills.

Darrow pulls no punches, but offers a starkly beautiful tribute to a life well lived.

M. L. Hamilton, best selling and award winning author of the Avery Nolan series, The two Peyton Brooks series, the Zion Sawyer Cozy Mystery series, The World of Samar series, and numerous stand alone books.

This is an amazing story of a strong and resilient woman's love for her children. I admire the bravery and courage she exhibited, no matter what life handed her. I especially loved that her mother's love and spiritual guidance strengthened her. It was difficult to put this book down, for I kept wondering how she would keep the family bond going, despite all the hardships she went through. This is a heartwarming and feel-good book.

Carolyn Radmanovich, award winning author of the Shape-Shifter's Wife series

Laura's journey through life was not an easy one. Tough decisions were made out of love and for the safety of her family. The authors description of places and events will leave you wanting more and praying for the best. I loved my own thought provoking journey through this series. Worth reading.

Marlene Meincke, Beta reader par excellence

HER TRIUMPH

Other Books
by Sharon S Darrow

Bottlekatz,
A Complete Care Guide for Orphan Kittens

Faces of Rescue:
Cats, Kittens & Great Danes

From Hindsight to Insight,
A Traditional to Metaphysical Memoir

Tom Flynn, Medium & Healer

Navigating the Publishing Maze,
Self-Publishing 101

She Survives, Laura's Dash Book 1
Strive and Protect, Laura's Dash Book 2
Desperate Choices, Laura's Dash Book 3

Short Stories appear in the following Anthologies:
Lizard Love, in Birds of a Feather
Introduction To Chickenese, in More Birds of a
Feather
Travel Means Flying, in Destination, The World,
Volume 1
First Solo Trip, in Destination, The World, Volume 2
Hanukkah Paper, in All Holidays 2020

Her Triumph

Sharon S Darrow

Samati Press

Sacramento, California

First Edition, 2021
ISBN-13 — 978-1-949125-26-9 (Print Version)
ISBN-13 — 978-1-949125-27-6 (Digital versions)
ISBN-13 — 978-1-949125-28-3 (Audio version)

Library of Congress Control Number: 2021921419

Edited by Black Cat Editing Service
https://blackcatediting.weebly.com

Publisher: Samati Press
Sacramento, California

Manufactured in the United States of America

Dedication

This book is dedicated to Shirley Gilbert, Leona Scannela, and June Azevedo—all amazing, strong women and invaluable resources for this series.

Shirley, still going strong at 92, shared many stories that helped me understand the times and daily lives of the family. Her father was Laura's only brother.

Leona was also a huge help in providing insight into the people and history. Her grandmother was the real Laura's oldest sister, who took over as mother to the children at the age of twelve after their mother died.

June is my incredible mother, and Laura's only daughter. Without her memories and encouragement, this series couldn't have been written.

I'm also dedicating this book to my brother, Jack Michael (Mike) Bowman Azevedo, who passed away on October 29, 2021. We were very close in age, and fought for most of our childhood. I'm incredibly grateful for his last visit, when we reconnected and realized how much we loved each other. I'm also thankful that he was greeted on the other side by our brother, James Patrick (Pat) Azevedo, who passed in December, 2016. Heaven will never be the same now that they are back together.

Contents

Chapter One

Hold On A Little Longer

Friday, August 11, 1939
Aurora, Missouri,

Laura's jaw and fists were clenched tight. She licked her lips, took a deep breath, and stared across the street at the gold-veined glass double doors of The Hillside. The three-story hotel, grandest in the county, was red brick with tall, narrow, white-framed windows. Laura had never been inside before, but forced herself to march straight to the entrance and push through the doors.

"Good afternoon, madame," said an elderly gentleman standing behind an ornate teak and gold leaf podium labeled *Concierge* on the left side of the foyer. "Welcome to The Hillside. How can I assist you today?"

Laura hadn't expected a greeting and was caught unaware by the slender man wearing a black suit, starched white shirt, and a black and gold bow-tie. "I, um, I was told that the Aurora Women's Auxiliary meets here each Friday at noon."

"Yes ma'am, in the Ruby Conference Room." The man looked Laura up and down, taking in the out-of-style day-dress that hung on her thin frame, and the lack of make-up and jewelry. Her dark hair, threaded with silver strands, was pulled back and clipped at the nape of her neck. Her shoes and handbag were worn and well past their prime. His voice was polite but cold, his expression disdainful. "Only members and invited guests may attend."

Laura tamped down her feelings so they wouldn't show on her face. "I need to speak to one of the members, Mrs. Chloe Zimmerman. Is there a way to send her a message?"

"We don't like to disturb our guests, but I suppose you could leave your name." The voice was less polite, more supercilious. "I'll try to get the message to her when their business meeting ends."

"Thank you. My name is Mrs. Webber, Laura Webber. It's important or I wouldn't interrupt."

Thin lips compressed into a tight line. "I wouldn't dream of interrupting them, ma'am. I'll try to catch her when the meeting is over." He put his hand up, palm toward Laura to prevent a reply. "You can wait over there." He pointed toward a backless bench to the left of the door. It was upholstered in the same pattern as the ornate carpeting, and was almost invisible at first glance.

"It's really important for me to speak to Mrs. Zimmerman. I don't want to miss her."

The concierge flicked his fingers toward the bench, then turned his attention and a big smile toward two couples headed for the door, followed by a porter pushing a cart loaded with bags and trunks.

Laura sat, seething inside. What a pompous jackass. It was embarrassing to have to depend on him to get to Mrs. Zimmerman. If only there was someone else who could help her.

Gold hands on a huge white marble clock mounted above the entrance to the foyer ticked off the passing seconds and minutes in what seemed like slow motion. The concierge never glanced at Laura, but greeted each guest entering or leaving the hotel.

Anxious about speaking with Mrs Zimmerman, Laura thought about the first time they'd met. The knock on the door had startled Laura, who was resting on the couch while two-year-old David napped. Exhausted from cleaning three apartment building basements, she had no idea who it could be.

The striking woman at the door was dressed to the nines, hair and make-up perfect, designer pocketbook tucked into the crook of her arm. "Hello, I'm Chloe Zimmerman. Mr. Charles Johnson suggested I introduce myself to you," she'd said. "My mother-in-law, Phoebe Zimmerman, lives below you on the second floor."

Laura lived on the third floor, but had never met the lady below her. She'd been told by her landlord, Charles Johnson, that her downstairs neighbor was both hard of hearing and unfriendly.

Laura's visitor had gotten right to the point. She wanted to hire Laura to help her mother-in-law with cleaning, laundry, and personal care, since she and her husband were much too busy to spend time with his mother.

Laura recalled her shock at meeting Mr Zimmerman after his mother died—he was just as cold and unfeeling as his wife, not at all like his sweet mother. Remembering all the hours she and her children had spent with the neighbor they'd learned to love brought a smile to Laura's face. Poor thing, everybody thought she was a mean old lady, but she was just feeble and lonely. Every morning after the three oldest children left for school, Laura took David to Mrs. Zimmerman's apartment. Her face always lit up with a smile as her arms opened wide to hug the little boy.

Laura blinked, shaking her head to clear away the memories. No use looking back. Mrs. Zimmerman was dead, poor thing. They all missed her. David still cried and begged for his friend, Mizerman, to come back. Laura couldn't help feeling guilty that losing the five dollars a week she'd earned caring for her was even more devastating to the family than missing her company.

≈⊱

There she was.

Mrs. Chloe Zimmerman stepped out of the elevator across the lobby with another woman, headed toward the foyer. Laura gasped and stood, determined that nothing would stop her from talking to her now. Laura hurried to the lobby entranceway, ignoring the disapproval that radiated from the concierge, focused only on the women coming towards her. Both looked elegant and professional in suits with tailored jackets that hugged their waists and flared below the hip above straight skirts.

"Excuse me, Mrs. Zimmerman," Laura said. She cleared her throat to get rid of the slight quiver in her voice. "May I speak to you for a few minutes?"

"Mrs. Webber? What are you doing here?" Mrs. Zimmerman pulled her shoulders back, then turned to her companion. "This is the woman we hired to help with John's mother before she passed away."

"I'm sorry to interrupt, but didn't know any other way to reach you. You told me about your Friday meetings and your active charity work." Laura tightened her fingers around her pocketbook shoulder strap and tried to find the right words. "I apologize for turning up like this, but didn't know of anyone else with your connections who might be able to help me."

The other woman snorted, then said, "She's got you there, Chloe, you know everybody who's anybody in town." She glanced at a slim gold and diamond watch, then patted Mrs. Zimmerman on the arm. "Oh dear, my driver is waiting for me. We can talk later." She glanced at Laura, then leaned in close to her friend for a quick hug and whispered in her ear.

Mrs. Zimmerman's smile disappeared when her friend left. She turned to Laura, eyes cold. "Rupert, do you have a private space where Mrs. Webber and I could talk for a few minutes?"

The concierge jumped to attention. "Of course, Mrs Zimmerman, you can use the Topaz Room. Do you know where it is?"

"Yes, thank you." Mrs. Zimmerman turned toward the lobby. "Come with me, Mrs. Webber."

Laura followed at a brisk pace, ignoring curious stares aimed her way. The hotel was cool, but sweat dampened her armpits and slicked her cold palms. This had to work, just had to. There was no one else she could turn to.

Mrs. Zimmerman opened the door into the Topaz Room, hit the light switch, and marched inside. She headed straight to the nearest chair tucked against a long oval table, pulled it out and sat down, then tossed her handbag on the table. "So, Mrs. Webber, what's this all about?"

Laura's gaze circled the room as she sought the perfect words to plead her case. No inspiration here, just windows covered with heavy burgundy drapes, bare walls with gold-flocked paper, and no furniture except for the carved teak conference table and eight teak and leather chairs. "Thank you for talking to me." She sat, leaving one empty chair between them. Laura clasped her hands on the edge of the table and leaned forward. "My husband has been gone for a year after having a breakdown at work. The doctor called it shell-shock from the war, but wasn't able to fix him."

Mrs. Zimmerman glanced at her wristwatch. "I'm sorry to hear that, but what can I do about it?"

"Nothing, ma'am, I'm just trying to let you know what's going on. Please, I won't take much more of your time." Laura took a deep breath and cleared her throat. "Our doctor took Glen, my husband, to the hospital in Springfield for treatment. My children and I figured he'd get better in a couple of weeks, then come home and everything would be back to normal." Laura looked down, rubbed her eyes, then continued. "He's still not home. They transferred Glen to a different hospital in Illinois, and the doctors there told me they have no idea when, or even if, he might be released."

"Mrs Webber, I'm a busy woman and I still don't know what you want from me."

"A job, Mrs. Zimmerman." Laura stared into Mrs. Zimmerman's eyes and pressed her hands flat on the table top. "I need a job. I have four children to feed, not one dime coming in, and less than a hundred dollars to my name."

Mrs. Zimmerman leaned away from Laura and pulled her pocketbook into her lap. "I'm sorry, it does sound like you're in a bad way, but what about your family? Surely your husband's family would want to step in and help you and your children while your husband is away?"

"He only has one sister, and she can't help. Everyone in my family lives in Ardmore, Oklahoma, and they all have problems of their own. I don't have a car or a phone, so have to find a solution here in Aurora."

"Mrs Webber, I don't know anybody who can pay your expenses, although several local churches might help with food and clothing."

"Please, Mrs. Zimmerman, at least one of the women in your group might have some ideas. I'm not asking for myself, since I was brought up not to ever take charity. But my children need to eat, to go to school, and just be kids without worrying about where their next meal will come from. I'm a hard worker and a fast learner, and I'll do anything." Laura stopped to take a breath. She blinked away the sting of tears forming. "I'm begging you, for my children, please see if anyone you know might be able to help us."

Mrs. Zimmerman looked at her watch again, grimaced, and stood. "All right, I'll see what I can do. No promises, though. Be here at noon next Friday. If any of our members want to talk to you, we'll have Rupert bring you in. Otherwise, I'll talk to you after our meeting." She didn't wait for Laura to thank her, just headed out the door with a nod.

Laura followed her out of the room and down the hallway. One week, one whole, long week before she might have a solution.

🦇

Laura exited the lobby and breathed a huge sigh of relief. She glanced back at Rupert— such a snobby little man. You'd think he owned the hotel instead of just working there.

It was a long walk across town to Magda's apartment where Laura had left the children. Her thoughts careened back and forth from fear of their uncertain future to hope that Mrs. Zimmerman would have some suggestions for her. She kept her head up as she marched, trying to hide her inner turmoil so she could present a cheerful face to her children. Laura tried her best, but she couldn't prevent anger at Glen from creeping into her thoughts.

Why had a young man's accidental death at his job-site thrust Glen back into the memory of the day his brother had died at his side during the war? Sure, it was horrible, but Bobby had been killed years ago. Dr. Farnsworth called it shell-shock, but that didn't help. Other men suffered awful things during the war, but they were back with their families, not stuck in an institution for the criminally insane with almost no hope of ever getting out.

Guilt and shame for blaming Glen brought a flush to Laura's face. It wasn't fair to blame him for something beyond his control. People didn't blame someone with consumption for being sick, so she shouldn't blame Glen for being sick in his mind. But it wasn't fair to her either. No income, almost no money left, trying to raise four children by herself. Glen had always been a great provider for them—that was his job. Now she had to do everything, and was so worn down and scared that she just wanted to run away and hide.

Tears started to fill Laura's eyes. She brushed them away, determined not to cry. "Stop it. Just stop it," she whispered to herself. One more block to the tailor shop below Magda's apartment. She could hold on a little longer.

Chapter Two

No Magic Answers

Magda opened the door with a finger against her lips. "Davit's sleeping." She backed into the room, then closed the door behind Laura.

"Thank you so much for watching the kids for me," Laura whispered. She glanced at her son sprawled on an area rug in the tiny living room, surrounded by kitchen utensils, blocks, and pans. "Looks like he wore himself out." She followed Magda to the kitchen and sat next to her at the table. "Are June and the boys at the park?"

Rich, dark brown curls bobbed around Magda's face as she nodded. "Oh yes, zey headed zere right after you left. Zee boys ran down zee stairs and up the shtreet, vile June and Helga valked and gossiped togezer behint zem." Magda paused and pursed her lips. She reached out and rested her hand on Laura's arm. "Vat's wrong, Laura? I know sings are difficult for you and zee children, but today you seem so tense.

Laura blinked, then crumpled and wrapped her arms around her torso. She'd been able to stay strong against Rupert's contempt and Mrs. Zimmerman's cold condescension, but Magda's loving concern pierced her emotional armor. Her entire body shook, and she moaned through clenched lips. "I'm so scared, Magda, I don't know what we're going to do. If Mrs. Zimmerman's charity group doesn't come up with something to help me, I just don't know."

Magda leaned closer and rubbed Laura's trembling shoulder. "I don't understant, liebchen, tell me vhat's wrong. You know Harvey and I vill help any way we can."

Laura took a deep breath and cleared her throat. "I told you I was getting five dollars a week to take care of sweet, old Mrs. Zimmerman. But I didn't tell you that was all the money I had coming in. Now that she's passed on, I have nothing coming in at all. Glen and I saved money through the years, but now that's almost all gone. Today I met Chloe Zimmerman, the daughter-in-law, and begged her—begged her—for some help. When we first met, she bragged about how busy she was with all her charity work, and about how much time she devoted to the Aurora Women's Auxiliary. I didn't know any other way to contact her, so I went to The Highlands and caught her after their meeting was over."

"I'm so sorry. Vill she help?"

"I don't know. She told me to go back to The Highlands at noon next Friday and wait. She said that one of the members might be able to help me with a job or something. No promises, of course. She told me to try to get free food and clothes from some of the churches in town, but that doesn't solve the problem of an income to live on."

"Mama, you're back," whooped David. He stood, ran to Laura, then wrapped his arms around her waist, pressing her into the chair.

"Yes, little man, I'm back." Laura kissed the top of his head and inhaled his sweet little boy scent of soap and sweat. "Why don't you go potty after your nap?"

While David went to the bathroom, Magda whispered, "I hope zose vomen fint help for you. But vat about rent? Has zat been comink out of your savings?"

"No, thank goodness. I clean the basements of my landlord's three apartment buildings. It's a lot of work, but that covers our fifteen dollars in rent each month. If they find me a job, I'll still have to take care of those basements."

Magda squeezed Laura's hand as David came barreling out of the bathroom, tugging at his suspenders. "Look, Mama." He swept his arms wide, encompassing all the items strewn about on the floor. "I made a giant mountain, then it fell down."

"I see. Could you make another one for me?"

David nodded, then dove to the floor and started scooping everything together.

"He's such a sweetheart," Magda said, watching David as he began stacking wooden blocks. "Harvey and I love your kids." She turned her attention back to Laura. "You know you can alvays leave zem vith me ven you neet to."

The door burst open before Laura could reply. Four children, two boys and two girls, shot across the room. "I'm first, gotta go bad." The smallest boy grabbed the doorknob just ahead of his brother.

"You better be fast, Jimmy, or I'm coming in after you."

The two girls giggled, attracting David's attention. "Elga, Elga," he yelled, then clambered to his feet and hurled himself toward Helga.

"Gotcha, little man." She swept him up into her arms, then plopped on the sofa with him and started tickling his ribs.

David shrieked with delight, which only egged Helga on. "I'm goink to steal you, and tickle you every day."

"Steal him? You don't need to steal him. Heck, I'd give you all three of my brothers for nothing."

"June!" Laura scolded her daughter, but couldn't stop the corners of her lips from creeping up. "That's not very nice."

"What's not nice?" Raymond said, closing the bathroom door behind himself.

"Never mind, honey." Laura grinned at Magda and the girls. "I hate to break this up, but we need to head home. Magda has put up with you guys long enough today."

～✦⁓

The boys skipped and bounced back and forth on the sidewalk ahead of Laura and June all the way home. Raymond and Jimmy kept David amused by swinging him between them, then running circles back and forth around him.

June stayed at her mom's side. "We're really lucky, aren't we?"

After the day she'd had thus far, lucky was not the word Laura would have used to describe them. "What makes you say that?"

"Helga and I talked a lot today about what it was like in Germany before they escaped." June stared down at her feet, her soft voice hard to hear. "She loves going to the park and playing without being afraid all the time. She told me they used to visit a big park, the name sounded like tear-garden, when she was little, but then things started changing."

Laura yearned to pull June close and hug her shoulders, but didn't want to interrupt the narrative.

June paused, then looked up into Laura's eyes. "Mama, Helga saw awful things. Before her family left Berlin, soldiers called SS were everywhere, dressed in black uniforms and carrying guns. She had to wear a yellow star on her clothes with the word *Jude*—that's German for Jew—in the middle of it, and after a while she couldn't go to school or to the park anymore." June's voice quivered. "Helga saw soldiers hurt people—even shoot them—on the street for no reason, and nobody could do anything about it."

"I'm so sorry you had to hear that, but Helga must feel very safe with you to open up and talk about such things." This time, Laura wrapped an arm around June's waist for a hug.

"I know. She said she's never told anyone else before today." June brushed a tear away. "Mama, Helga said that some bad men killed her grandpa and would have killed her and her parents if they hadn't run away."

"I know, Junebug, Magda told me. I wish there was a way to protect you from hearing about such terrible things, but the truth is, awful things are taking place in the world today."

June stopped walking and clung to Laura. "I'm so glad we live here. It'd be terrible to be afraid all the time. Helga says she still has scary nightmares and wakes up screaming sometimes."

"No need for you to be frightened, honey, you're safe here." Laura kissed her head, then released her. "Come on, let's catch up with the boys and get home."

When they arrived at their run-down apartment building, June's words rang in Laura's mind. Lucky, yes, compared to conditions for Jews in Berlin, but awful compared to the farm they'd been renting before. Peeling paint, filthy windows with torn or missing screens, and overgrown weeds instead of grass—the landlord hadn't changed a thing on the outside of the rundown, three-story structure since they'd moved in.

Once inside, eight-year-old Raymond and seven-year-old Jimmy sped up the steep, narrow stairs to the third floor. David followed, not wanting help, trailed by June, with Laura bringing up the rear. When Laura made it into the room, she found the kids gathered around the scarred, stained kitchen table where pieces of their favorite puzzle were spread out. They'd put it together many times before, and always commented on how much it looked like the farm where they'd lived before. Some pieces were pretty ragged, but they still enjoyed seeing how fast they could put it together.

"I'm hungry." Jimmy pushed away from the table and opened the tiny refrigerator.

"What can we eat? There's no milk left, and I'm thirsty."

Laura sighed. "I'll fix something. Go help with the puzzle until it's ready." She pulled a housedress off a wall hook and headed into the bathroom to change. No milk, no eggs, almost no meat, and the bread was stale. Fixing lunch would be a challenge.

She stared at her wavy, speckled reflection in the mirror above the sink, noting the gray threads at her temples and the deepening lines on her face. She always used to smile and laugh. When had she turned into this gaunt-looking, grim-faced old woman? Laura leaned closer to the glass and attempted a grin. It looked fake, but would still be better for the kids to see than her sad funeral face.

Tummies full of mayonnaise, fried bologna and cheese sandwiches washed down with water, the boys sat around the coffee table in front of the sofa where Laura and June perched.

"Sure wish we were still on the farm. You used to make the best sandwiches in the summer," Raymond said, his head tilted to one side with a lock of light brown hair hanging in front of his eyes. "Remember? You made fresh bread every week that made the house smell so good. You'd pile juicy red tomato slices, onion, and lettuce from the garden on top of leftover meatloaf. That was my favorite."

"I loved bacon and egg sandwiches with fresh cheese," Jimmy chimed in. "Or just egg salad with lots of those sweet pickles you made."

"Those were good," June said. "But my favorite was when you made us roast beef with mashed potatoes? That was the best."

"Um hmm. And I also recall how much you guys loved helping me weed the garden and pick off the bugs, too." Laura raised her eyebrows and looked down her nose.

"We helped. We brought in the eggs and fed the chickens," Raymond said, looking at June for support.

"Yeah, and we helped pick stuff and bring it inside for canning," June agreed, then turned to David. "And we took turns taking care of David so he didn't get into trouble."

"I not trouble." David shook his finger at his sister.

Laura grinned and ruffled David's hair. "Of course not, no trouble at all."

"I wish we still lived on the farm." Jimmy's voice sounded wistful as he rubbed his fingers in a circle on the table. "I miss the animals and the garden. I miss playing and running outside all day." He glanced up at Laura, then looked back down. "And more than anything, I miss having Papa with us."

"I'd pick bugs all day if we could get Papa back," Raymond said. "Then we could sing silly songs and play games with him."

"That would be so much fun." June's voice was soft and wistful. She looked at Laura and asked, "Do you think he'll ever get to come home again?"

"Oh honey, I wish I knew." Laura gazed at each of her children's faces in turn. "I know your papa wouldn't want you moping around, sad all the time." She paused, searching for the best words. "He'd want you to always remember how much he loves you, and all the special times you had together. No matter how long he's away, those will never change."

The mood for the rest of the evening was somber, but there were no tears. Laura remained awake long after the children fell asleep. Unable to still her mind, she went into the bedroom to check on the boys. As usual, Jimmy was on his back, legs and arms spread-eagled, with Raymond and David on the edges of the bed on either side of him. Their faces were damp in the hot room, and the top sheet had been kicked to the foot of the bed. Laura stroked their foreheads and wished them sweet dreams.

June was curled up in her place on the couch, a soft snore emerging from half-open lips. Laura didn't touch her, fearing she'd wake up. "Sleep well, Junebug," she whispered.

Laura tip-toed to the end of the couch past June's feet and knelt on the mattress resting on the floor. She sat down and pressed her back against the wall. Not ready to sleep, she closed her eyes and relaxed her tired body.

"Let the worries go for tonight, and deal with what you can in the morning." The voice was commanding, but full of love. It reverberated in her mind and felt like a soothing balm surrounding and penetrating every cell of her body.

"Ma?" Laura said, careful to stay quiet and not wake June. "I've missed you. It's been so long since you've talked to me. I need your help." The words tumbled over each other in Laura's mind as she sought to engage with the mother who'd died when Laura was only three years old, but who'd communicated with her throughout her life.

"I've missed you too, sweetheart, but time doesn't work the same from this side, just like I've told you before." The words were clear inside Laura's mind, but the love they conveyed came through with even more force.

Laura wiped her eyes free of unwanted tears. "Ma, I'm so scared. The truth is—"

"I know what you're feeling and what's happening. Sad to say, there is no magic answer. You must always focus on what is best for your children and do it, no matter how hard."

Laura's eyes were closed in the dark room, holding on to the sensation of being enfolded by her mother's energy. "But I don't know what I can do." Laura wanted to cry, but knew it wouldn't help.

"You will, when the time comes."

"I don't understand." Laura wanted to say more, but knew her ma was gone. The all-encompassing warmth of her presence had disappeared in an instant.

Chapter Three

Jimmy's Hurt Bad

The next morning

"Why do I always have to use the bathroom in the middle of the night?" Laura flushed the toilet, then decided to check on the boys and get a drink of water. Just enough moonlight filtered through the dirty screens to show her way. The boys were dead to the world, and she could hear June's soft snore from the hallway.

Wait a minute? There's another sound, scritch-scratch-scritch, coming from the walls in the gloomy, shadow-filled living room. Doggone rats. She hated them, and couldn't tell where the disgusting things were in the dark. Darn things were getting trap-wise and more aggressive every day. She had two baited traps on the exposed rafters that ran across the ceiling, and two in the bottom kitchen cupboards, but fresh droppings appeared almost every day. The nasty rodents ignored them. If only she could use poison, but she didn't dare risk it—David was too young.

Laura filled a glass from the kitchen faucet, leaned back against the counter and swallowed the cool water—then almost spit it out. Not even three feet away, a huge brown rat stood upright under the table and stared at her. The sharp tips of his yellow incisors showed when he hissed.

"Don't threaten me, you filthy thing," Laura hissed right back at him. She reached behind her and grabbed the handle of a heavy wooden rolling pin off the counter, then swung it as hard as she could toward the rat. She was fast, but the rat was faster, and disappeared into the shadows across the room. At least it hadn't gone toward the boys' bedroom. Guess she'd have to look for more rat holes in the walls and close them up. But every time she sealed new holes with steel wool and caulking, the darn rats would chew fresh ones—and they squeezed through tiny spaces that looked way too small to accommodate their bodies.

It was too early to stay up, not much past midnight, so Laura settled back down on her mattress. Sleep was slow in coming, though, since she jerked awake at every tiny sound.

"Mama," David's soft voice breathed in her ear. "Wake up." He patted her cheek and poked at her eyelid.

Surprised to have slept later than David, Laura hugged him and ruffled his hair. "I'm up, little man. Give me a few minutes and I'll start breakfast."

The smell of fried potatoes sizzling in bacon grease brought the children to the table, still in nightshirts and bare feet, disheveled hair spiking in all directions. Laura pan-fried toast with a tiny amount of melted butter in a second skillet, the perfect way to make stale bread palatable.

"June, please fill the glasses with water." Laura scooped potatoes into a bowl, stuck a spoon in it, and popped it in the middle of the table. "Raymond, stop kicking Jimmy's ankle under the table. And Jimmy, you quit too."

Raymond and Jimmy stared at each other, wide-eyed.

"How does she do that?" Jimmy whispered in Raymond's ear. "She's not even looking at us."

Raymond whispered back, "Magic. Or maybe she really does have eyes in back of her head."

Laura smirked as Jimmy's eyes widened.

June grinned, then set the water pitcher next to the potato bowl. She sat down just as

Laura brought the toast and started filling plates.

"I have to do the basements this morning, so you guys need to gather all the dirty clothes and bedding. David can help me in the basement while you drag laundry downstairs. Do that first thing so I can get the washing started while I'm working." She stopped the groans and complaints by adding kitchen clean-up to the laundry chore, with the promise of more if they kept whining.

Laura started toward the door with David in tow. "Hold on, little man. Go to the bathroom first before we head down the stairs. I don't want to make an extra trip up here just because you forgot to go first."

Even at David's slow pace on the stairs, Laura had started work before the laundry tumbled down the last flight of steps. She shook her head and grinned when the laundry reached the floor. The kids had done as she'd asked and gotten it all together, but hadn't yet mastered the art of tying the corners of a sheet with the dirty clothes inside. It might have started that way, but by the time the bedding and clothing reached the basement, everything was loose—a fabric cascade down the steps.

"We're all done," June said, hands on her hips. She peered over the side of the rickety wooden bannister, a few steps higher than the messy mountain of dirty clothes on the floor.

"Can we go to the park now? I'll pick Helga up on the way."

"Park, park. Me too." David left his toys on the folding table and ran toward the steps.

"Sorry, honey. I need your help in the basements." Laura winked at June, then motioned for her and the oldest boys to leave. "Besides, I'd be awfully lonely without your company."

Placated and hugged, David went back to his toys and Laura filled the two washers. She secured the heavy, round lids in place and pushed the buttons to start the machines. Next, she wrapped a broom with a cleaning rag, pinned it into place, and started sweeping dust and webs off the walls and ceiling. By the time the washers had finished the wash cycle, she was ready to do the floors and counters.

"Go potty," David announced, climbing down from a chair and heading for the stairs.

Laura groaned, and dropped the dirty rag off the broom. Laura hurried after him. "Hold on, little man. You know better than climbing stairs by yourself." She grabbed him by the back of his pants before he hit the third step. "You went before we came down here. Can't you wait a little while?"

David shook his head, hair flying in his eyes, and pressed his hands in front of his pants. "Now, Mama, now."

Laura opened her mouth to protest, then sighed and followed him. No way to win in an argument with a two-year-old.

By the time they were back in the basement, Laura's legs were trembling. "Six flights of stairs, just for you to go potty," she said. "I swear, if you need to go again before we're done I'll hold you up over the washbasin and let you pee there."

David turned toward her, a huge grin on his face.

"Forget it. I was just kidding." She ruffled his hair and patted his bottom. "Go play while I finish." Laura opened the first washer, swung the wringer out over the washbasin, and flipped the switch to turn it on. One by one, she pulled each item from the washer and ran it through the wringer, then dropped it into the basket at her feet. Her mind wandered while she finished wringing the contents of both machines, reloaded them, and started them again for the rinse cycle. When they finished, she repeated the process and hung the wet things on the lines strung across the room to dry.

What must it be like to have one of the newfangled washers she'd seen advertised that didn't need wringers? That would be like heaven. Laura shook her head to clear it. Who was she kidding to even think about such things? At the rate they were going, she'd be lucky to not end up doing laundry on a washboard again. It was a waste of time to daydream about stuff she'd never have.

🦇

"Oh, my poor feet." Laura plopped down on the sofa, kicked off her shoes, and stretched her legs out on the table.

"My feet poor too." David sat next to her and pulled off his shoes.

Laura grinned and rolled her shoulders. "Those tenants in the third building are slobs."

David nodded and repeated, "Slobs."

"You'd think a bunch of pigs lived in that basement, spreading trash and dirt everywhere."

"Pigs," David said, throwing his arms in the air, "pigs and slobs."

Laura leaned over to tickle David, but stopped when she heard a loud clatter on the stairs outside the front door. All of a sudden, it was shoved open so hard it slammed into the wall.

"Mama, Jimmy's hurt bad." June and Raymond held their brother up between them, copper smears on their skin, while Jimmy's face and the front of his shirt were covered with blood.

"Oh, my word," Laura said as she leaped off the couch. She picked Jimmy up and put him on top of the table. "Hold on, sweetie, let me take a look." The side of his face was bruised and scraped, with a gash on his cheekbone that poured blood. Jimmy's nose was swollen, with drops still leaking over his lips and chin. He held his left forearm and hand cradled against his body. "Oh boy, let's get this dirt and blood off so I can see better. June, hand me a wet dishtowel. Raymond, tell me what happened."

"We were just playing, taking turns climbing on and off that big old cannon with a couple of other boys. Jimmy tried to jump off the barrel and slipped. He hit the wagon wheel first, then the cement slab under the statue."

June jumped in after handing Laura the wet towel. "It was an accident. Jimmy jumped okay lots of time, but then he slipped."

Laura bit her lip and wiped Jimmy's face. "Sorry, sweetie," she said when he flinched. Fresh drops spilled from his nose as she tried to clean off the thick streaks. The cheekbone was worse. The edges gaped apart and blood sheeted down in a steady flow, covering the side of his face and neck. "Lay back, honey, we've got to stop the bleeding before we do anything else." She supported him with one arm, then eased him onto his back. "Hold still." She held one edge of the wet towel against his upper lip and nostrils, with the rest of it pressed tight along the length of the cut.

Silent tears coursed down Jimmy's face. His eyes scrunched closed while Laura worked—then he screamed.

"What? I'm so sorry." Laura leaned back and looked over Jimmy's body. "What's hurting?"

"My arm. My arm, you leaned on my arm." Jimmy's body curled around his left arm. The visible skin on his face, chalk white, shone in stark contrast with the bright red bands and streaks of blood.

"Okay, honey, I'm sorry, but I need to look." Laura turned to June, who stood at her right side. "June, put your hands where mine are over these two wet towels and keep them tight against Jimmy's nose and cheek. We've got to stop the bleeding. I need to look at his arm, so you have to keep the pressure on."

As soon as June's hands were in place, Laura took a deep breath and eased Jimmy's right hand away from his left arm. She could see a swollen bump just a few inches above his wrist, and an abnormal curve where the bones should be straight. No question. His arm was broken.

"Jimmy, we're going to have to get you to the doctor. I think your arm is broken, and your cheek might need stitches." She ignored his complaints, protests, and tears while fighting to remain calm. If she broke down, it would only frighten him more. In a matter of minutes, David remained in the care of June and Raymond, while Jimmy and Laura made their way down the stairs. It was an awkward, slow trip. Laura held Jimmy around the shoulders with one arm and pressed a bloody towel against his cheek with her other hand, while she murmured encouragement with every step.

꙳

In minutes, Jimmy and Laura were ushered into a small treatment room where Dr. Farnsworth lifted Jimmy up on the examination table and inspected his face and arm. After Jimmy explained what happened at the park, the doctor grinned. "You're not that old cannon's first casualty, and I'm sure you won't be the last. But don't worry. We'll fix you up good as new."

Jimmy's eyes glistened and his voice quivered as he asked if it was going to hurt.

"You won't feel a thing, young man. My nurse is going to put a rubber mask over your mouth and nose. You'll smell something kind of funny, then drift off to sleep. When you wake up, I'll be finished."

Laura stayed in the room until Jimmy was under, then headed back to the waiting room. She paced back and forth, rubbing her crossed arms, until Dr. Farnsworth came out.

"Relax, Mrs. Webber, your son will be fine. He has a cast on his left forearm and three stitches in his cheek. Nurse Bolton is cleaning him up, then will bring him out when he's awake. She'll give you some medicine for pain, a list of instructions, and information on a follow-up appointment." He tossed his rumpled white coat into a hamper, and patted Laura's shoulder. "Boys are quite resilient. He'll be showing that cast off like a trophy in no time. I'll need to see him in ten days so I can remove the stitches. He'll have a scar, but it shouldn't be too bad."

The doctor started to walk away, then swung back around. "Did you two walk here from your apartment?" When Laura nodded, he said, "Have Nurse Bolton come get me as soon as she finishes up and I'll drive you home. Your boy'll be pretty woozy and he's too big for you to carry."

"Okay. Thank you." Laura's cheeks flushed. How could she have come to this? Unable to even take her own child home without help. She'd been raised to never take charity—and had worked hard and taken pride in taking care of her children on her own since Glen had been taken away. "I really appreciate your help." She hoped her smile, which felt more like a grimace, conveyed gratitude instead of shame.

Her pa would have taken his belt to any of his kids for accepting a ride home, no matter how sick they were. She didn't approve, but the lesson was hard to put aside.

Nurse Bolton eased Jimmy into the room, a hand on each of his bare shoulders. "Just another couple of steps, young man, then you can sit on the chair while I talk to your mother."

Jimmy's eyes looked glassy, not fully focused as he sat and leaned back. "Hi Mama."

"Hi, sweetie. Where's your shirt?"

"It was torn and covered with blood. I threw it away," Nurse Bolton said. "Mrs. Webber, I have two sheets of paper for you." She settled herself on the groaning chair behind her desk. "The first is a list of instructions for caring for your son's stitches and his cast. There is an appointment date at the bottom for when you need to come back and have him checked." She put the first paper aside, cleared her throat, and lifted the second one. "The second sheet is your invoice for today. It includes Dr. Farnsworth's examination, anesthesia, cleaning and stitching the facial wound, an X-ray of your son's arm, manipulating the bones back into place, and application of a plaster cast." She paused and looked up at Laura. "Your total is seven dollars and thirty-five cents."

"I didn't bring my pocketbook with me. I'll have to pay on Monday." Laura could feel her pulse pounding after hearing the amount. "Why did you throw his shirt away? I could have cleaned and mended it. Now I'll have to buy a new one, and that costs money." She refused to look away and stared at Miss Bolton until the nurse huffed and handed her both pieces of paper without another word.

"Mrs. Webber, my car is out front." Dr. Farnsworth entered the front door and picked Jimmy up. "Come on, son, let's get you and your mother home."

Laura sent one last glare at the silent Miss Bolton before she left the office.

When they arrived at Laura's apartment building, she thanked Dr. Farnsworth, but insisted on helping Jimmy upstairs by herself. Exhausted by the climb, he stretched out on the sofa and was asleep in minutes.

Chapter Four

You Goofy Little Owl

Monday, August 14, 1939

Laura stood in front of the tiny refrigerator, examining the almost empty shelves.

"Morning, Mama," June said.

Laura whirled around, grabbing the edge of the kitchen counter. "Oh my word, you about scared me out of my skin, sneaking up behind me. I thought you were still in bed asleep."

"I was until the sink pipes made that loud clanging noise. Who could sleep through that?"

"You and your brothers." Laura put her arm around June's shoulders. "You can keep me company while I fix breakfast."

"Not much to fix. We're about out of everything," June said. "Good thing you're going food shopping today."

Laura's mood dropped to her feet. Food shopping, Dr. Farnsworth's office to pay the doctor's bill, a new shirt to replace the one Nurse Bolton had thrown away—all money that had to be spent today. She'd have to count the money in the mason jar, but she was afraid to. She didn't want to talk about the money situation in front of the kids. They'd seen their living situation change so much in the last year, there was no need to make things worse.

Laura took Jimmy and David with her for the errands. Jimmy hadn't wanted to go, but agreed when she told him he'd be in charge of keeping David entertained. "Okay, boys, Dr. Farnsworth's office is our first stop. I need you two on your best behavior."

"I don't like that nurse," Jimmy said. "She's mean, and she never smiles."

"SShhh." Laura put her finger to her lips, glanced down at David, who was skipping ahead of them, and shook her head. "Remember that little pitchers have big ears. Don't say things like that around your brother since he might repeat it where Nurse Bolton could hear." Laura whispered to Jimmy. "Even if I agree with you."

Jimmy giggled, then made the sign of zipping his lips.

Two women were seated in the doctor's waiting room, but Nurse Bolton wasn't at her desk. Laura took the last empty chair and pulled David into her lap. Jimmy stood beside her, looking around the room.

"Mrs. Green, Dr. Farnsworth will be ready for you in just a few moments," Nurse Bolton said as she came into the room from the hallway that connected with the examining rooms. "Mrs. Adams, you'll be next after Mrs. Green." She smiled at both ladies, then stepped behind her desk. "Well, Mrs. Webber, I guess you're here to pay your bill." No smile this time, just a bit of a smirk as her glance slid from Laura to the other ladies. "Next time be sure to bring your pocketbook since we expect people to pay when the doctor cares for them, not days later."

"I'll certainly remember that, Miss Bolton, the next time one of my children breaks a bone or requires stitches. How rude of me to worry about his bleeding wounds instead of my handbag," Laura snapped. One of the women snickered as Laura strode to the desk with her open coin-purse in hand. She pulled out eight dollars and dropped them on the desk. "I'd like my change and a receipt."

Nurse Bolton counted each bill, then pulled out an accounting ledger and entered the payment. Next, she counted out the change and pushed the coins toward Laura, then wrote a receipt and tossed it on top of the money, all without saying a word.

"Thank you." Laura put the coins away and read the receipt, then held it towards the nurse. "Would you mark that 'Paid in Full' please?" She could feel the intense stares of the women in the chairs behind her, but didn't care.

"That's not necessary," the nurse said, but Laura remained standing with the receipt in her hand. Grimacing, Nurse Bolton grabbed the paper out of Laura's hand and scrawled the words across it. "There."

Holding her back straight and her head high, Laura picked up the receipt, called the boys, and marched out of the office.

"Can I talk about her now since she was mean to you too?" Jimmy said.

"Who's mean?" David said. "Who? Who you talking about?"

Laura ruffled David's hair. "Nobody, you goofy little owl, nobody at all."

🦇

Next stop was All Faith Thrift Store, a second-hand shop maintained and run by the Blessed Trinity Catholic Church, together with the Lutheran and Methodist churches of Aurora. Laura hoped Sister Mary Rachel would be there, since they'd become friends the first day they'd met. Laura smiled, remembering that day—her first thrift store and the very first time she'd ever spoken to a nun.

They were in luck, since Sister Mary was sorting clothes on a table just inside the door. "Mrs. Webber, how nice to see you again." Sister Mary clasped her hands under her chin, then leaned forward toward the boys. "David, welcome, young man. Did you come to enjoy our play area today?"

David whirled around and looked to Laura for permission. When she nodded, he pulled his hand free and threaded his way through hanging racks of clothes toward the right wall. Hidden by shelves laden with household goods was a small area with a bright red rug where small chairs, a table and bookshelf, and a brimming toy-box awaited him.

"And you must be David's big brother." The sister tilted her head to the side and looked Jimmy up and down. "My word, what in the world happened to you?"

Jimmy's eyes were wide, never having met the sister before, or anyone dressed in such strange attire. "I'm Jimmy. David's my little brother." He glanced at Laura, obviously for reassurance. "I was climbing on a cannon in the park and tried to jump down, but I fell off. It was an accident." He peeked at Laura again. She smiled. He took a deep breath and grinned. "I cut my face, and the doctor had to sew it up. And I broke my arm too."

"My goodness, you're a lucky fellow. And a brave one too for the doctor, I'll bet."

Laura watched Jimmy's nervousness with Sister Mary melt away. She'd won him over with her words and warm smile. "You're so right, Sister Mary. But now we need to get him a new shirt since the other one was ruined."

"Jimmy, why don't you go join your brother? I'll bet he'd love to show you everything in the play area. And while you two enjoy yourselves, your mother and I can look at shirts."

Without a backward glance, Jimmy ran to join his brother. "Your boys are lovely," Sister Mary said. "You should be very proud of them." She patted Laura's shoulder.

"Ouch." Laura pulled her arm away.

"I'm so sorry. Did I hurt you?"

Laura shook her head. "Just a bruise on my arm, Sister, nothing serious." Sister Mary looked concerned, so Laura explained. "I let Jimmy sleep with me the last two nights, and he smacked me with his cast. He moves so much it's like sharing the bed with a combination eggbeater and starfish. I swear, his future wife will need to wear armored nightgowns."

Peals of laughter burst from Sister Mary's lips and continued all the way to the shirt racks.

❧

Twenty minutes and ten cents later, Laura and the boys were back on the sidewalk on their way to buy groceries.

"That place was fun," Jimmy said. "Next time you go there, I want to go too." He paused, then cast his glance sideways. "Mama, that Sister Mary was really nice, but she dresses kind of weird. And why did you call her sister? You said your sisters live a long way away."

"I'm glad you enjoyed it. You can go with me as long as it isn't during school." She took a deep breath and gathered her thoughts. "Sister Mary is both a name and a title. She belongs to a special part of the Catholic Church, just like the priests."

"Priests?"

"Yes, remember Pastor Brighton from the Baptist Church? Well, Catholic Churches don't have pastors, they have priests. When the church members talk to their priests, they call them Father."

"Father?"

"Yes. They also have women who are sort of like lady assistant pastors, but they're called nuns. And when you talk to the nuns, they're called sister."

"That doesn't make sense. Calling a church man father and a church lady sister?" Jimmy said, scratching his head.

"Honey, it doesn't have to make sense to us, just to the members of the church."

Jimmy kicked at the sidewalk and hunched his shoulders. "I guess, but why the funny clothes?"

"Again, honey, it's part of the church. I've been told that Catholic Churches are a lot fancier inside, and the priests and sisters wear special clothing that is part of their religion. We don't have to understand other churches, but we do have to respect their beliefs."

Laura hugged Jimmy, who then raced to catch up with David. That stuck-up Pastor Brighton and his nosy wife might not like her teaching her boys tolerance for other religions, but she was determined they'd learn that God didn't care how you worshipped—just that you were a good person and treated other people the way you wanted them to treat you.

Shopping with two little boys instead of just one was both easier and harder. Easier because David walked close to his brother instead of riding in the shopping cart and complaining about not being able to get down. Harder because the two boys talked and played in the aisles and asked for lots of things that they couldn't afford to buy. Laura was worn out when they left the store with a tired David riding in the cart piled high with bags and Jimmy walking next to her. She wished she could buy in larger quantities to save money, but that was impossible with their tiny, rat and bug infested kitchen.

When they reached their building, Laura parked the shopping cart at the base of the stairs, grabbed two bags, and sent the boys up ahead of her. Jimmy leaned on the wall and held David's hand as they climbed. Once they reached the apartment, June and Raymond helped Laura carry the rest of the bags up the stairs.

"Thanks, all of you, for your help today." Laura dropped into a kitchen chair, kicked off her shoes, and rubbed the bottom of her feet. "I still have to take the cart back to the store. Could you guys please put everything away for me? Remember that all the dry goods boxes and bags have to be poured into the empty Crisco cans so the rats can't get into the stuff." Laura had always saved the Crisco cans and lids, a habit inherited from her big sister, Ruth, who'd raised all the children after their ma died when Laura was three. "It shouldn't take me too long. And when I get back, we can have a decent dinner tonight."

The kids cheered and got right to work. Laura headed to the stairs, wishing her legs weren't already trembling. Sure, she'd figure out a good dinner for tonight, but how many more could she make? If those women in Mrs. Zimmerman's club didn't come up with some help, what in the world would she do? Four more days until she'd know—and four days sounded like an eternity.

Chapter Five

Alone, What An Ugly Word

The kids were excited about helping Laura prepare their feast. "June, keep stirring the spaghetti sauce so it doesn't scorch on the bottom. Raymond, set the table and fill the glasses with milk."

"I get to do the margarine," Jimmy said, grabbing the unopened package and a bowl. He loved dropping the white, lard-looking block in a mixing bowl, then dumping the package of yellow dye in. It took a lot of work to mix the dye through the greasy mound of margarine, but somehow, turning the thick stuff yellow made it taste better.

"David, keep your fingers out of that bowl," Laura said. "Jimmy doesn't need your help."

The kids declared dinner a feast— spaghetti with meat sauce, salad, milk, and bread smeared with margarine sprinkled with garlic.

Sated, they played with a big box of domino pieces spread out on the kitchen table while Laura did the dishes. All four of them worked together, creating a tall structure, then knocked it down and started over again.

After the last dish was dried and put away, Laura leaned on the counter and watched the domino fun. If she commented on how good they were being, it might jinx them, so she headed for the sofa instead. Once settled, she reached for the radio perched on a wooden box next to the couch and turned it on.

Screeching sounds of a car crash blared out of the speaker. "Shoot, I missed the start of *The Ellery Queen Show*," Laura mumbled, then closed her eyes and leaned back. Oh well, she'd only missed a few minutes, and would be on time for *Abbott and Costello*. The kids enjoy that program too, and might be ready to join her by the time it started.

When the theme music for *Abbott and Costello* came on, the children swept the domino pieces back into the box and climbed up next to her to listen. David, of course, pushed his way onto her lap.

"I love *Abbott and Costello*," June said. "They're so funny."

"Me too, "Jimmy chimed in. "*The Lone Ranger's* my favorite, but they're my second favorite."

"SShh," Raymond hissed. "I can't hear over you guys."

Laura turned the volume up a little. Soon, only giggles interrupted the dialogue and sound effects. By the time the show was over, the kids' eyes were closed. She stood and lifted David in her arms. "You're all falling asleep. Off to bed."

The three boys dropped onto their bed and were comatose in minutes. June took a little longer, since she had to spread the bedding out on the sofa, but her soft snoring began mere moments after her head curled into the threadbare pillowcase.

Laura carried the radio into the kitchen, put it on the table and plugged it in with the volume way down. She sat and leaned her chin into her hands to listen to the news. Her cheery mood from *Abbot and Costello* grew somber as world news replaced local stories and commercials. German troops were mobilizing on the Polish border, threatening to invade. She shook her head and pressed her hands together, thinking about the awful carnage she'd seen in Glen's dreams when he relived—endlessly and repeatedly—the battles he'd experienced in the Great War. The worst was the one when his brother died right next to him as they fought together in a furious battle along the Maginot Line.

She was relieved when an Alka-Seltzer commercial interrupted the news, and got herself a glass of water. The glass trembled in Laura's hands, and her pulse thumped at double its normal speed. She closed her eyes and prayed. Please God, don't let Glen hear this news. The prospect of another war, of more soldiers dying, would terrify him, and he might never get well and come home.

Laura sat back down at the table when the commercial ended. The announcer said that there had been no results yet from the tripartite negotiations about a military alliance between France, the United Kingdom, and the Soviet Union. The discussions had begun with high hopes, but didn't seem to be going anywhere.

"What's the matter with those people?" she hissed, clenching both her fists. "They've got to work together and stop Hitler now. If they can't figure out how to work with one another, how can they expect their armies to fight together?"

When the news ended, Laura turned the radio off. She rubbed her forehead with icy fingertips, thumbs pressed into her cheekbones.

"Oh Glen, I wish you were here," she whispered, then groaned. Her chest ached with the pressure of remaining silent. "I know the news would be hard for you, but at least you wouldn't hear it all alone."

Alone, what an ugly word. And the reality was so much worse. The kids didn't count, even though they kept her busy all the time. She needed to talk to her husband, for him to help with all the decision making, even laugh or cry with her. It'd been so long since she'd been able to reach out and touch him, be held by him, take comfort in his quiet presence. Tears leaked down the sides of Laura's nose, one by one, painting her face with wet streaks before plopping down on the table between her elbows.

So many times when she thought about Glen, Laura let anger take over, furious at his leaving the family in such desperate straits. This time she wasn't angry, just feeling abandoned and forlorn. They'd been through so much together, but he'd always been her rock. She opened her eyes and headed to the bathroom to blow her tear-stuffed nose.

"That's enough," Laura whispered when she could breathe again. "I can't keep falling apart like this." She turned on the faucet, filled her hands with cold water, then rubbed it on her sweaty face. "I need some fresh air."

She padded on bare feet into the dark living room, drawn by the sight of the moon shimmering through the dusty glass.

"Oh Lord, I miss our front porch."

Laura shoved the living room window halfway up, then pressed her forehead against the cool glass. Her fingers gripped the sill, but she didn't care that the outer portion was rough and splintery. A slight breeze caressed her hands as the air slipped inside the stale, dark room. She shoved the window all the way open and leaned outside, resting her forearms on the dirty sill. Narrow strips of torn screen material wafted in at the sides of the frame and hung down from the top.

Not much of a view, only the building next door and the overgrown grass that separated the two structures. Laura closed her eyes and imagined herself back in time, sitting on the front porch of the farmhouse where they'd lived for five years before moving to the apartment. She ignored the scent of the air coming through the window, perfumed by caked dust on the screen fragments and exhaust from the occasional car passing by on the street. She pretended the air was fragrant with the clean smell of grass, trees, and flowers in their old yard. Sure, there was a slight undertone of hay and animals from the barn, but it only added a touch of spice to the earthy smell.

Laura's eyes remained shut. With every deep breath, her memory strengthened. Not just the smell of the air, but the sounds that had surrounded her when she rocked back and forth on the porch glider. She remembered how the tree branches moved in the breeze, and the sound of a nightbird's chuckle from the top of a pine tree next to the driveway.

The image in Laura's mind shifted, the colors rippled for a fraction of a second as she slid from memory into a vision. The scene was the same, but was no longer a mere memory. She was now immersed in an altered reality. It felt different, too. Instead of imagining a familiar scene, she was in it with no separation of time or place.

Laura's eyes remained closed, but all of her senses were hyper-aware of everything around her—the slight shake of the glider's frame, the way her dress hem moved on her legs as she rocked, the irritating itch of a mosquito bite on her ankle. Her left hand, resting on the wooden surface of the glider seat, was now cupped in a warm, large hand, fingers interlaced with hers. She felt the warmth of Glen's body next to her, their arms pressed together, as his thumb stroked the top of her hand.

Laura opened her eyes and stared at their fingers. "You never could get your nails perfectly clean." She wasn't sure if she spoke out loud or only in her mind.

"Working man's hands, honey." His words surrounded and filled her being. She didn't hear them; she felt them.

His hand felt warm and strong. She stared at the faint dark lines at the base of each nail, and the white crescent-shaped scar on his thumb just below the first knuckle. She treasured the clarity of each mark, wrinkle, and bluish vein. With a deep sigh, she rested her head against his shoulder, inhaling his scent from the flannel shirt.

"I don't want to move. I wish we could stay like this forever."

She felt Glen lean against the top of her head, and knew he was pressing a kiss against her hair. "I know. I love you and the kids more than anything in the world. I'm sorry things have been hard, but I'm so proud of you."

His voice lingered in her mind and in the atmosphere around her, but his presence faded away like shadows at dawn. Her hand rested, once again, against the wooden seat of the glider, as his warmth and scent disappeared.

The canopy of stars blurred as tears filled Laura's eyes. She blinked and found herself leaning on aching forearms out of the apartment window.

Chapter Six

Explain Yourself

Friday, August 18, 1939

The walk from Magda's place to The Hillside Hotel was a long one. Laura's mind swung back and forth from wanting to hurry and find out what Mrs Zimmerman had come up with, to slowing down to delay her arrival in case the news was bad. Those snooty women probably never had to worry about money or where their next meal was coming from in their whole lives. How could someone like that understand what she was going through?

As soon as the imposing edifice of The Hillside came into view, Laura's heart began pounding. This was it. Somehow, she had to make these women understand and want to help her. She couldn't beg or they would look down on her. But she couldn't come across as proud or uppity either, or they'd think she didn't know her proper place. When she reached the heavy front doors, Laura swallowed what felt like a huge lump in her throat, composed her face into the most dignified expression she could manage, and walked straight to the concierge desk.

Rupert, once again greeting guests with his unctuous simper, looked up. His smile turned into a cold grimace as he gazed at Laura. His expression made it clear that she didn't measure up to his standards.

"I have an appointment with Mrs. Zimmerman at noon." Laura was pleased that her voice was firm, with no tremor. "I know I'm a few minutes early. She'll be calling for me either during or right after the Aurora Women's Auxiliary meeting." Laura crossed her arms, fingers clenched around her handbag strap. "She told me you'd let her know when I arrived."

Laura stood her ground, looking straight into Rupert's eyes. When he looked away first, a small victory, she walked to the backless bench by the door and sat down.

The concierge began writing on a notepad, then looked up. "Spell your name so I can let Mrs. Zimmerman know you're here."

"Mrs. Webber, Mrs. Laura Webber, W E B B E R."

No thank you or acknowledgment. Laura watched him call a bellboy over, hand him a folded paper, and send him off into the main lobby.

The second hands on the giant marble clock ticked by one by one, seeming to take hours between each tiny jump. After what seemed like an eternity, the concierge called her. "Mrs. Webber, Neville will take you to the Ruby Conference Room now."

Turning his attention to Neville, the bellboy, the concierge cleared his throat. "Take Mrs. Webber to one of the chairs in the hallway by the conference room, then let Mrs. Zimmerman know she's outside, waiting. I'll expect you right back here when you're finished."

Neville tipped his hat. "Yes, sir." Then he turned to Laura. "Right this way, ma'am."

The gold-edged plaque on the door read Ruby Conference Room in neat black letters. The door was closed, but a faint buzz of conversation leaked out into the hallway. Neville knocked on the door once he'd seated Laura against the wall in an armless wooden chair, and he slipped inside. Mere moments later, he came back out. "They'll send someone for you in a few minutes," he whispered, then hurried down the hallway.

Laura studied the hallway while she waited, memorizing the ornate carpeting pattern, the doors with name plaques—Topaz, Diamond, Emerald, Opal, and Sapphire—just like the one on the Ruby room. She counted the frosted white, gold-trimmed glass sconces on the walls, two between each pair of doors.

"Mrs. Webber, please join us."

Startled, Laura nodded and followed the short, round woman in a pink and white dress into a room almost three times as large as the Topaz room she'd seen the previous week. Four tables, covered with white tablecloths, and the remains of a meal, were arranged in a hollow square. More than twenty women were seated, all staring at Laura with greedy, predatory expressions.

Her escort pointed to an empty chair at the foot of the square opposite the head table where four women sat, with fancy nameplates in front of them. "Mrs. Webber, please sit here. Mrs. Zimmerman told us about your dilemma, but we'd like to ask you some questions."

Laura sat and stared at her lap. This must be what a plain brown sparrow feels like in a room full of beautiful, exotic birds. The women were different sizes, shapes, and ages, but all were dressed and groomed to the highest standards and latest fashions. How on earth could she make these women understand her plight? She cleared her throat, afraid that she wouldn't be able to speak.

"Mrs. Webber, thank you for coming in." The speaker, an imposing woman dressed in bright yellow, leaned forward with both hands on the table. Her gray hair was swept up in an elaborate style, and looked like not a single hair would dare try to escape. "I'm Mrs. Comstock, President of our club. For many years, we've tried to help less fortunate members of our community through local churches, schools, and other organizations. Your request that we help you find a job is unique, but we're willing to consider assisting you once we have a better idea of the specifics. So, please explain your circumstances and why you're asking for help."

All eyes in the room swiveled from Mrs. Comstock to Laura. The women's facial expressions varied from curious to bored. Laura blinked and looked around the room. "I, uh . . ." She cleared her throat and coughed into her fist, searching for words to begin. "Excuse me. I need a job so I can support my four children until my husband is released from the hospital. He's been away for over a year. I have no income and our savings is almost gone. My youngest is just two years old, so I've always been at home to care for them, but I've got to find a way to earn money. Before my husband and I were married, I worked in the housekeeping department at a hospital in Tulsa, but I'm willing to do anything." Laura's face and neck burned, and beads of sweat formed at her hairline. "I'd like to work at a hospital again, but it's too far to travel to Springfield each day."

"That's right." A tall, slender woman in a gray suit with black lapels smoothed the ends of the white silk scarf around her neck. "Mrs. Zimmerman said something about your husband being in a mental hospital." She rolled her eyes toward the woman next to her, then back at Laura. "Can you explain that please? I certainly hope he doesn't have some dangerous mental malady, or something that might be passed on to your children."

The skin on Laura's face warmed even more, drawing tight across her cheekbones. "My husband is a good man and a great father, and he does not have a mental disease. He suffers from shell-shock from his service in the Great War. The doctors say they don't know why some men are struck with it, and they don't have any cure. They can only try various treatments, since people respond in different ways."

"Hmph" The sound came from a small woman with wispy white hair and reading glasses on a chain around her neck. "My Henry and both of our sons have served in wars, and none of them had any problems when they came home. They all saw fighting. George, my youngest, even received a medal. Every one of them went right back to work when they came home. Henry said soldiers that claimed shell-shock were weak-minded and lazy."

Laura bit her lip to hold back an angry retort. "With all due respect, ma'am, our family doctor and the specialists at the hospital disagree. I understand that most soldiers saw horrible things on the battlefield, but my husband saw his baby brother shot down right next to him. That awful memory comes back over and over, so Glen relives that terrifying experience every single day."

"That's an awful thing for him to endure," Mrs. Comstock said. "I would think your support should have helped him. Do you take your children to see him so he can concentrate on their needs instead of on his brother?"

"When Glen was first in the hospital in Springfield, I did take them, hoping that would help him snap out of it, but it didn't work." Laura twisted her fingers together on the edge of the table and took a deep breath. "We haven't seen him in quite a while now because we don't have a car or a phone. And when he was transferred to the hospital in Illinois, the rules changed. They don't allow children to visit at all, so even if I could find a way to get there, I have no one to leave them with."

"How can you take a job if you don't have anyone to leave your children with?" Mrs. Comstock stared at Laura, then she glanced around the room. "Our primary concern has to be you children's welfare, you know."

"As is mine. Visiting my husband would require half a day's travel time each way, and their instructions are to allow at least two days in case something causes the visit to be delayed.

I have a friend who will watch my children while I work, but I can't ask her to take all four for days at a time." Laura clasped her hands together in her lap so the women couldn't see them shake. "My children are the most important thing in the world to me, which is why I'm here begging for help." Laura bit her lip and blinked. "I was raised to never take charity, but I will take any position, and do any kind of job, to care for my children."

The questions continued until Mrs. Comstock raised her hand and said, "Thank you, Mrs. Webber. I believe we have all we need from you. You can go back to the lobby now. Mrs. Zimmerman will join you after we've had time to review our alternatives."

Laura's heart hammered as she waited in one of the overstuffed chairs in the lobby. Should she have said more in Glen's defense? Had she said too much? Her legs trembled, so weak that she wasn't sure she'd be able to stand when Mrs. Zimmerman came. Laura fidgeted, played with her pocketbook strap, and tapped her toes, but nothing made the time go by faster.

After what seemed like forever, the woman who had led her to the meeting room approached. "Mrs. Webber, Mrs. Zimmerman will see you now in the conference room. Can you find your way or do you need help?"

Laura leaned on the chair arms and pushed herself up. "I'm sure I can find it. Thank you for your help."

"You're welcome." The woman bobbed her head, started to turn away, then looked back at Laura. "Mrs. Webber, I hope things work out for you and your family."

Before Laura could respond, the lady headed toward the foyer at a brisk pace, and never looked back.

Chapter Seven

Abandon Your Children

Her legs shaking, Laura fell back in the chair and pressed her forehead into her fingers. This was it. The only chance she had. After a couple of deep breaths, she stood, straightened her back, and set off toward the conference room.

Mrs. Zimmerman, the only woman still in the room, snapped her compact closed when Laura entered. "Take a seat, Mrs. Webber, so I can explain what we've come up with."

"Thank you very much for your consideration, Mrs. Zimmerman. I hated to ask, but didn't know where else to turn."

"You're welcome. Now, first of all, none of the ladies were able to find a job opening for you." She put up her hand to stop Laura from replying. "And even if there were positions available in town, men always have priority in hiring because they're supporting families. I know you're trying to support your family as well, but many people prefer hiring men because women are more likely to quit or take time off to care for their children."

Laura tilted her head and squished her eyebrows together. "I don't understand. If there aren't any jobs available, how can you help me?"

"As Mrs. Comstock emphasized, our concern is for your children's well-being. We want to be sure their needs are met, that they have food, shelter, and are in school, but no programs exist to help a married woman with children. To tell the truth, Mrs. Webber, if you had divorced your husband when he was committed to the hospital in Illinois, it would be much easier to assist you. The thinking now is that by staying with him, you chose him over the welfare of your children."

Laura's head jerked back with a sharp intake of breath, but Mrs. Zimmerman kept talking.

"Aurora doesn't have an orphanage or children's home; however, there are families and local organizations that sometimes take in underprivileged children. We believe we can find placement for them, but only under special conditions."

"My children are not orphans! They have two parents who love them more than anything in the world. We need temporary help, not for the family to be broken up."

"Mrs. Webber, if you cannot feed and clothe your children, you could be declared an unfit parent and have them taken away from you."

The sharp tone and ugly words stabbed Laura's heart as her nails dug into the skin of her palms. She pressed her lips together, then said, "I understand, and appreciate your offer of help." Each word she uttered cut like ground glass in her mouth. "What would you need from me?"

"I know this sounds harsh, but the only way we could take the children and place them without lots of time and red tape would be for you to abandon them."

"What? You're asking me to give up my children?"

Mrs. Zimmerman glanced at her watch and tightened her lips. "That's the only way. If we ask the county to declare you unfit, it takes time and wouldn't help your immediate needs. If you abandon them—and you will have to leave town for the county to believe us and declare the children wards of the court—then we can take steps right away."

Hot tears gushed from Laura's eyes. "Are you sure there's no other way? I want my children cared for, but doing this would break them." She sniffed hard and cleared her throat, but the tears kept flowing. "I'd have to tell them what was happening. After losing their father, if I disappeared without saying anything, they'd be destroyed. I can't do that."

"Mrs. Comstock didn't say anything about you having to sneak away—and her husband is the judge—so I suppose you can talk to them. But don't make any promises about getting the family back together, since you'll have to prove your financial stability before you could even think of having your parental rights returned. Your kids will be taken care of, but not by you."

Laura wrapped her arms around her torso and tried to hold herself together. She wanted to scream and cry. Instead she shook so hard it was almost impossible to breathe. "Can I give you an answer tomorrow?"

"Yes," Mrs. Zimmerman said, pulling a card out of her purse and handing it to Laura. "You must call me before noon tomorrow so they can make arrangements." She stood and looked at her watch again. "I've got to run. My driver is waiting."

Laura didn't watch her go. She collapsed back onto the chair, her legs unable to support her. It took all of her energy and strength to hold herself together and not fall to the floor and curl up into a fetal position. Her clenched jaw hurt, but held in the screams and moans that threatened to erupt. Her eyelids weren't strong enough to stop the flood of hot tears that poured down her face, dripping off her nose and chin unheeded.

"Excuse me, ma'am, I need to clean the tables." The voice came from behind Laura, soft

and polite. "I'm sorry to bother you, but I need .
. ." An unseen hand touched Laura's shoulder,
shaking her. "Are you sick? Should I get you
some help?"

"No! I'll be okay." Laura's voice sounded
so thick and guttural, she didn't recognize it as
her own. She uncurled her body, pressed her
hands on the tabletop, and stood. She grabbed a
napkin and wiped her eyes. "Thank you, but I
don't need help." She made a strange sound,
something like a cross between a chuckle and a
groan, and shook her head. "It's nice of you to
ask, but I'll be okay."

Laura walked out of the room on stiff,
wooden legs, reminding herself to breathe with
each step. She'd lied to the bellboy. She'd didn't
think she'd ever be okay again. And it was clear
that the help she needed wasn't coming.

After she trudged through the hotel and
pushed through the front door, Laura realized
she didn't know what to do or where to go.

Her children were in the park with Magda
and Helga. If they saw her now, they'd know
something horrible had happened, and she
wasn't up to explaining or pretending she was
fine. She needed some time alone to process
what Mrs. Zimmerman had said. She also
wanted to get her emotions under control.
Laura wiped her eyes once again with her
fingers, tightened her fists together around the

handbag strap, and forced one foot after the other at a steady pace toward the apartment.

Chapter Eight

The Children Deserve Better

Turning the key and opening the door sapped the last vestige of Laura's energy. She sank to the floor, handbag forgotten at her side, her legs stretched out straight, and her arms hung limp at her sides, as if she were a discarded marionette. Then she wailed, a deep guttural howl that tore from her throat. The painful sound continued, ripped from her open mouth that was fixed in a rictus of agony. Tears poured from swollen red eyes and filled her nose, which overflowed as mucus that covered her lips.

"Are you done feeling sorry for yourself? Or have you already given up?"

The words filled Laura's mind, but, lost in her torment, she ignored them.

"Laura, listen to me. If you care about your children, stop this."

Laura stopped screaming and cleared her throat. "Ma?" She didn't have the energy to speak out loud, but knew her mother heard her thoughts. "How dare you ask if I care about my children. They're everything to me."

"Then act like it! You have to make a decision and have a plan before you call that woman tomorrow. Crying like a baby accomplishes nothing, except to maybe let them take your children under their terms. Look at yourself, tears and snot all over your face. You're stronger than that. And the children deserve better." The voice was insistent and powerful.

Laura raised a hand to her face, then grimaced when she touched the slimy wetness of her skin. She pulled herself up to her knees, then stood. Her shaky limbs carried her to the kitchen sink where she turned on the water. She could feel her mother's approval as she washed and dried her face.

"That's much better." Now the voice, still strong, was also infused with love that wrapped around and through Laura's being. "This is real, honey, and only you can decide what to do."

Laura blew her nose, then sat at the table. "I can't desert my children. Somehow, some way, I have to find a plan for us to stay together. There has to be a better strategy."

"Laura, look at your hands."

Laura swallowed and stared at her palms. "Look at my hands?"

"Yes, turn your hands over and look at them, really look at them."

Confused, Laura examined the back of her hands. Her wedding ring hung from her finger, held in place by a thick layer of thread she'd wrapped around the band. Her knuckles stood out like skin-wrapped knobs, connecting bones that were thin and fragile looking. The rough skin was wrinkled with scars and dark spots, with every vein standing up in sharp blue relief. The nails were ragged and very pale with rough ridges running from base to tip.

"When I was young I had pretty hands." Laura folded them together in her lap.

"Now touch the back of your neck."

Laura's hand crept under the hair at the nape, feeling the edges of a wide, round scar that was tender to the touch. "The carbuncle's healed, Ma. It took a long time, but it's okay now."

"The carbuncle got so bad and took a long time to get well because you didn't go to the doctor. The same way you've lost hearing in one ear because you didn't get it treated when an ear infection caused the drum to burst."

Laura started to protest, to defend her lack of treatment because of the need to save money, but her ma ignored her attempt.

"When's the last time you ate enough to feel full? And I don't mean full from drinking water to ease the hunger pangs."

Laura crossed her arms over her chest and leaned back in the chair. "Ma, I eat enough. It's more important for the kids to eat what they need. I can't afford fancy food, but I make sure they have enough to fill their bellies."

"You're starving yourself, Laura. Look at that belt—the buckle is secured through the tightest hole and still sags way down. And if you get sick or hurt, who's going to take care of the children? If they matter most, you've got to be strong and healthy for them—and you're not right now."

Laura stood and shoved the chair back. She wanted to get away from her ma's voice, but there was no way to do that. She paced back and forth in the room, her ma's words reverberating in her mind. "What are you saying, Ma? That I have to give up my children? Are you accusing me of neglecting my babies? I'd do anything for them. I'd die for them."

"School starts in a couple of weeks. Can you get them clothing and supplies? How about shopping for groceries? You went a week ago and now the cabinets and refrigerator are empty again."

Ma's words hurt, but Laura felt the love they conveyed surround and sooth her.

"I'm not telling you what to do, only that you have to make a decision and the plans to implement it. I have no doubt you would die for your children, but will you live for them? Can you accept the unimaginable pain of letting them go if it means saving them?"

The last sentence repeated in Laura's mind, over and over, and hurt just as much each time. Could she do this? Did she have the strength to do this if it meant her children would be safe and cared for?

She stopped pacing. Her ma was gone, but Laura didn't feel alone. Somehow she'd find the courage to do what was best for the kids, and she'd make sure they understood why. They needed to know she'd never loved them more, and would be back with them as soon as she could. She looked around the dingy room and took a deep breath. "Thank you, Ma. Stay near, please. I'm going to need your help."

She grabbed her pocketbook and headed out the door.

✼

When Laura arrived at the park, she was relieved to see that Magda was sitting alone on one of the park picnic table benches, with her back leaning against the edge. She eased down next to her. "Hi, how are they doing?"

"Zey're all fine." Magda squinted at Laura. "But how are you doink? You don't look so goot. I know somezing is goink on. Can you tell me?"

Laura hadn't planned on saying anything yet, but couldn't resist the kind concern in Magda's voice. The whole story poured out, in sudden stops and starts, as Laura sought to control her emotions.

Magda didn't say a word, just wrapped her arms around Laura and rocked her like a child. "Oops, here come the kids. I zink zey just noticed you're here ant are vorried."

Laura straightened up and moved a little bit away from Magda. She smiled when the children joined them. "Hi kids. Looks like you've all been having a great time."

June and Helga looked at each other. "Are you alright, Mama?" June peered at Laura, then glanced back at Helga. "Your eyes are kind of red."

"I think I'm catching a cold, Junebug, but it's not too bad." Laura reached out and tucked June's hair behind her ear, out of her face. "Nothing to worry about."

"Do we have to go home?" Raymond held a scarred old soccer ball under his arm. "Jimmy and me want to play a little more."

"Helga and I aren't ready to go either, but can David stay with you? We've been watching him forever."

Laura glanced at Magda, who nodded her head, then brushed curls out of Helga's face. "Okay with me."

The four big kids took off running, but David plopped down on the grass next to the concrete base under the table. He opened a small cardboard box full of lead soldier figures and started to play.

"I can't imagine being away from them, no matter the reason." Laura took a deep breath, then curled over when she exhaled. "You must think I'm a horrible mother—in fact, I think I'm a horrible mother—to even consider leaving them."

Magda patted Laura's hand. "Let me tell you a shtory about a voman named Ursula. She vas my rabbi's wife's sister-in-law. She lived in Shpandau, a part of Berlin zat vas a long vay from Pankow vhere we vere. My fazer was killed on November ninth, the first night of vhat is beink called Kristallnacht, ant ve shtarted our journey out of Germany zat fery night. Ursula's husbant, Felix, zought the fiolence vas over."

Magda paused and took a drink of water. She smiled at David, then turned back to Laura. "He vas wrong. Zee same awful gangs filled the shtreets the next evenink, breakink vindows, schooting and beatink any Jews zey found outside, ant breakink into homes and schops. As soon as zhey heard the sounds of gunfire and shoutink, Ursula and her eight-year-old daughter, Gerda, hid in a cramped hole under the floor in the livink room. Zey had just enough room to curl up togezer in the space, vhich locked from the inside. Felix pulled a heafy couch over the shpace, zen hid zeir twelve-year-old son, Rolf, at the back of a closet behint some shtacked boxes."

Laura's hand flew over her mouth. "Oh no, that poor family."

Magda nodded and cleared her throat. "Ursula had varned Gerda not to make a sount, no matter vhat she heart, just as Felix had varned Rolf. Ursula kept her hant over Gerda's mouz, just in case. Zee sounds were awful. Zey couldn't move or escape zee zhem as laughink men broke in zhrough the vindows and beat Felix. He triet to reason viz zem, zen yelled and cursed at zhem ven zey began tearink zee room apart, tellink zem to take vhatever zhey vanted. Zen Felix began screamink vhen zey found Rolf and dragged him out of zee closet. All of the screamink shtopped after Ursula heard two gunschots."

"Oh my God, oh my God. That poor woman."

"Ursula helt Gerda tight, one hand clasped over her mouz, stiflink any possible sount, long after the room vas silent. Vhen it vas safe, sche unlocked zee cover and climbed out after makink Gerda promise to shtay in hidink until sche came back for her."

"I can't even imagine what she suffered. Losing her husband and her son, and needing to shield and protect her daughter. What on earth did she do?"

"Sche made Gerda promise to keep her eyes closed, zen pulled her out of the hole. Sche also grabbed a small cloth bag zat had been hidden in the hole. Zee sack contained jewelry, Felix's gold pocket vatch and its chain, as vell as the last of zeir money. Zen Ursula covered her daughter's eyes and valked her out of the apartment. Zey never returned. Zey ran to a friend's place—vhich vas damaged but not as bat—ant took schelter vith zem."

"Ursula's story makes me ashamed of my tears. At least my children are healthy and safe."

"But zat's not the ent of the shtory. Ursula vas frantic to save her daughter. Sche learned about a group zat vas takink Jewish children out of Germany, most of zem to England. Zee Germans didn't care because zey charged a lot of money for each child zey let leave. Sche sold every piece of jewelry ant spent all the money sche had on passage for Gerda's train ticket out. Sche prayed for her daughter's safety, and zat zey might be reunitet someday."

"What a brave woman. At least she can wake up each morning knowing her daughter is safe."

"You're right, for a little vhile." Magda took another sip of water. "Four days after Gerda left, Ursula was rounded up vith hundreds of ozer Jews from Spandau. Zey were crammed into cattle cars and taken avay." Magda looked at Laura and brushed a tear from the corner of her eye. "Now, vould you say Ursula was a good mother for sending her daughter avay? Or shoult sche have found a vay to hide her so zey could stay togezer?"

Laura started to protest, then leaned toward Magda and hugged her instead. "Thank you."

Chapter Nine

Tell Me What To Do

The next morning, Saturday, August 19, 1939

Mr. Niedermann, resplendent in his signature green suspenders, waved and smiled at Laura from behind the post office counter. His pipe, cold as always, rested in an ashtray at his elbow.

Why did there have to be a line this morning? Talking to Mrs. Zimmerman was going to be hard enough, but people overhearing the discussion would be awful. Laura walked over to the counter next to the pay phone and pretended to read the notices on the bulletin board.

FBI Most Wanted posters shared space with official post office bulletins and ads from local businesses. She didn't retain a single word she read, concentrating instead on the conversations behind her. She wished they would hurry up and leave, but the number in line stayed about the same with new people replacing those that finished their business and left.

Laura tried to look busy, touching Mrs. Zimmerman's card over and over, then checking and rechecking the coins in her coin purse.

"Excuse me, folks." Laura heard Mr. Niedermann say. "I'll be right back."

She heard the distinctive sound of the latch in the counter divider open, and footsteps approached her.

"Good morning, Mrs. Webber. You look a little peaked. Would you like to rest a moment in the back?"

Laura glanced at the line, where all eyes were staring back at her. Mr. Niedermann touched the base of the phone, then tilted his head and glanced toward his office door behind the counter. "Thank you, I am feeling a little faint."

Mr. Niedermann was such a kind friend, not only helping her with some privacy, but protecting her from the stares and gossip that would follow the speculation after they heard her half of the conversation with Mrs. Zimmerman.

He ushered her into his tiny office and cleared a stack of papers off the chair next to his desk. "Go ahead and use the phone. Just don't make any long-distance calls. And if it rings, don't answer." With a wink and a reassuring pat on her shoulder, he left and closed the office door behind him.

Alone, staring at the phone, there was no reason to delay any longer. Laura placed Mrs. Zimmerman's card next to the heavy round base of the telephone, lifted the receiver from its cradle, and listened to the buzzing dial tone. She took a deep breath and dialed the numbers.

"Zimmerman residence. How can I help you?"

"Mrs. Zimmerman? This is Mrs. Webber."

"Hold on a moment, ma'am, and I'll get Mrs. Zimmerman for you."

Laura's anxiety level increased as she waited. How dumb of her to expect that woman to answer her own phone. That was probably the maid.

"Good morning, Mrs. Webber. Have you made your decision?" The voice was clipped and businesslike.

"Good morning, Mrs. Zimmerman." It was hard for Laura to force the words out. "Yes. For the sake of my children, I think I have to accept your offer." Laura heard her voice crack and pressed her hand against her eyelids to prevent threatening tears. "Tell me what I have to do."

"I think this is the best decision for your children, Mrs. Webber, even though it might seem harsh right now." There was a sound like paper shuffling. "All you need to do is leave your apartment before ten in the morning on Wednesday. Mrs. Atherton will pick up your children sometime after ten. She's an employee of the Children's Bureau, and will be responsible for their placement with foster families or other acceptable locations. Her brother is Judge Comstock, our club President's husband. She's been briefed on your case, and is ready to handle everything on an emergency basis."

"What about their things? Their clothes and toys? Should they be packed and ready for her?"

"She knows the children have been abandoned, and how to handle their needs."

"But how can I contact her? And can the children contact me?"

"Mrs. Webber, the children will no longer be your responsibility. They'll be placed right away, but it will take a couple of weeks to complete the transfer of their guardianship to the Children's Bureau. During that time, you cannot be here, or nobody will believe that you've left the children alone. After the process is complete, we can discuss contact. Keep my phone number and call me after two weeks. It may take longer, but I'll provide news when I can. Do you understand?"

Laura nodded as tears streaked her cheeks. "Yes, ma'am."

"Good. Do what you need to do and make sure you're out of your apartment early Wednesday morning."

The dial tone cut off Laura's reply. It was really happening. Three days together, then her children would be with someone else. And where was she going to go? She couldn't go to her sisters in Oklahoma, but that only left Willa's family in California. Thank goodness the Missouri Pacific train station was in town since she'd have to travel by train, but how much would a ticket cost? What if Willa and Isaac didn't want her to come? What about all their stuff in the basement? Would the landlord let her keep it there until she came back? Should she, could she, sell Glen's tools and things since there was no way to carry it around if Mr. Johnson wouldn't let her leave it for a while? Would the little money she still had be enough to pay for a ticket and her expenses while she was away? She still had to buy food for the next few days. Somehow, she had to get some money.

Laura sat frozen in place at the desk, paralyzed with fear. She jumped, startled, when Mr. Niedermann entered.

"Are you okay?" He bent down and peered at her ashen face. "Looks like maybe you ought to sit awhile. I'll close up for lunch in forty-five minutes. I brought enough to share if you'd like to relax and rest a bit before you go."

"Thank you, but I'm not hungry." Laura felt nauseous at the thought of food. Her white knuckles hurt from the pressure of holding her hands locked together. "I need to go." She stood on shaky legs and stepped away from the chair.

"I've still got a bunch of people out there. You'd think I was giving away money today." Mr. Niedermann chuckled at his little joke, but Laura didn't respond. "Why don't you go out the back door so Mrs. Brighton won't bother you on the way out?"

Laura grimaced at the thought of meeting Mrs. Brighton. No way she could handle the worst busybody in town. Her husband, the church pastor, might preach against the evils of gossip, but his wife was the town's absolute rumor queen.

"I'd appreciate that." She followed Mr. Niederman through the storeroom to the delivery door. "Thank you so much." She tried to say more, but could only manage a nod. Desperate to get away before she fell apart, she patted his arm and hurried out the door.

Burning eyes and blurred vision blotted out the quiet street. Laura stared down at her fast-moving feet, arms wrapped around her torso, trying to hold herself together. She paid no attention to where she was going, knowing only that she couldn't face Magda or her children. If she went to the apartment, she might collapse and never get up again. So she walked, almost running, block after block and turn after turn.

The loud screech of tires and smell of rubber stopped Laura where she stood. "Hey lady," the red-faced driver shook his fist at Laura. "You stepped right in front of my car. Watch where you're going."

"I'm sorry," Laura said, shocked to find herself in the middle of the street, mere inches in front of a car. "I'm so sorry." She finished crossing the street in front of him, then looked around to figure out where she was.

"Jackson Street, there's the barbershop Glen used to go to," Laura mumbled. "And the auto mechanic's service station is just a couple of blocks down. Glen liked him a lot." She remembered how nice he'd been when the truck broke down. Since she couldn't afford to repair it, he'd bought it for parts. I wonder, maybe he might buy Glen's tools." Her shoulders pulled back and her body straightened. She marched now with a purpose.

Laura heard whistling from the open bay door at the service station. When she stepped inside, she saw a man leaning under the hood of a car. "Excuse me. Mr. Giddings, is that you?"

"At your service." The man grabbed a rag and rubbed his hands as he stood upright. When he saw Laura, he squinted and tilted his head. "I'm sorry. You look familiar, but . . ."

"Mrs. Webber, Glen Webber's wife," Laura said. "You helped me by buying our truck when the engine blew last year."

"Oh my goodness, of course." Mr. Giddings' eyes narrowed, and his gaze flickered from her head to her feet and back again. "Sorry I didn't recognize you, but it has been a long time. How's Glen doing? Is he back? I haven't heard anything about him, but you never know."

Laura realized her ma's assessment was right. She must have changed a lot if this man didn't recognize her. It hadn't been that long, but she'd lost a great deal of weight.

"No, Glen's not back." She crossed her arms. "They moved him to a different hospital in Illinois, and to tell the truth, nobody knows if he'll ever recover enough to come home."

"That's terrible. Glen's a good man and a terrific mechanic. I liked working with him a lot."

"Thank you for saying that. He is a good man. I just wish the doctors could help him." Laura stopped, uncrossed her arms, and rubbed her hands on the sides of her skirt. "Actually, since he can't come home, I wondered if you might be interested in buying his tools. There are a lot of them, and they're just taking up space. We may have to move again, and might not have a place for them."

"You're not still on the farm?"

"No, Mr. Woltz sold his place and moved to New Orleans to be near his son and grandchildren. We're in an apartment on Walnut right now, but may be moving." She paused to take a breath and choose her words. "I didn't think I'd ever sell Glen's things, but we don't have a choice. I hate to ask, but I need to sell them as fast as possible."

The expression on Mr. Giddings' face softened. He shook his head and rubbed his chin. "Well, a man can't have too many tools, and Glen always took good care of his. How about if I come by later this afternoon and look at them?

Laura's shoulders dropped. "That would be perfect. The address is 98 Walnut St., and we're on the third floor."

"I'll close up about five, then clean up and drive on over," he said.

Laura nodded, thanked him, and left, thankful that he could come soon before her courage waned.

The plan worked just as she had envisioned, except for the empty feeling in the pit of her stomach after Mr. Giddings left with all of Glen's tools and machine parts in the bed of his truck. He'd even taken the bicycle for his own son. She received more money than she'd expected, and knew that his generosity was based in large part on his friendship with Glen and pity for the family's situation.

That night, once the children had fallen
asleep, she stood in the bedroom doorway and
watched her sons. Raymond and David had the
outside positions in bed, with Jimmy in the
middle. David curled against Jimmy's body,
beneath his outstretched arm. The boys had
kicked the sheet down to the foot of the bed to
escape the heat, but their bodies still looked
damp in the muggy air.

Laura couldn't help grinning at the way
the boys were arranged on the bed with Jimmy
spread-eagled in the center. All of a sudden, he
scrunched up his face, pulled both hands in to
rub his eyes, then flung his arms straight out.
When the plaster cast whipped toward David,
Laura almost yelled, but he was down just far
enough in the bed for Jimmy's arm to clear the
top of his head. Raymond was not quite so
lucky. Jimmy's arm landed on his shoulder, but
Raymond brushed it off without waking up.

Laura watched her sons sleep, memorizing
the sound of their breathing, the look of the
suntanned skin on their torsos, and the freshly
bathed little-boy smell of their warm bodies. She
begged God to watch over her boys, if he was
really out there.

June was a lighter sleeper, so Laura didn't
touch her as she slept on the couch. Instead, she
sat on the coffee table in front of the couch and

watched the slow, subtle movement of the sheet as June slumbered. Poor June, old enough to understand much more than she should have to deal with. She'd always been her papa's girl and still blamed her mama for Glen not coming home. Laura knew she'd be sad and hurt, but she'd also be angry. Laura just hoped that, in time, June would understand and forgive her for what she had to do.

Chapter Ten

Don't Leave Us

Three days later, Tuesday, August 22, 1939

"This was the best day and the best dinner ever." Raymond curled up on the sofa with the family. Baths were over, teeth were brushed, and the kids in their night-clothes surrounded Laura on the couch waiting for *The Lone Ranger Show* to start on the radio.

"Sure was," Jimmy said from his position between Raymond and Laura. "I ate so much spaghetti I might pop." He pushed his flat tummy out and patted it. "We haven't had that in a long time."

"SSShhh." June pressed her finger against her lips. "It's starting."

The children listened with rapt attention. No talking, but gasps and cheers at appropriate times during the story. Laura didn't hear a word, lost in her own world. She held her kids close, touching them, kissing their hair, trying to absorb their very essence. She wanted the program to go on forever, since when it ended, she'd have to tell them she was leaving.

"That was a good one," Raymond said, pulling Laura out of her reverie. "I wish we had one of those televisions they have at Hamilton's Furniture. It would be so cool to see the Lone Ranger and Tonto catch all the bad guys, instead of just hearing them."

"It sure would," Jimmy said. "Maybe someday we can get one."

June harrumphed and shook her head. "Televisions cost a lot of money. We'll never be rich enough to have one."

Laura leaned across Raymond and turned the radio off. "Maybe someday." She moved off the couch and sat on the table facing the kids. "I need to talk to you guys about something very, very important." Her voice sounded shaky, and her hands, clasped together in her lap, were clammy and cold.

The children looked at one another, then focused on Laura.

"This last year has been awfully hard since your papa went to the hospital. But you've all been so good and so brave, even though it's been tough waiting for him to get better and come home." Laura cleared her throat, which seemed to close up to block the words. "Well, it doesn't look like that's going to happen."

"Don't say that." June's voice was steely. "He got better once. You told us he got better but they wouldn't let him go. If he got better once, he can do it again."

Laura reached for June's hand, but she pulled it away. June crossed her arms and sat in stony silence. "June, your papa did get better. And you're right, they wouldn't let him go. The doctors wanted to wait and make sure he wouldn't lapse and get sick again. Glen was worried about us, and that's why he escaped and tried to come home."

"So why isn't he here? If he was awake enough to get away, couldn't they just send him here?" Raymond's innocent questions sounded so logical.

"Honey, I wish it was that easy," Laura said, "but your papa hurt a guard really bad when he escaped. When the guards chased him down and caught him, they were angry at what he'd done. They beat him when they captured him, and injured his head."

"Is that why they moved him to the new hospital? So they could take care of him and make him better?" Jimmy's innocent face broke Laura's heart.

"No, sweetie, I wish that was why, but it wasn't. All they cared about was that your papa hurt someone and escaped. The new hospital is much stronger and filled with police, along with the doctors. They put him there because they thought he was dangerous and might hurt someone else."

June snorted and leaned away from her brothers. "That's crazy."

Laura nodded in agreement. "I know, Junebug, but now we have to face the fact that your papa is not the same and may never get out again."

Shocked faces proved that the three oldest children hadn't even considered this possibility.

"And because Papa isn't coming home anytime soon, our family is in serious trouble." Laura stopped and looked at each child in turn, praying that they would understand and accept what she had to tell them. "This apartment is awful, but it was supposed to be temporary, just until he came home and could start working and supporting us again. Now, it's the only place we could afford—and that's only because I clean the basements in all three of Mr. Johnson's apartment buildings. Since Mrs. Zimmerman from downstairs died, no money is coming in at all."

Laura's throat burned and her chest ached. The children stared at her in silence. She could see fear competing with trust on their faces, and decided to plunge in and get the worst out of the way.

"Tomorrow morning when you get up, I won't be here." The children's expressions changed. Shock widened their eyes. Before they could speak, she continued. "A lady from the Children's Bureau will come at ten to take you with her. You'll be with a different family for a while, where you'll have plenty of good food and be well taken care of."

"No, don't leave us," Raymond threw himself off the couch into Laura's arms. "If you go, I'm going with you."

Laura held him tight and kissed the top of his head, and tried to blink away the tears that sprang from her eyes. "Honey, I don't want to leave, but I have no choice. There is just enough food left for you guys to have breakfast tomorrow. I've tried everything I could think of to find a job, but nobody will hire a woman, especially a married woman."

David and Jimmy joined Raymond and clung to Laura.

"Maybe we could help." Jimmy looked at Raymond.

Raymond nodded back at his brother. "Yeah. I could deliver papers or something." He looked at David. "We could take turns watching David and doing odd jobs."

"You boys are wonderful, but you're much too young to be under that kind of pressure. Your job is school, and just being kids." Laura couldn't help the tears that started. Her chest hurt from holding in sobs. "Your father and I talked about how important it was to make sure you were well fed and educated, and that's what I'm trying to do."

June jumped down from the couch and circled around to the end of the table. "You're just running away from us," she spat. "Why couldn't it have been you in the hospital and Papa here with us? He'd never leave us just because of money."

"Well, like it or not, I'm the one that's left here with you. Your papa is in the hospital because he's the one who had the mental breakdown and attacked somebody." Laura could feel her own temper rising to meet June's rage. "He left us, whether he meant to or not, and I'm the one who has to deal with that."

Laura could see that June was almost vibrating with rage. "Papa would never leave us. It must have been you. He got mad at you, not us. I'll bet you did something that caused him to get sick." June jumped forward and pounded her fists against Laura's chest. "It's your fault. I hate you."

Raymond leaped in front of Laura and shoved June to the ground. "Don't you hit Mama and don't say those things."

David screamed and yanked at his hair with both fists until Jimmy picked him up. Laura thrust herself between June and Raymond. "Stop it, both of you. Just stop it."

Raymond shoved his hands in his pockets while June jumped to her feet and ran to the bathroom. She slammed the door so hard the wall shook, then wailed and called for her papa, over and over.

Laura took David from Jimmy and soothed him. Raymond and Jimmy both stared at the bathroom door.

"She'll be okay, boys, just give her some time." She led the way into the bedroom. Come on, let's get you guys settled down for the night.

Both boys followed her and climbed onto the bed. "Stay with us, please." Raymond grabbed her hand.

"Mama, don't leave us. I love you. Don't go." Jimmy started crying, which made David start again.

Laura sat at the foot of the bed. "I love you too, more than anything in the world. I need you to stay strong while I'm gone, and remember that I'm thinking about you and sending you love every single day." She helped each boy settle into their spots, rubbing their legs and feet. "I'll stay right here until you go to sleep." She sang and hummed to them until, exhausted, they dropped off. When she was sure they were sound asleep, she leaned down and kissed each forehead and whispered. "I love you."

The bathroom door was open when Laura left the boys. She saw June's body curled in a ball under a blanket on the sofa, face turned away and pressed into the back cushion. Her uneven breathing showed she was still awake. Laura unrolled her mattress at the end of the couch, sat down, and leaned against the wall. The inches that separated her from June felt like a giant chasm.

Laura smiled and spoke just above a whisper. "I remember the day I told your papa that I was pregnant with you. He grabbed me in his arms and swung me around in our tiny kitchen, laughing and singing. Then he stopped and carried me to the nearest chair and put me down like I was made of glass." She paused and listened to June's breathing, which was a little more regular.

"The whole time we waited for you, he made a point of cupping his hands around my belly and talking to you. And then the day you were born, we both thought you were the most perfect, most beautiful baby in the world." Laura could feel June's attention. "And we both have loved you from that first moment. Your papa would never have left you on purpose, but he suffered brain damage when the guards caught and beat him, sweetheart. He can't come home because he's not the same man anymore. I didn't say that to your brothers, but you're old enough to understand, even if it hurts." Laura waited a moment when she thought she heard June say something. "I'd give anything to not leave, but this is the only way the women would help. And honey, if I don't do this, we literally won't even have food to eat. I cannot do that to you and your brothers, no matter how hard it is—and trust me, leaving you is the hardest thing I've ever had to do."

June cried out, slid off the sofa, and crawled into Laura's lap. "I didn't mean what I said, Mama, I'm just so scared. With Papa gone, you're all we have." June wrapped her arms around Laura's neck. "Promise you'll come back, please Mama. You've got to come back to us."

"I promise, baby, nothing on earth can keep me away from you." Laura held June tight, rocking her as if she was an infant. When the shaking and sobbing stopped, Laura stretched out on the mattress and spooned her body around her daughter, until, at long last, June fell asleep.

Chapter Eleven

You Probably Hate Me

Wednesday Afternoon, August 23, 1939

The bench-seat rocked in time to the clickety-clack sound of steel wheels moving on the twin rails. Laura was exhausted, but wide awake. She kept her eyes closed to discourage conversation from the couple who sat next to her.

Their voices were animated, interspersed with laughter, but sounded like a formless buzzing in Laura's ears. The scenes from last night when she put the children to bed, through this morning when Magda and Harvey picked her up and drove her to the train station, kept playing over and over. Thank goodness, Willa and Isaac had agreed to have her come stay with them in Stockton, California, for as long as she needed. It had been years since they'd met, but she couldn't ask for better friends.

She was too keyed up and hadn't slept at all. While the children were awake, she didn't want to miss a single minute with them. After they fell asleep, she kept watching them, studying the way they looked, the sounds they made, even their scents—committing everything about them to memory, saving it up for while they were apart.

As soon as they were asleep, Laura retrieved her suitcase from the basement, then moved all their kitchen things, except for bowls, spoons, and cups for the kids' breakfast, into the storage cabinet. Selling Glen's tools, supplies, and his bicycle had left a lot of room, so when she returned for the children, they'd have some of their things to start over with. But Lord, it was hard to let Glen's bicycle go.

She'd hoped to see the boys riding it someday when they had a safe place to learn, but feared it would have disappeared if she'd left it behind. Mr. Johnson, the landlord, had agreed to keep the storage cabinet full of her things since she'd been such a good tenant. Besides, nobody else had wanted to rent the third floor apartment for years, so it shouldn't create any problems for him.

Packing hadn't taken long, since Laura had very few clothes or personal items. She'd included a small wooden box with their family photographs and letters. One big problem was how to carry her money. Laura had thought about putting most of it in the suitcase, but was afraid of losing it. And if all of it was in her handbag, she might forget or misplace it. She decided to put most of the bills in an envelope and pin it inside the waistband of her slip. Her ticket and ten dollars, much of that in change, rested at the bottom of her pocketbook in a coin-purse.

"Excuse me, ma'am." The lady seated next to Laura touched her shoulder. "Excuse me?"

So much for playing opossum. Laura opened her eyes and turned to her seat-mate.

"I hate to bother you, but we're headed to the dining car. Would you mind saving our seats until we come back?"

The couple looked so young. He was tall with dark hair, while she was tiny with porcelain skin and strawberry-blonde curls. Must be newlyweds, the way they looked at each other and held hands. Lord, had she and Glen ever been that young and in love?

"Sure, no problem. Enjoy your meal."

Laura pulled Glen's pocket watch from her handbag and checked the time. Ten-thirty. That Mrs. Atherton is probably at the house right now, getting ready to take the children away. I hope she's gentle with them and lets them take their things.

Laura squeezed her lips tight, holding in the scream that fought to escape her chest. She imagined David clinging to June, with Jimmy on his other side. She didn't think Raymond would say much. He'd just stand with his hands in his pockets and a stoic expression on his face. Unless, of course, the woman said something negative about his parents or his brothers and sister. Then his face would turn red and he might lash out.

Please don't, Raymond, she prayed. Just ignore any remarks and do what the lady says. Let this whole, awful thing be as easy as possible.

Two days later, Laura stepped off the train and walked through the Stockton train station, wishing her suitcase could sprout wheels and follow her.

"Laura." The voice came from her right. She turned toward it and spotted Willa waving at her as she approached.

Laura ran to meet her, then dropped the suitcase and opened her arms. "Willa, I've missed you so much." Her throat closed up, not letting any more words out.

Willa held on tight, patting Laura's back. "Come on, honey, let's go." She dropped her arms, and moved her hand onto the shoulder of the tall, handsome young man standing next to her. "Ruben will take your bag to the car."

Laura gasped, eyes wide, as she looked closer at Willa's son. "Ruben? My word, you're all grown up. I wouldn't have recognized you."

Ruben ducked his head and grinned. He reached for Laura's suitcase, then led the women out to the car. Ruben drove them through the bustling downtown, then parked in the driveway of a small, single-story house with a deep front porch shaded by a pair of large elm trees.

"Ruben, take Laura's suitcase to the guest room, then let your father know we'll be in the dining room." Willa took Laura's hand and led her down a door-lined hallway. "Isaac's office and his waiting room is through that door." Willa pointed to a small sign that read York Accounting Company on the left side of the hallway. "Our living room and parlor are on the right, and the kitchen and dining room are on the left, just after the office. The bedrooms and bathroom are at the end of the hall."

In minutes, Laura was ensconced on a thickly-padded kitchen chair while Willa started heating water for tea.

"Thank you so much for letting me come." Laura picked at her handbag strap and swallowed. "I honestly didn't know where to go. Just let me know how I can help because I don't want to make extra work for you."

Willa sat down next to Laura, then reached for her hand. "We're happy to have you. We've been friends for a long time now, helping each other through thick and thin. You're welcome to stay as long as you need to."

Just then Isaac entered the room. "Laura, it's so good to see you," Isaac said in the same deep, rich voice Laura remembered. "Ruben is going to the bank and post office for me, so I can visit with you two."

"He's grown into quite a good-looking young man. You both must be very proud of him." Laura wrapped her hands around the steaming cup of tea that Willa placed in front of her. "I didn't recognize him until he smiled and blushed. Looks like he's still as sweet and shy as he was at twelve-years-old when we met."

We are proud of him," Willa said, placing a cup of tea in front of Isaac before seating herself, "just as you must be proud of your children."

Isaac sipped at the hot brew. "How are they doing?"

The simple question drilled into Laura's mind. Her entire body started shaking as she pondered the answer. "I . . . I . . . I don't know." The whispered words sliced their way out of her throat like razor blades.

Isaac and Willa responded at the same time.

"What do you mean by that?"

"How can you not know?"

Laura flinched as if from blows. "They made me leave them. The people at the Children's Bureau refused to help us, even though I didn't have money left to buy food, unless I left them." Laura wanted to cry, or yell, but her throat felt like it was closed tight. "I tried, really I did, but they left me no choice." She stared down at the table, her shoulders hunched tight against her neck. "I couldn't let my children go hungry. They promised to provide for them and see that they got to school. They swore my babies would be well fed and cared for, as long as I abandoned them and stayed away for a while."

She glanced up and saw the horrified expressions as Isaac and Willa looked at one another. She stood up, spilling tea into the saucer beneath the cup. "I shouldn't have come here. I don't deserve to stay here. You probably hate me for what I've done." The torrent of words poured out as Laura fumbled with her pocketbook.

Willa reached her first. "We know how much you adore those children. Sit down and tell us what's been going on."

Isaac joined in, "Of course, you should be here. Tell us what's happened and maybe we can find a way to help."

Laura lowered herself back down onto the chair. She had to tell her story to someone or it would eat her up inside. She focused on the cooling tea in her cup and started.

"I wrote you about Glen's breakdown and commitment, but I didn't tell you all of it." In a strangled monotone she filled them in on all the things she'd left out of her letters, such as his recovery, escape, brutal capture, and transfer to the Marshall Rubenston's Asylum for the Criminally Insane in Galeston, Illinois. "With no car and no money for the train or bus, I have no way to go there and talk to the doctors. Besides, children are never allowed and I couldn't leave them alone. The letters say he has to stay until a judge decides he's no longer a danger to himself or others, but he suffered severe brain damage from the beating when he was captured." Laura stopped a moment to swallow some of the tepid tea. "He's not our Glen anymore, so lord only knows if he'll ever get out. Our family doctor told me to divorce him, and the women that took the children said I could get more help if I was divorced, but I just can't do it. The only reason he's in this predicament is because he wanted to come home and take care of us."

"I'm so sorry," Isaac said. "I liked Glen a lot. He seemed like a fine man."

"He is . . .he was. But he's still my husband and the children's father. How can I just throw him away?"

"How have you been living without him?" Willa's eyes shone and she wiped at them.

"It hasn't been easy, but Glen and I promised one another that if things ever got tough, we'd try our best to handle things ourselves rather than worry the children about money. We also had been saving money from every paycheck. He didn't trust banks, so our savings was in a mason jar that we kept hidden."

Laura was brutally honest, no longer skipping over the problems like she had in her letters. She told Willa and Isaac about the difficult decision to move from the farm to the horrible, rat and bug infested apartment in Aurora. Then about caring for the elderly Mrs. Zimmerman for five dollars a week until she died, leaving her with children that needed food and clothing. But at that point, there was no way to pay for those necessities except with the last few bills and coins in the mason jar.

At last she reached the end of her story—the day she begged for help from Mrs. Zimmerman's daughter-in-law, which resulted in the horrific choice she was given by the Children's Bureau.

Willa stood and wrapped her arms around Laura. "I'm so sorry. I wish we'd known and could have helped you."

Isaac stood and cleared his throat. "We have to figure something out to help so you and your children can get back together."

"Thank you." Laura tried, but couldn't say another word.

"Come on," Willa said, helping Laura out of the chair. "You must be exhausted. Let me help you to your room"

Chapter Twelve

You Need An Attorney

Two weeks later, Thursday, September 7, 1939

"I don't understand what this is for." Laura stared at the two dollars Isaac had given her. They were parked outside of a small building with a brass plaque above the front door: Arthur Dillard, Attorney at Law,.

"Arthur Dillard is not only a client of mine, he's also a good friend and an excellent lawyer. Like I told you, I took the liberty of making an appointment for you to meet with him about the situation with you and your children." Isaac, seated in the driver's seat next to Laura, leaned toward her and pointed at the money in her hand. "Everything you tell your lawyer is in confidence, but you have to hire him first before you tell him your story. That money covers your meeting today."

"I can't take money from you. You and Willa have done too much already. I've been working for a week now, so I can pay him on my own."

"You're not taking money. You're accepting a loan." Isaac glanced at his pocket watch, then opened his car door. "You need to go inside or you'll be late. I'll be in the cafe across the street. If you hire him, I'll pay his retainer, then have you sign a note for that amount plus the two dollars. If you don't hire him, you can pay this money back from your first check."

Isaac shut his door and hurried around the car to open Laura's. She followed him to the office, where he waved her inside the door. "Good morning, Mrs. Prentice. Would you please let Arthur know Mrs. Webber is here for her appointment? And remind him that if she hires him, I'll write the check for the retainer since she doesn't have a local bank account yet."

Bank account? Laura hadn't thought about needing one since she'd been using her tiny amount of cash for personal expenses. Tomorrow was payday and she wouldn't be off again until next Wednesday. She'd have to open an account today. She sure hoped there was a bank nearby.

Mrs. Prentice kept her eyes trained on her typewriter, keys moving so fast that Laura couldn't imagine how she did it. "Of course, Mr. York. Always a pleasure to see you." She slid her glasses off and let them drop, tethered by a glass bead chain, to her chest, then pulled the sheet of paper out of her machine with a flourish. Only then did she turn to Laura. "Mrs. Webber, please make yourself comfortable. Mr. Dillard should be ready to see you in just a few minutes."

Laura didn't have much time to worry or speculate after Isaac left. She'd never talked to a lawyer before, so had no idea of what to expect.

A short man, impeccably dressed in a crisp white shirt, dark blue tie, dark gray vest and matching trousers with knife-edge creases, popped through the door.

"Mrs. Prentice," he said, handing her a stack of papers. "I signed all of these, so they're ready to go out. Would you please drop them at the post office for me on your way home?" He wheeled toward Laura the minute the paperwork left his hands. "Mrs. Webber? Come on in."

Laura stood and followed the man through the door into a large inner office.

"It's a pleasure to meet you, Mrs. Webber. I'm Mr. Dillard." He gestured toward a ladder-back chair in front of a glass-topped mahogany desk. "Mr. York told me you're a good friend of the family, but are in a pickle and need an attorney."

Laura sat at the same time the lawyer dropped into his chair and steepled his hands on the desk. "Um, I've never talked to an

attorney before, but Isaac told me I need one."
She opened her handbag and pulled out the two
dollar bills. "He also told me I needed to give
you these so our conversation would be
confidential."

A quick smile flashed on a face made up of
angles—prominent cheekbones, sharp chin, and
deep-set blue eyes—under thick, dark brown
hair, all warmed and softened by the smile.
"Thank you, Mrs. Webber, but there is no
charge for this initial consultation. Everything
you tell me is still privileged." He watched Laura
place the bills on the surface of the desk in front
of her. "Now, tell me why you're here."

Laura pulled her hands into her lap and
interlaced the fingers. She took a deep breath,
focused her gaze on Mr. Dillard's eyes, and
explained what led up to her leaving her
children.

"It's been two weeks, but when I called
Mrs. Zimmerman, she told me she wasn't
keeping track of my children. She was pretty
curt, and said she didn't know how to reach
Mrs. Atherton, or even if she's the one in charge
of them now. She said it's up to me to handle
things from here." Laura swallowed and
blinked. "I need to know what's happening and
how I can get back with my kids. I don't know
what to do."

"That's quite a story." Mr. Dillard leaned
back in his chair and crossed his arms. "Mr.

York was right, you must have an attorney if you want any chance to reunite your family." He raised his hand, palm out, when Laura started to speak.

"I believe you, but unfortunately, you've been misled about how the system works. I know the Children's Bureau here will be somewhat different from the one in Missouri, but the basic framework will be the same."

He stood and stepped toward a long cabinet against the wall to his right. A pitcher of water rested on a tray with four empty glasses. He filled two glasses, carried them to the desk and placed one in front of Laura before he sat back down with the other.

"The big problem, Mrs. Webber, is that the Children's Bureau staff doesn't know or care about anything you've told me." He ignored her gasp, and kept going. "The only thing they know is what Mrs. Atherton wrote in her report. I'll bet that her report has some true, but very ugly sounding statements." He stopped to drink from his glass, wrapped both hands around it, and continued. "Her report will probably say that four children, including a toddler, were left alone in an apartment with virtually no food in the cabinets or refrigerator, no way to reach their mother or even knowledge about where she went. She'll describe the apartment as dim, located up three dangerous flights of stairs, and with signs of rodent and insect infestation. I'm sure she noted that the children appeared clean and healthy, but she'll still make a big deal about the fact that one of the boys had fading bruises on his face and a cast on his arm. She'll also say that, according to the children, their father is incarcerated in a mental hospital for a breakdown after a violent attack on one of the medical staff."

Laura pressed her hands against the chair arms, squeezing hard. "You make everything sound so awful, and so simple. Mrs. Zimmerman and all the women in her club know the whole story. They said they wanted to help me, and that this was the only thing I could do."

"I've no doubt, but even if they passed that information on—which is unlikely—only the report matters to the agency. The question now is, do you want to get back with your children? If so, you need to let me handle this."

"Can't you just find the name and number of the person I need to contact? I'll call them and explain."

Mr. Dillard interrupted. "No, Mrs. Webber, you don't want to do that. You are, in their mind, the neglectful mother that ran away from her children. Why would they believe you? The report will have prejudiced them against you. And if you just called up, wanting to see the children, they'd think even worse of you. You'd look like a woman that ran off for a little vacation from her children and now wants to come back."

Laura's shoulders dropped, and she buried her face in her hands. "Oh my god, what have I done? I need them, and they need me too." She wiped at her eyes, then gripped the desk edge with her fingers. "Isn't there anything I can do?"

"No, there's nothing you can do alone," Mr. Dillard said. "However, they will pay attention to an attorney, and they'll give you more respect because you hired one. The first thing I'll do is find out all I can about the case, the case manager, and the status of the children. I'll also have to research the steps required for reunification of your family, and get them to commit to that goal. This will take time, though, so we need to get started as soon as possible."

Laura, face ashen at the news, whispered. "Okay, just tell me what to do. I love my children, Mr. Dillard, and I can't live without them."

Mr. Dillard nodded, then walked to the lobby door and opened it. "Mrs. Prentice, please bring us a new client packet."

When Laura, after what seemed like hours, joined Isaac at the cafe, she was trembling and glassy-eyed, but hopeful for the first time since she had crept down the stairs away from her children.

"Will he be able to help?" Isaac pulled a chair out for Laura, then sat back down at the small table. "Let me order you some tea. You look like you need it."

Laura nodded, then took a deep breath. "Thank you so much for sending me to Mr. Dillard. I could never have done anything on my own." She held up a manila envelope. "You were right about the retainer. I've signed a retainer contract. And there's a receipt for the two-dollar down payment."

"Good, now you can relax a little. Arthur doesn't waste time, that I can promise you." Isaac glanced at his watch. "We'd better finish our drinks so I can get back to the office."

"I have to ask for another favor. Since tomorrow is payday at the hospital, I'll need a bank account. Is there one near your house?"

"You're right. We'll stop on the way."

Chapter Thirteen

Remember Their Happy Lives

Friday, September 8, 1939

Laura reached for the door handle of the housekeeping supply room near the time clocks, ready to stock a cleaning cart.

"Mrs. Webber, hold on please." The voice came from behind her.

"Yes?"

"Mrs. Webber?" Andy Ballard was a long-time housekeeping worker at the hospital, and had helped Laura get settled into the job. "I was told to send you to Mr. Jeffries's office first thing today."

Laura swallowed and bit her lower lip, trying to figure out what she might have done wrong. "Do you know why?" Mr. Jeffries was the Housekeeping Department head. It wasn't ever a good sign to get called in by someone in his position.

"No, but I wouldn't keep him waiting."

"Okay." Laura's mouth was suddenly too dry to say more. She proceeded down the hallway to the elevator, a single phrase repeating over and over in her mind: please, please don't let me lose this job.

॰॰॰

Mr. Jeffries was on the phone when she entered his office, but waved her toward a chair in front of his desk. Laura tried not to fidget, but found herself rubbing damp palms on her skirt, over and over.

"Good morning, Mrs. Webber," Mr. Jeffries said after placing the phone receiver back on the cradle. "How are you doing in Housekeeping?"

Laura cleared her throat. "Fine. I'm doing fine. Everyone has been very helpful and nice."

"That's good to hear." He dropped his gaze to a folder on his desk. He opened it, then glanced at the top page of the thin stack. "Your supervisor says you're a fast learner and a hard worker. She has no complaints at all about the job you're doing or how you relate to other members of the department."

Laura smiled and nodded, but sensed something more was coming.

Mr. Jeffries closed the folder and tented his hands on the desk, fingers under his chin. "I'm sorry to say that I've received some complaints from the nursing staff about your interactions with the patients." He sat back in his chair and folded his arms. "Have you ever worked in a mental hospital before?"

"No sir," Laura said. "I worked in housekeeping at a regular hospital in Tulsa several years ago. I got along well with the patients as well as the nurses and doctors there, so I'm not sure what I've done wrong."

"Our job here is quite a bit different than what you've experienced before. Our patients don't have physical ailments to treat, they're mentally ill. Patients are committed to this hospital only after they've been deemed dangerous to themselves or to the community."

Laura tilted her head and rubbed her hands together in her lap. "I understand."

"I don't think you do, but I'm not blaming you." Mr. Jeffries leaned forward, elbows on the edge of his desk. "In the Tulsa hospital, I imagine you worked with the medical staff to make sure patients' needs were met, right?"

"Yes, sir. The nurses were always busy, so sometimes if a patient needed a pillow fluffed or something simple like that, I'd take care of it. Other times if a patient needed something, I'd let a nurse know."

"Exactly," Mr. Jeffries said. "But here, it's not part of your job to assist patients or carry their requests to the nurses. Your job is housekeeping, period."

Laura felt a flush creep up her neck. "Then I should ignore a patient who asks me for help?"

"Yes," he answered. "Our patients requests may be tied to their delusions. A woman who asks you to help to find her husband may have been widowed for a decade. A man complaining because he fell and thinks he broke his arm in the bathroom may have been repeating the same false story for weeks. Our medical staff knows the patients. If you try to help, you may be wasting everyone's time and even interfering with a treatment plan."

"I'm sorry, sir," Laura said. "I thought I was helping."

Mr. Jeffries nodded. "From now on you need to stick to housekeeping and limit your interaction with patients to a smile or wave. Leave them to the medical staff." He stood and walked around the side of his desk. "Now that you understand, I'm sure you'll do well."

"Yes, sir, I do understand." Laura stood, then left the office. It sounded so simple, but could she ignore someone begging for help?

Laura started her cleaning in one of the women's wings. She breathed a sigh of relief each time she entered a room and found it empty. What a difference from the awful place Glen had been taken. Most of the patients in residence here spent much of their time outside, walking the paths or enjoying the vegetable and flower gardens. Only the most severe patients stayed inside, and many of those were treated the same way Glen had been, with hours-long water baths, straight-jackets, and electroshock therapy.

When the women's rooms were all clean, Laura replenished her cart and headed to the common room, which was full of women sitting at tables scattered about, moving back and forth in rocking chairs that lined the walls, or meandering around the room.

"Miss, can you help me? Please, I need help." The speaker sat in a rocking chair near the entry door.

"I'm sorry, ma'am. Let your nurse know when she comes in." Laura cringed inside, but moved toward the nearest trash basket.

She concentrated on emptying all the trash bins, then began wiping down the tables. Several times she smiled when women accosted her, then referred them to their nurse before moving away from them. Laura noticed three orderlies in the room, two standing at the doors and one roaming throughout the room. All three were focused on the women and looked ready to handle any problems that might occur.

Then loud, anguished sobs burst from one corner. Laura whirled toward the sound and saw a thin gray woman—gray hair a messy nimbus around her head, washed-out colorless dress and sweater, pale grayish skin—rocking in a chair, holding her head in her hands. Her cries were loud and full of despair, but no one in the room, including the orderlies, attempted to approach her or pay her any attention other than a quick glance. Laura pressed her eyes closed and clenched her hands around the cart handles, unable to ignore the awful sound.

As soon as her eyes closed, Laura was transported to a different place and time. The same woman, decades younger, came out of a barn with two pails of frothy milk, and screamed. She stared at her house, about a hundred yards away, fully engulfed in flames, then dropped the buckets and ran toward the flames.

"No, no, no! Jim! My babies!" she yelled as she sprinted toward the back door, only stopping when the skin on her face began to sear in the heat. Desperate, she rushed around the house as close as she could, praying that she'd find her family safe outside in the front yard. But the front door was burning as well, and no one waited for her. With one final agonized howl, she collapsed on the ground, imploring God to take her too.

Laura opened her eyes to escape the pain she felt pouring from the crying woman. She saw one orderly staring at her, so she dropped her gaze and finished cleaning an empty table, then ducked down at the side of the cart as if she were searching for something. She closed her eyes again, and was sucked back into the vision.

The woman was unconscious on the ground in front of the smoldering building. All Laura could do was pass on the thoughts she was receiving from the woman's family. "Jim and the girls are fine in the hands of God, and are happy and perfect. They want you to know the fire was not your fault, and there was nothing you could have done. They love you, and want you to remember their happy lives, not how they died." The words kept repeating in her mind, a powerful, soothing mantra, and through her to Claire, the woman in the corner.

This time when she opened her eyes, Laura was at peace. The episode had only lasted a minute, but felt much longer. No one noticed what she had done, but Claire no longer sobbed in the corner. She leaned back in her chair, head resting against the wall, with a faint smile on her face.

"You did well today." The voice was warm and calming, like a scented bubble bath. It wrapped around Laura, filling her body and mind while refreshing her spirit.

"Ma?" Laura couldn't help looking around her bedroom, hoping that somehow she might catch a glimpse of her mother. "Thank you. I couldn't stand Claire's crying, especially with everyone ignoring her obvious pain."

"They've become accustomed to hearing her. No one knows the reason she cries, and the doctors have no idea of how to help her. They've given up and hope that she'll snap out of it by herself someday."

"I don't really know what I did. I was trying to help her without getting in trouble." Laura shrugged her shoulders. "Somehow she seemed to hear my thoughts and understood the message came from her family."

"Yes, she did. And that helped her."

Laura lifted her chin and threaded her fingers through her freshly washed and brushed hair. "I'm glad it helped. But will the communication from me stay with her?"

"Most likely she'll see that awful past again, but perhaps remembering what you told her will make it less frightening and help her through it."

Laura nodded, leaned forward where she sat on the edge of the bed and stared at her slippered feet. "Ma, I saw all of Glen's awful dreams. Why couldn't I help him like I helped Claire?"

"The Second Sight is a strange gift, and one that does not obey those that have it. When someone with the gift tries to help a loved one, their mind often gets in the way. Your love and intimate knowledge interferes with the spiritual information you receive. Sometimes you can confuse your desires for the person as the message, instead of what comes from the spirit guides."

Laura opened her mouth to ask another question, but felt her ma's presence disappear. As always, the space around her felt empty, but her heart was at peace.

Chapter Fourteen

Focus On The Future

One month later, Wednesday, October 11, 1939

"Good morning, Mrs. Prentice." Laura closed the office door behind her and walked to the desk in the small lobby. "I have an appointment with Mr. Dillard."

"Yes you do, Mrs. Webber," the secretary said, already typing from a notepad covered with curvy lines. "Mr. Dillard will be ready for you in a few minutes. Please take a seat. There's coffee on the side table, if you'd like a cup."

Laura sat down, hands in her lap, and played with her purse strap while she waited.

Mr. Dillard burst out of his inner office, nodded to Laura, then leaned down and riffled through some typed pages on the side of Mrs. Prentice's desk. Straightening up, he welcomed Laura and motioned her to his office door. "Come on in, Mrs. Webber," he said, walking around the desk and dropping into his chair.

"Thank you. Have you heard anything about my children?"

"Yes, I have." He opened a folder on his desk and lifted a multi-page letter. "I've learned quite a bit, actually. The best news for you is that the case worker has approved contact with your children, so you will be able to write to them. If you were still in Missouri, they would have approved visits as well."

"Oh, thank God." Laura whispered. "I'll write them as soon as I get home." Then she pursed her lips and shook her head. "I don't understand them saying I could visit if I was in Missouri, since I was told that if I didn't leave the way I did, no one would have helped us."

Mr. Dillard raised one hand, palm out. "Let's not revisit the things you've been told. Instead, we need to go over the information on the children's current status, the conditions attached to the letters, and the next steps you have to take."

"Yes, sir. I'm sorry." Laura pressed her hands together and leaned forward, not wanting to miss a word.

"First of all, let me bring you up to date on the children." Mr. Dillard glanced down at the letter and smoothed the papers out on his desk. "Your daughter, June, stayed with a foster family in Aurora until it was time for the school term to begin. She is now enrolled at a boarding school near Springfield, Lake of the Ozarks

School. She'll attend there through High School."

"June? Is she all alone there? Why isn't she with her brothers?"

"Hold on, Mrs. Webber, let me get through all this. The Children's Bureau keeps siblings together when they can, but that is not always the case." Mr. Dillard stared at Laura, then looked back down at the papers.

"Your oldest son, Raymond, was sent to Ozark Home for Boys outside of Springfield. It's similar to Boys Town, but a local version."

"But Boys Town is for delinquent boys. Raymond has never been in trouble."

"It is also for poor and neglected boys whose families can't care for them properly." Mr. Dillard sighed. "Please, Mrs. Webber, let me finish without interruption."

Laura tipped her chin down and swallowed hard. "I'm sorry."

"Raymond was a problem at first. He ran away twice, but seems to have settled down." Mr. Dillard looked up, pausing a moment before going on. "James and David are living at The Mountain View Men's Home, but that's considered a temporary placement. Living with elderly men is not ideal for young boys, but the caretakers watch out for them and make sure James gets to school each day. They care for David while Jimmy is away, but report that the boys stay together the rest of the time. The

Bureau is looking for a more suitable home, one where they can remain together, since the boys both get very stressed when they're separated. In fact, David refuses to sleep alone and clings to his brother at night."

Tears pooled in Laura's eyes, and her lips trembled. "What have I done to my babies?"

"You did what you thought was the only thing you could do." Mr. Dillard removed his glasses and laid them on the papers. "I know it's difficult to hear about what they are going through, but now you need to focus on the future."

Laura wiped at her eyes and pulled her shoulders back. "Okay, just tell me what I have to do."

～✎～

When Laura got off the bus two blocks from the Yorks' house, she was in a daze. She carried a manila envelope filled with papers from her attorney and a small bag that contained a box of stationery and envelopes from a shop near the law office. Discouragement alternated with determination as she kept going over the information Mr. Dillard had given her, and the list of things she needed to do.

First, write letters to each of her children, but they had to be full of love and hope. She mustn't say anything negative about where the children were living or make any statements or promises about when they'd be together again. She had to figure out a way to find work to satisfy the Children's Bureau regarding her fitness as a parent and provider. Finding a place to live near her job was critical, since she'd have to walk or depend on local bus lines.

The apartment had to be cheap, but clean, and with two bedrooms. Mr. Dillard told her that if there wasn't adequate room for the children, they wouldn't be permitted to stay with her.

She could share a room with June, but there had to be space for the boys if they were ever to be allowed to stay with her. How in the heck all of that could be accomplished from California was a mystery, but somehow she had to figure it all out.

Chapter Fifteen

It's A Good Start

Five weeks later, Wednesday, November 15, 1939

Laura's emotions were a mixture of fear, hope, and excitement as the train pulled out of the Stockton station, headed for Nixa, a small town not too far from Springfield, Missouri. She'd been gone for twelve long weeks, way more than she'd ever imagined. Twelve weeks was an eternity for children.

Laura reached into the large pocketbook tucked between the side of the train compartment and her hip and patted the three envelopes in a zippered section. The envelopes held letters from her children. The paper was soft from handling, and the words were memorized from repeated reading.

They'd sounded stiff and uncomfortable the first time she'd read them, but she'd taken slight comfort in the knowledge that they'd been written under their case worker's supervision. She'd been given strict guidelines for her letters, and imagined the children had been as well. Each included the same pat phrases—they were being treated fine, the people were nice, and school was okay. And each child said "I love you" above their name. Jimmy, of course, wrote for both himself and David.

Laura's musings were interrupted by two women, who looked like a mother and adult daughter, settling into the bench seat next to her.

"Delilah, put your suitcase under the seat in front of you, dear." The oldest woman positioned her feet in perfect alignment on the floor, squared her shoulders, then turned to stare at Laura. "Hello, miss," she said, craning her neck, but couldn't see Laura's left hand since it held her purse between her side and the wall. "Or is it missus? I'm Mrs. Penelope Winthrope and this is my daughter, Delilah. We're heading for Los Angeles to meet with her fiance's family." She patted her daughter's hand. "Planning a wedding is so exciting."

Laura kept her hand tucked out of sight, not ready to answer nosy questions about her husband or children. Perhaps she should remove her wedding ring? But then would come the inevitable interrogation about why a woman of her age wasn't married. "Congratulations,

Delilah, I hope your wedding will be everything you've dreamed of."

Delilah nodded, but her mother inhaled and leaned in, eyes gleaming. "Oh yes, it will be quite grand."

"That's lovely. I hope you two can excuse me, but I have a terrible headache. I need to take a nap to try and get rid of it." With that, she closed her eyes and leaned back against the headrest.

The next two-and-a-half days passed in a haze as the train chugged its way across the country in spurts.

A succession of people occupied the seats next to Laura, but she exchanged only the shortest of polite responses, feigning the need for sleep when someone was too inquisitive. How could she answer common questions when she didn't know the answers?

Everything about her destination and immediate future was unknown beyond the barest of facts. The only solid thing to hold on to was her determination to reunite with her children.

~⁖~

When the train stopped in Nixa, only a few people stepped down onto the platform with Laura. So this was her new home? There were just a few cars parked in a lot to the side of the small, tidy train station building. An elderly couple approached through the double-doors, waving their hands.

"Mrs. Webber?" The gentleman wore a heavy overcoat and a wool hat, while the woman with him clutched at his arm with hands muffled in thick gloves. "We're Mr. and Mrs. Schroeder, from the synagogue in Springfield. Magda and Harvey Cohen asked us to meet you and take you to your new home."

When they arrived at the apartment, Mr. Schroeder insisted on carrying Laura's bag from the car. Mrs. Schroeder opened the door, then said, "Welcome to your new home, Mrs. Webber. We hope you'll be happy here." She handed Laura the key, then gave her a fast tour of her new place.

After Laura said goodbye to Mr. and Mrs. Schroeder and closed the front door behind them, she leaned against the door, exhausted, alone in her new apartment.

How could she ever thank Magda and Harvey enough for all they'd done for her? She never expected them to elicit help through the members of their synagogue in Springfield, yet both her job at the Ozark Rivers Sanitarium and her new home came through those contacts.

And the biggest surprise of all, the family's things from the storage cabinets in Aurora were stacked in the living room.

The Schroeders had even provided a hand-drawn map of the area between her apartment and the Sanitarium, showing the bus stops and local shops she might need. And a bus schedule was paper-clipped to the map so she'd know how to get to work and back.

"It's a good start, honey. Now get up and get busy. You start work on Monday, and have a lot to do before then." The disembodied voice, so loving and strong, filled Laura's mind and heart, feeling like a hug from the inside.

"Ma, I'm so glad you're here." Laura stood in the center of the small living room, glanced around, and wished there was some physical sign of her mother's presence, even though she knew it was pointless.

"Don't waste time. Get comfortable in this place, so you'll be ready to explore tomorrow before work the next day. The faster you're stable here, the faster you can prove yourself and work on seeing the children."

"Thank you . . ." Laura stopped speaking. Her ma's presence was gone as abruptly as she had appeared.

Energized, Laura took a deep breath. "

"Okay, time to check this place out."

The ground-floor apartment was small, but clean, with a faint smell of Pine-sol. A quick walk-through revealed all white walls, but with patterned linoleum floors that added light blue and soft rose colors. The furniture throughout was worn, but comfortable and spotless. The kitchen was small compared to the farm they'd lived in before Glen's breakdown, but twice as large as the place in Aurora. Both bedrooms were tiny, with just enough room for a double bed, an armoire with a top section for hanging clothes, and four drawers at the bottom, and a narrow dresser at the foot of the beds. The bathroom was basic—sink, tub, and toilet, but it did have a storage cabinet under the sink as well as a mirrored medicine cabinet above it.

Laura grabbed her bag from the living room and put her things away, but decided to leave the storage boxes until another day.

"I'd better make a shopping list." She pulled a small notepad and pencil from her handbag, moved to the kitchen, and opened the refrigerator.

"Oh my goodness."

Tears stung her eyes as she stared at the milk, eggs, fresh vegetables, cheese and meat inside.

"I don't deserve such amazing, generous friends."

She turned around and checked the cabinets. Sure enough, all the basic food staples were there, together with a small supply of dishes and a couple of pans. and cleaning supplies under the sink.

"I guess tomorrow will be the shortest shopping trip ever."

Laura fixed a can of soup and some fried toast, then sat down to review the papers from

Mr. Dillard once again. Settling into the corner of the couch, she stretched her legs and feet out, wiggling her liberated toes. She tossed the envelope onto the coffee table after dumping the contents on her lap.

"It's too quiet in here. I wish there was a radio to listen to." She swung her legs around and stood, pitching the papers on top of the envelope. "Our old radio has to be in one of those boxes and shouldn't be too hard to find."

It wasn't in the first box, but her kitchen things were. Laura found her pressure cooker, cast-iron skillet, double-boiler, and two saucepans. Touching each one brought back family memories of meals cooked in every place they'd lived or stopped at on the road when they lived out of their old truck. The pressure cooker was the newest, but it triggered the most vivid pictures of all from the evening when the pressure valve slipped off and beans shot out of the vent like bullets, coating the kitchen ceiling with beans and juice. She and the kids had laughed until they hurt at the way they looked covered with the mess. And for weeks afterward, just mentioning beans would set them off laughing again.

The second box was also for the kitchen, with dishes, utensils, dishtowels, tablecloths, napkins and dishrags.

"Not many left from our original sets, most of this stuff came from the thrift store."

Laura found the radio in the third box, together with towels and washcloths wrapped around it for protection. She lifted it out, uncurled the cord, and plugged it into the electrical outlet behind the end table nearest the wall to the fireplace. Laura twisted the dial until she found a local station playing a commercial for Dreft detergent. "At last." She grabbed the papers off the table and burrowed into the corner cushions. "I don't care what's on, just company while I read through this stuff again."

Mr. Dillard had coordinated with an attorney in Springfield, Mr. Brian Cooper, who would handle everything from now on.

"I wonder how big my file is?"

Laura flipped through the papers, but found only the information sheet and contract with Mr. Cooper, the rental agreement for her apartment, the employment papers for her job, and the latest letters from her children's case worker, Mrs. Penneyworth.

"Mr. Dillard said he sent the whole file to Mr. Cooper. I guess he didn't think I'd need the whole thing."

Laura closed her eyes when the first notes of "*Somewhere, Over the Rainbow*" in Judy Garland's amazing voice poured over her. She sang along, soothed in spite of herself, wondering if Glen ever heard music in the hospital. Music had brought them together and had carried them through the toughest of times.

Did he ever sing anymore? Or was his poor, damaged brain too far gone to respond to it?

Chapter Sixteen

I'm Doing My Best

Tuesday, December 5, 1939

Laura's hands shook and she could feel sweat under her arms in spite of the biting cold. She stared at the administration building's front door, the words Lake of the Ozarks School engraved on the lintel above it.

"Get going," she told herself. "You're finally going to see June. What are you waiting for?"

One foot, then another, each step closer to a reunion she'd been praying and dreaming of. Laura muttered under her breath. "But will she even want to see me after so long? Will she be happy or angry at me? Will she believe that I've been trying? And what about the person who'll be watching us?"

The door was heavy, but the warm air inside was worth the effort. The room had six chairs arranged against three walls, with a large secretarial desk on the left side.

"Good afternoon. May I help you?" The girl at the desk looked like a high-school student. She appeared to be arranging a stack of papers in some type of order.

"Yes, thank you." Laura felt a warm flush creeping up her neck at the thought of explaining her business to a child. "I'm Mrs. Webber, and I have an appointment to meet with my daughter June."

The girl picked up a note next to the typewriter on the desk's side extension, read it, glanced at Laura, then said, "Excuse me, I'll be right back."

She hurried through a door behind her desk. She reappeared, followed by a tall, very thin woman. "Mrs. Webber, this is Mrs. Bailey, our Vice Principal. She'll take you to the conference room."

The room was small, furnished with an oblong table at the far end with six armless chairs around it, and four overstuffed chairs with wide padded arms grouped together near the door. Mrs. Bailey sat in the one nearest the entrance, and gestured for Laura to sit with her. "June should be here in just a few minutes, but I wanted to go over some things first."

"What things? I don't mean to be rude, but I haven't seen my daughter in a long time, and want all the time with her that's possible."

Mrs. Bailey sniffed. "Then let's get to it. Because of the circumstances of your case, all visits right now have to be supervised, as you've been told. When the Children's Bureau feels comfortable with your behavior toward the children, the supervision requirement may be removed. I'll sit at the table to give you two some privacy, but will be observing your interaction. Do you understand?"

Laura fought to keep her expression neutral as she nodded, but was burning inside with embarrassment and anger. Thank goodness Mr. Dillard and Mr. Cooper had both briefed her on what to expect and how to respond, or she'd be sorely tempted to pop this woman in the nose.

"Mama?" June's voice broke the spell, releasing Laura and Mrs. Bailey from their dueling stares.

"June," Laura said, opening her arms wide and reaching out. "Oh, Junebug, I've missed you so much."

Mrs. Bailey stood and moved to the table. Neither June nor Laura paid any attention to her as she pulled a notebook and pen out of her satchel and placed them on the polished surface in front of her.

June broke the hug, pulling back. "What took you so long? I thought you'd come get us long ago. You said it would be a couple of weeks, and that was months ago. It's not too bad here, but that other place was horrible." June took a fast breath and barreled on. "The woman, Mrs. Pritchett, was mean and made me work all the time. She made me do dishes every single day with Dreft and my arms broke out in a horrible red rash. It burned, Mama. I told her and told her, but she didn't care. I even showed her the pictures on the box that showed the stupid soap was for laundry, but she made me use it, anyway."

Laura tried to wipe tears away from June's face, but she stepped out of reach. "I'm so sorry, honey," she said, glancing at Mrs. Bailey, "but I'm here now."

"Can we leave now that you're back?" June looked at the door. "Where are the boys? I didn't see them. Are we picking them up on our way?"

Laura could feel Mrs. Bailey's eyes on her, and knew she could hear every word. "I wish that were possible, but this is only a visit. The Children's Bureau people say they need to make sure I can support us and provide a good home for our family." She sighed and took June's hands in hers. "I haven't been able to see the boys yet, but hope to soon. I'm doing my best, honey."

June plopped into the chair and crossed her arms. "I haven't seen my brothers since the day you left. I miss them. And David's so little, I'm afraid he won't even remember me."

"Of course he remembers you," Laura said, hoping it was true.

June was quiet for a long time, rubbing her hands on the upholstered chair arms. "Mama, why is Mrs. Bailey staring at us and writing?"

"Uh, I think she's taking notes. She's supposed to make sure we behave well together, and then she'll report back to the Children's Bureau case worker."

"You mean she's spying on us?" June's eyebrows rose almost into her hairline. "I don't want to talk in front of a sneaky tattletale." She jumped up and moved to a different chair with her back to Mrs. Bailey. "I'll stay over here and whisper."

Laura kept her voice at a normal pitch, but was unable to convince June to speak up or move back to the chair facing their dour chaperone.

"Tell me what the school is like? Where do you sleep? What subjects are you studying? Do you have some new friends?" Laura tried, but getting information from June was a struggle. She'd start opening up, then glance over her shoulder at a staring Mrs. Bailey.

Instead of providing more than one-sentence answers, June wanted to know all about California and why Laura had stayed there so long. Then she wanted descriptions of the sanitarium and the apartment.

"Two bedrooms? Why do you have two bedrooms all by yourself?" June said.

"Only one is for me. I have two, so the Children's Bureau will see that I have room for you children." Laura leaned forward, hands on her knees, staring into June's eyes. "Every single thing I've done from the day I left has been focused on getting our family back together."

"What about Papa?" June squeezed her hands together. "He's part of the family. Are they going to let him come home too?"

Laura closed her eyes and dropped her chin. "Oh honey, I wish that was possible. I've written to the hospital several times, but the doctors say there has been no change and don't expect any improvement. Miracles do happen, but right now your papa is not the man he was."

June tightened her lips, but before she could speak, Mrs. Bailey sang out. "I'm afraid your time is up. You two need to say goodbye so June can go to class."

June jumped out of the chair, glared, and planted her hands on her hips. "Nobody likes a bossy tattletale. I'm not done talking to my mama. I go to class every day."

Laura stood and wrapped her arms around June's shoulders. "Hush, Junebug," she whispered. "If she writes a bad report they might not let me see you again. Please, honey, please apologize so I can come back soon."

June's tense muscles relaxed, but tears pooled in her eyes. "I'm sorry, Mrs. Bailey. I shouldn't have talked back." The lump in her throat made her voice sound thick, and the words were forced out between trembling lips. "It's just that I've missed my family so much. Please don't write anything bad. I need to see Mama and my brothers. I promise to be good, I promise."

The emotional dam broke. June turned her face into Laura's chest and sobbed, holding on as hard as she could. Laura rubbed her back and whispered soothing words.

Mrs. Bailey cleared her throat. "It's okay, I understand. I know you need each other." Her voice sounded shaky, too. "If we don't go out on time though, somebody may notice and say something to the Bureau."

Laura nodded, hugged June, and kissed her forehead. "I love you, honey, and I'll come back as soon as they let me. Please be good and be as happy as you can."

Laura stabbed the key into the apartment door lock and hurried inside. She didn't know whether to break something or scream. Instead, she sat on the couch and dialed the Children's Bureau.

"Hello. May I speak to Mrs. Penneyworth, please?" She took several deep breaths to calm herself. "My name? I'm Mrs. Webber, Laura Webber, and Mrs. Penneyworth is my case worker. She asked me to call this afternoon."

When they connected, the case worker seemed delighted that the visit with June had gone well. She wasn't surprised that June had begged to go with Laura, saying that was a normal reaction. But she wouldn't commit to a date for the next visit, saying only that she'd follow up with the school first.

Laura's knuckles were white, wrapped around the telephone cord, when she broached the subject of visiting her sons.

"Well, they need a chance to settle into their new placement first. I'd say let's wait two to three weeks."

"Two to three weeks? What do you mean, new placement?" Laura tried to keep her voice level, but knew her fear and impatience came through.

"Well, you should be happy that we've moved all three boys into a place together. Raymond kept trying to run away from the Ozark Home for Boys, and David just wasn't gaining confidence, and cried every time Jimmy was away from him. Now all three are at a ranch with an experienced foster couple, Mr. and Mrs. Stinnett. They don't usually take boys as young as David, but agreed since we felt the three would do better together."

Tears leaked out of Laura's eyes, and her chest hurt with each breath. "Thank you for putting them together. We've always been a close family, which is why I want to visit them as soon as possible."

Mrs. Penneyworth sighed into the phone, then said, "I'm sure you do, but they need to get comfortable with the Stinnetts first." Papers rustled during a pause. "Actually, Mrs. Webber, we've had an inquiry from a young family that would like to adopt David. He's the perfect age, and this would be an excellent alternative for him."

"NO!" Laura tasted blood from biting her lip. "David is my son! I will never give up one of my children. Do you have any idea of what that would do to his brothers and sister? You might as well just shoot us all."

"Calm down, Mrs. Webber. I just proposed that because the couple asked and because our job is to do what's best for the children."

"What is best for my children is for us to get back together. I have a good job and a nice apartment with two bedrooms. I've done everything you've asked of me thus far." Laura spoke one careful word at a time, aware that she was talking to someone that held power over her children. "I left my children in the first place because I was told it was the only way for me to get any help, not because I wanted to leave them. I'm back now, and love them more than anything. I'll do whatever I have to do in order for us to get back together. But please, please don't even think about asking me to give one of them away."

When the call was over, Laura curled around herself on the couch and wailed, hurting as if a part of her had died. She pulled her hair, deserving the pain, and bit deeper into her lip as she cried.

Her raw throat produced a harsh, hoarse sound when the keening stopped.

"Mr. Cooper," she said, snapping her fingers. "I've got to get hold of him. He's my attorney, so he can make sure nobody takes David away from us." She grabbed the phone, but realized that his office was closed for the day. "Tomorrow, then. I'm off again tomorrow, so I'll call him first thing. I can walk to his office if necessary. I've got to protect my kids."

Chapter Seventeen

Can They Take My Son Away?

The next morning Laura crawled out of bed long before her alarm went off, unable to stay under the covers any longer.

"I'll call Mr. Cooper the minute his office opens."

She stumbled to the bathroom, soaked a washcloth with cold water, and rinsed her puffy face. "Mmmm, that feels good." The words echoed in the small room, but speaking out loud made her feel less alone. Her swollen, sticky-edged eyes stung when she turned the light on, so she wrung the cloth out and pressed it against her eyelids. She sank down on the lid of the toilet and leaned sideways against the wall, soothed by the cool touch against her skin.

By the time the clock crept to eight, Laura had finished getting ready in the bathroom, eaten breakfast, cleaned the kitchen, fixed her hair, and dressed for a trip to the attorney's office just in case he wanted her to come to see him. Her fingers trembled when she picked up the telephone receiver, so she cleared her throat and straightened her shoulders.

"Cooper and Goodwin, attorneys at law. How can I help you?" The greeting was clipped and efficient.

"Good morning. This is Mrs. Webber, and I need to speak to Mr. Cooper." Laura's heart raced and her fingers gripped the phone hard enough to ache, but her voice sounded normal.

"Mr. Cooper is on another call. I'll let him know you're waiting. May I tell him what this is about?"

"Uhh, I'm calling about a conversation I had with my Children's Bureau caseworker, Mrs. Penneyworth, yesterday afternoon." Laura missed Mrs. Prentice, her California attorney's secretary. Mrs. Prentice was always super busy, but still conveyed warmth in her voice when they talked. This person sounded like a machine.

"Well, that's not much for him to go on." When Laura didn't add any new information, the secretary sighed, then continued. "Hold on and he'll pick up as soon as he's off the other phone."

Laura had rehearsed what to say for hours, but all the preparation disappeared when Mr. Cooper came on the phone.

"Good morning, Mrs. Webber." Mr. Dillard, her attorney in Stockton, had assured her that Mr. Cooper had an excellent reputation, but she wasn't as comfortable with him. "How can I help you?"

"Well, I had my first visit with June yesterday, and called Mrs. Penneyworth when I got home just liked she asked."

"How did the visit go? The supervised visit reports are very important for the case workers."

"Seeing her was wonderful, but it was awful when I had to leave." Laura's voice broke as she remembered June sobbing against her chest. She took a deep breath. "The problem I'm calling about came afterward. Mrs. Penneyworth told me a couple wants to adopt David, and she said it would be a good thing for him. I refused in no uncertain terms, but I'm scared to death that she might try to do it behind my back. Can they take my son away?"

"Whoa, no wonder you're concerned. In some cases, children can be taken away by the court, but the circumstances are pretty rare and they have to have solid reasons. Why don't I review your file and then find out what I can from the Children's Bureau? I'll contact the supervisor and do some research on what's happening, then get back to you."

"Thank you, but please, I'm begging you, we've got to make sure and stop this from going any further."

After Mr. Cooper agreed to get back to her before he hung up the phone, Laura sat with her head in her hands, trying to breathe.

~🦇~

The next two days were torture as Laura yearned for word from the lawyer. She forced herself to focus at work, but alternated between jumping at every sound and drifting in a mind-numbing fog. By Friday afternoon, she couldn't stand it anymore, and used the payphone in the employee area as soon as she clocked out.

"Cooper and Goodwin, attorneys at law. How can I help you?" Still annoying as ever.

"Good afternoon. May I speak to Mr. Cooper? This is Mrs. Webber."

An audible sigh came through the phone. "He's in a meeting. I'll try to have him call you before he leaves for the day, but most likely you won't hear from him until at least Monday."

"Please, miss, I just want to know if he's learned anything about my case since I talked to him on Wednesday."

"I'm sorry, but I can't interrupt him. I will let him know you called."

"But..." The dial tone buzzed in Laura's ear. She started to slam the receiver into its cradle, but couldn't because she wasn't alone in the room. Instead, she put the handset back, grabbed her handbag and coat, then walked out as fast as she could. Just in case Mr. Cooper called before he left for the day, she had to get home so she could answer the phone.

Weekends were always busy at the sanitarium. More guests visited the residents who were allowed to receive them, which made additional work for the housekeeping staff. Rest and a total lack of stress was the recognized treatment for consumptive patients, so visitors were required to stay quiet and calm. Those guests that had progressed far enough in their treatments to be ambulatory for short periods enjoyed sitting in the large common area.

Holiday decorations adorned the walls and windows, warm fires crackled in the two fireplaces that faced each other from opposite ends of the room, and music played in the background on a Victrola monitored by a young nurse. The atmosphere was both festive and soothing, but it was hard for Laura to escape her worry about what her lawyer might have learned.

Sleep Sunday night was elusive, so Laura looked worse than some of the patients on Monday. She took an early lunch and ran to the phone in the isolated timeclock area. As soon as her call to Mr. Cooper's office was answered, she was surprised to be put straight through.

"Good morning, Mrs. Webber. How are you?"

"Fine, I guess," Laura said. "Were you able to find out anything about David?"

"Actually, I did, but I think we need to talk in person. What time do you get off work?"

"I leave at two-thirty." Fear tightened Laura's throat.

Paper flipped in the background. "Could you get here by three-thirty?"

"Yes, that would be fine." Laura felt a sheen of cold sweat forming on her face. "Can you give me an idea of what you learned?"

"That's what we'll discuss this afternoon." Mr. Cooper's voice was neutral, no hints at all. "See you then, Mrs. Webber."

"But should I be worried?"

Laura's words were cut off by the dial tone. This time she slammed the receiver back in place, then rested her face in her hands. She took a deep breath and looked at the clock. Five hours to go. Five hours to find out what was happening. Sounded like forever.

Laura walked into her attorney's office fifteen minutes early, out of breath and anxious. She played with the strap of her pocketbook, running her hands up and down, while staring at the closed door to Mr. Cooper's office. At long last he ushered a couple out, shaking hands with the portly, elderly man, then nodded to Laura. She leaped up from the chair and followed him inside the door, then sat down.

"Well, Mrs. Webber, it's a good thing you mentioned Mrs. Penneyworth's comments to me when you did." Mr. Cooper settled himself behind the desk and opened a file. "The couple she mentioned are serious about wanting to adopt David, and don't want to accept your refusal as the final word."

"But he's my son. How can they just take him away from me?" Laura leaned forward, fists resting on the edge of the desk.

"Hold on, I didn't say it would be easy for them," Mr. Cooper said, holding his palms out toward her. "There are a lot of steps. Please calm down and hold on while I explain what the law requires."

Laura sat back and intertwined her fingers. Her clenched knuckles turned white.

"First of all, the couple has to undergo a thorough investigation about their character, their financial situation, and their standing in the community. The Children's Bureau needs to be satisfied that they'd make stable, loving parents with a suitable home for a child."

Laura started to interrupt, but a stern glance from Mr. Cooper stopped her.

"They shouldn't have any problem qualifying, since they're a stable married couple that has wanted to adopt for some time, and have already completed many of the preliminary steps." Mr. Cooper put the paper down and looked straight into Laura's eyes.

"But the Bureau knows you've been working hard to rebuild your life. As the mother, you do have priority, so as long as you keep doing whatever is asked of you, that makes a big difference."

Laura let out a long breath and relaxed her shoulders. "So I don't need to worry?"

"Well, it isn't quite that simple. You have one major vulnerability—your husband." Mr. Cooper pulled a clipped stack of papers from the open folder on his desk. "I understand that he's incarcerated in the Marshall Rubenston's Asylum for the Criminally Insane in Galeston, Illinois."

Laura nodded. "I don't understand why that matters. I'm a good mother and I can take care of my children."

"But what if he's released? He's your husband, so the Bureau would expect you to take him back into the home. That means the children would be exposed to a violent, mentally unstable man."

"That's not right. If he's released, it would be because the medical and legal staff believe he's not dangerous," Laura said, incensed at the unfairness. "Besides, the doctors said he suffered severe brain damage when he was captured after his escape attempt and will most likely never be able to come home. My children and I love him, and what happened to him was because of the war."

"Mrs. Webber, your husband's original breakdown may have been because of the war, but the Children's Bureau only cares about who he is now, and whether he could pose a danger to the children. That might not be fair, but it's the truth. And given that possibility, they could consider your home potentially unsafe," Mr. Cooper said. He rubbed his cheek with one hand, then continued. "And even if he's never released, your connection to him could be construed as your putting his needs and your relationship to him above the safety of your children."

Laura cocked her head to the side and scrunched her eyebrows. "I don't understand."

"I'm afraid that the only thing that might eliminate the Bureau's reservations about your choices as a mother would be for you to divorce him."

"Divorce him?" Eyes wide, Laura stared at Mr. Cooper, not sure she'd heard him right. "My children love their father. If I divorce him, what does that teach them about the sanctity of marriage? About the importance of family commitment?"

"Those are good questions," he retorted, "but my concern is making sure the Bureau doesn't think your son would be better off placed with a new family. A two-parent, stable family that has never had financial or mental illness problems. A family with solid community ties and a long-term church membership." Mr. Cooper leaned forward, forearms resting on the desk. "I didn't say it would be easy, and I can't guarantee anything either way. But my considered best legal advice to you, if you want to prevent the Bureau from taking steps toward approving an adoption for David, is for you to start the divorce and the termination of your husband's parental rights immediately. I can start the process right away and tell Mrs. Penneyworth's supervisor, but you need to make that decision by tomorrow and let me know."

Chapter Eighteen

I've Missed You So Much

Monday, December 11, 1939

It was a long walk home from Mr. Cooper's office, but Laura couldn't face sharing the bus with people crowding her on either side. She paid no attention to the icy air that burned with every inhale or the small clumps of snow that survived in the shade of fences and trees.

Her focus was on taking one rhythmic step after another, and replaying Mr. Cooper's words in her mind. The awful reality was settling in, but even though a part of her had almost accepted the fact that Glen would never be the same man again, never come home and be the wonderful, loving husband and father they missed so much, she had never imagined the finality of divorce. She didn't even know anyone who'd been divorced.

Mr. Cooper had seemed so sure of himself. He'd painted the people who wanted David as pillars of the community, folks who would be great parents. She clenched her fists in her coat pockets and hissed. "They can adopt a child if they want, but not my David. He belongs with me." By the time Laura's frozen fingers twisted the key to unlock her door, she knew what she had to do because she couldn't risk losing her son. But knowing didn't make it any easier or stop all the questions and pain in her mind.

Laura hung her coat on a rack by the front door, kicked off her shoes and padded to the kitchen. "My hands are so cold, probably nerves more than the weather." She filled the coffeepot and put it on the stove. "One cup won't hurt, and I need it."

She pulled a jar of left-over soup out of the refrigerator and dumped it in a pot to heat for dinner. "Better eat something, too, even if I'm not hungry."

She sat at the kitchen table, rubbed her eyes, and looked at the clock. "Mr. Cooper's office is still open. I might as well call now instead of waiting until tomorrow."

She turned the stove burners down, then moved to the sofa to use the phone. The conversation was short, since she was only able to leave a message for Mr. Cooper. She told the woman on the phone to tell Mr Cooper to start the divorce paperwork, but each word tasted like a bitter betrayal.

Sleep was slow in coming and brought confusing, painful dreams. She saw Glen's face on their wedding day and heard the tremor in his voice when he recited their vows, "for better, for worse, for richer, for poorer, in sickness and in health, to love and to cherish, till death do us part." Like a mantra, the words kept repeating. The scenes behind the words changed, swirling from one picture to another throughout their lives, illustrating different highs and lows of their lives together. The vows come to life.

Laura scoured her kitchen and bathroom the next morning, one ear tuned to the telephone. Did Mr. Cooper get the message? Could he get started today? The loud ring caught her leaning over the edge of the tub, Bon Ami in one hand and sponge in the other. She dropped them both and ran, grabbing the receiver on the third ring. "Hello."

"Mrs. Webber? This is Miss Watkins from Cooper and Goodwin. Mr. Cooper would like you to come in at two this afternoon, if that would be convenient."

"I'll be there," Laura said. "Do you know whether or not he's started on the divorce papers?"

"You'll have to ask him, Mrs. Webber. I'm just confirming the appointment."

Laura started to say something else, but the click of the phone cut her off. "That woman is so rude." She stood and glanced at the clock. "Oops, I'd better finish and get ready. Can't take a chance on being late."

The cold, wet wind tore at Laura when she got off the bus, one block from the lawyer's office. Once inside the door, she stuck the dripping umbrella into an ornate bucket next to the coatrack, then slid out of her coat and hung it up.

"Good afternoon, Mrs. Webber. Thank you for coming out in this weather on such short notice. Mr Cooper will be ready for you shortly."

Unable to concentrate on any of the magazines stacked on the waiting room tables, Laura sat and watched wind-whipped tree limbs thrash outside the office window until Mr Cooper ushered her into his office.

"Thank you for coming, Mrs. Webber." The lawyer settled into his high-backed chair, then selected a folder from the left side of his desk. "I need your signature on these divorce papers so I can file them with the court." He handed the pile to Laura, together with a ballpoint pen. "I'd like you to read them over, then sign where I've marked. Be sure to press hard so your signature will show up on the carbon copy."

"I've never seen divorce papers before," she said, lifting the first sheet. "The format was foreign to her, which made their names look even more out of place. Laura skimmed through the stack, not able to absorb much, except for ugly words that stabbed her heart—abandonment, insanity, violence. Her hands shook as she signed where Mr. Cooper pointed.

"Thank you," he said. "I'll have Miss Watkins prepare the cover letter for the court."

Laura nodded, not knowing what to say.

"I'll prepare a letter for your caseworker at the Bureau, and a copy for her supervisor and the local Bureau Manager." Mr. Cooper tapped his fingers on the desk to pull Laura's attention back. "Mrs. Webber," he said, his voice softer, "I'm also taking issue with your not being able to see your children on a regular basis. Even though they are not in your care right now, you are still a family. Your children need you and they need each other. I'm asking that you start having regular, biweekly visits with them. I also think that all of you need to have a day together since Christmas is right around the corner."

Laura's hands flew to her face as tears leaked from her eyes. "Oh my God, is that possible? I miss them so much."

"Of course it's possible. I can't guarantee anything, but I'll do my best."

Mr. Cooper's best worked very well. Tuesday, December 19th found Laura cleaning her apartment top to bottom in preparation for the children's visit the next day. She'd stocked the refrigerator and cabinets with their favorite foods and put up a tiny Christmas tree on top of a table in the corner of the living room. Underneath the tree there were several small, brightly wrapped gifts for each child.

The plan was for the children to be dropped off by Mrs. Penneyworth at ten in the morning and stay until four in the afternoon. And the best part would be no observers standing around watching them.

The next morning, Laura looked out the front window every few minutes from nine o'clock on, just in case Mrs. Penneyworth arrived early. When a cream-colored Ford sedan parked in front of her building, Laura couldn't move. She was transfixed by the sight of her children as they got out of the car and jumped down from the wide running-board.

"Oh my goodness, they're really here." She watched, frozen in place, as they stared at Mrs. Penneyworth, who seemed to be giving them instructions of some sort. When they started walking toward the apartment, Laura bolted to the door.

"Good morning, Mrs. Webber," Mrs. Penneyworth stood in front of the children when Laura opened the door. "I'll be back to collect the children at four. I hope you all have a lovely time." She turned to the side, then stared at each child in turn as she ushered them inside the door.

"Thank you, Mrs. Penneyworth," Laura's voice sounded strained as she spoke to the retreating woman's back.

When the door closed behind them, the children stayed in a tight group as they stepped further into the living room. David never let go of Jimmy's hand, and kept his little body pressed against his brother. Raymond's hands were tucked into his coat pockets, but he moved away from his brothers, glancing all around the room. June turned in a slow circle, taking everything in, then faced her mother.

Laura ached to grab her kids and wrap her arms around them. Their tense bodies and skittish expressions held her back.

"It's nice, Mama, real nice. Warm, too, with the fireplace." June removed her coat and carried it to the coatrack. "That's a pretty Christmas tree. I wish we had one in the dorm."

"That tree is for you kids. I put it up yesterday." Laura stepped over to the tree and touched the popcorn strings and colored paper shapes pinned to the branches. "It still needs tinsel if you guys would like to put it on."

The boys gathered closer to the tree. David let go of Jimmy's hand. He looked at the tree, then focused his eyes on Laura's face. He tilted his head, then reached out to touch her skirt. "Mama?"

"Yes, honey, it's me, your mama."

David's arms shot up in the air, fingers extended. "Mama! Mama!"

Laura swept him up and squeezed him tight against her chest, tears streaming down her face. "Yes, sweetheart, it's Mama. I've missed you so much."

Like a dam bursting, the pent-up emotions were released and all the children grabbed hold of Laura. She dropped onto the sofa with David still in her arms, and the other three nestled against her as close as they could. Eyes and noses both started running.

"You promised you'd be home in a couple of weeks. Where were you?"

"I hate all the mean people. I want to stay with you now."

"It's not fair that I'm all alone. At least the boys are together.

David kept his face tight against Laura's throat, one hand fisted around a handful of her hair.

"I'm so sorry, kids, but we're here together now." She leaned down and kissed the top of David's head. "Jimmy, don't you dare wipe your nose on my skirt."

When Jimmy lifted his sleeve to his face, Laura scooted out from under David and led the way to the bathroom. "Come on, we all need to wash our faces and blow our noses."

"It's pretty in here." June stroked a rose-colored towel that hung on a wall rack. "Everything looks bright and clean, much better than the old apartment."

"Thanks, Junebug."

"I wish we had a bathtub. The Stinnett's bathroom has a tub, but we're not allowed in there. We have to use a washroom at the back of the house, and it only has a dinky old shower.

The water never gets warm enough, and the towels smell sour," Raymond sat on the edge of the tub and spoke under his breath, glancing at Jimmy. "I'd love to take a real hot bath and duck my hair under to get warm all over."

"Yeah, me too. Seems like we're always cold," Jimmy said. Then his eyes opened wide as he stared back at Raymond. "But we'll get in trouble for talking about the Stinnetts."

June looked at Laura, then back at her brothers. "I know what Mrs. Penneyworth said, but you know Mama won't tell on us. So we won't get in trouble no matter what we say."

"Let's go sit down and talk. I think I need to know what Mrs. Penneyworth said to you guys." Laura led the way back to the living room. "And don't worry. I promise I won't tell her what you say." She glanced back at the bathroom once they were all settled back on the sofa. "And if any of you want to take a hot bath while you're here, it will be our secret."

Raymond and Jimmy cheered, then both looked at David. Their shoulders drooped and their smiles disappeared. "Thanks," Raymond said, "but I'll bet Mrs. Stinnett will ask David what we did today, and he'll tell her everything because he's still a baby."

"Am not." David pushed his fists against Raymond's chest. "I not a baby."

"It's okay." Jimmy patted David's back. "We know." Then he turned to Laura. "Raymond's right though. We have to be careful. David repeats everything he hears."

"You two are pretty smart, but it sounds like I need to know what your instructions were just in case." Laura looked around the room. "I know, why don't you kids open your gifts. Then June and I can have some girl-talk while you boys play for a little while."

That suggestion worked perfectly. The older boys each unwrapped wooden flutes and bags of marbles, while David opened nesting blocks and a toy truck. They started playing together, while June brought her new hair ribbons and a tiny musical treasure box over to the table in front of Laura.

"Thanks, Mama, these are really pretty."

"I'm glad you like them, honey." Laura hugged June's shoulders, then whispered. "Now, since David is occupied and can't hear us, I need you to tell me what Mrs. Penneyworth told you guys."

"I don't like her, Mama," June muttered. "We're all supposed to pay attention to what you say and do, and be ready to give her a full report after she picks us up. She wants to know if you yell or hit any of us. Also, if you ask us to do anything that we shouldn't, like to disobey the people we're living with." June crossed her arms and stuck out her lower lip. "I don't like tattletales, and I'm not going to be a spy against my own mother." June sighed and looked down at her hands. "But if I don't tell her all about our visit, she might think I'm hiding something and get mad at both of us. You're not supposed to ask about where we're living or what the people are like either—but if you do, we're not supposed to say anything bad. Even if they're not very nice, like the people the boys live with, we can't tell you we don't like them."

Laura didn't answer June right away. She mulled over what she'd heard, then said. "Junebug, I don't want you to stress over what Mrs. Penneyworth said another minute. You musn't risk getting yourself in trouble, or let that happen with the boys. Today we'll just enjoy every single minute we have together, but by our next visit, I'll figure out a way." She stroked June's hair and patted her back. Her daughter didn't need any additional burdens to carry.

Chapter Nineteen

Bubble Bath Might Be The Answer

Wednesday, December 20, 1939

Laura waved at Mrs. Penneyworth's car as it disappeared down the street, then dropped both her hands and the pasted-on smile.

"I can't stand that woman," she whispered under her breath. "But there's no way I'll say or do anything that might make it harder on the kids. I'd eat dirt if I had to in order to see them more often." She hurried inside and stood in front of the fireplace, warming her hands.

The apartment seemed so quiet and empty with the children gone, especially with the boys' unwrapped presents sitting underneath the tree.

"It's a crying shame that the boys had to leave their toys behind, but at least they'll have them when they come next time."

Laura walked to the little tree and stroked the clumpy, uneven strands of tinsel. It looked pretty sad, but David had been so proud of his job spreading it. He'd wanted to take his blocks and truck when they left, but Jimmy and Raymond told him they were leaving their presents because Mrs. Stinnett would find some reason to take the toys away. His little face was so sad, brightening only when Laura promised him the presents would be waiting for his next visit.

Laura hoped Mrs. Penneyworth didn't give the kids too much of a bad time. One last pat on David's truck, then she turned on the radio and headed to the kitchen to wash the lunch dishes. She hadn't asked the kids a single question about where they were living or what the people were like. But by remaining quiet and listening to the boys' talk while they played, Laura had learned a lot about the Stinnetts.

She learned that they'd taken in foster kids since the program first began. Sometimes the boys had overheard them laughing with their friends about getting paid to house kids as free labor on their ranch. The boys slept and ate in a drafty enclosed porch at the back of the house, with only a woodstove to keep them warm in the winter. There was a bathroom next to the porch with a toilet, sink, and shower for the boys to use, but they weren't allowed in the main family house.

The porch and bathroom had housed ranch laborers prior to the foster kid program. A school bus carried them to and from school each day, but they had chores before and after school. Any reading or homework had to be done at bedtime, before the lights were turned off.

Poor little David had the worst of it. Whenever Jimmy and Raymond were at school, David was locked in the porch room alone. He was only allowed to go outside with his brothers when they were sent to the fields or barn, where they were expected to care for him and keep him safe while they worked. Laura hated hearing that harsh physical punishments were frequent for talking back, shirking chores, crying, or any other reason.

The boys' casual remarks about the Stinnetts' cruel behavior sickened Laura, but she knew from her attorney that complaints about them would fall on deaf ears—or worse, earn bad reports for her. The Stinnetts were related to the mayor's wife, and nobody dared to mess with them.

"At least June is in a good, safe place." Laura draped the wrung-out dishcloth over the faucet, leaving the clean dishes in the drainer. "Boy, if I keep talking out loud to myself, somebody's going to think I'm nuts." She plopped down on a kitchen chair and rested her chin on her hands. "Poor June misses her brothers, and seemed jealous about how David clung to Jimmy. The school seems to agree with her, though, at least the learning part." Laura smiled, glad that her rambunctious daughter's spirit hadn't been crushed. "I'll bet anything she and her best friend, June Meyers, are getting up to lots of mischief in their free time."

Christmas passed, and New Year's Day. Laura worked both holidays after volunteering to cover for a staff member who wanted time off with his family. She didn't see her children during those weeks, but was notified by Mr. Cooper that the divorce papers had been delivered to the hospital where Glen was incarcerated. The Administrative staff would be reviewing and signing the papers on his behalf, since his mental condition rendered him unable to act on his own.

Laura wanted to keep the little Christmas tree until the kids could see it at least once again, but when the needles dried and started falling off, she had to take it down. She left the toys on the table, though, so they would know where to find them.

The next family visitation didn't take place until the Saturday after Valentine's Day. Laura was seething when Mrs. Penneyworth held the children outside the car for what looked like a lecture prior to escorting them to the door. Once the kids were inside, everyone watched Mrs. Penneyworth until she drove away, then sighed in relief.

June hung her coat and muffler on the rack by the door and placed her galoshes underneath. She helped David take off his coat and boots, then handed them to Laura to put away. David's face and hands were ice cold, and his lips looked chapped and sore. Raymond and Jimmy finished at about the same time, hugged Laura, and then ran to the table with the Christmas toys. June opened a shoulder bag and dumped the contents—a pile of coloring books and four boxes of crayons—on the kitchen table.

"Look what I brought for us to do," June said. She noticed Laura's raised eyebrows and added, "I earn a little money babysitting for Mrs. Duncan, the head librarian, and thought these would be fun for all of us."

"Cool." Raymond and Jimmy plopped into chairs and grabbed books and crayons.

David was a little slower, but soon was staring wide-eyed at the drawings in his book. June helped him open his crayons and showed him what to do.

Laura sat with them, delighted to see their smiles, and the joy June took in being with her brothers. June's hair was longer, past her shoulders, but looked freshly washed and shiny. Her clothes were also clean, as were her hands and fingernails. It was obvious that her school had high standards.

Laura was not happy to see the condition of the boys. Raymond's pants and shirt were much too short, leaving his ankles and wrists exposed to the elements. His shirt pocket was torn, with one side hanging down in a wrinkled triangle. Jimmy and David's clothes were the opposite, with rolled-up cuffs on both pants and shirt sleeves. Jimmy's shirt was missing a button, and David's pants were bunched up between the belt-loops. All three boys smelled sour, a combination of unwashed bodies and hair, bad breath from cruddy teeth, combined with dirty clothes stiff with old sweat.

Soon the children were engrossed, choosing each color with care, teasing and laughing at the funny combinations they chose, leaving Laura to figure out a way to help her boys without creating problems with the Stinnetts. She'd love to wash and mend their clothes, but there wasn't enough time for them to dry.

Bubble bath—that might be an answer. "Hey boys, how would you guys like to take a nice, warm bubble bath? I bought some that smells kind of like trees in the woods and it foams up like crazy. You could wash you hair and swim in the tub with the bubbles."

"How could we swim? The three of us would fill your tub up," Raymond said. "Sure sounds nice, though."

"You don't have to share the bath. You can take turns. By the time you're all done, June and I could have lunch ready. How does salad, spaghetti, and garlic bread sound?"

The idea was a huge hit. Laura poured the bubble bath in and ran the water for Raymond, who was getting the first bath.

"Toss your clothes outside the door so you don't splash them with water," Laura said, thinking bubble bath splashes could only help the grimy garments, but Raymond couldn't put wet things back on. Besides, she wanted a closer look at the clothes while he was in the tub. "Here's a washcloth to scrub with, and a towel for when you're done. You can wrap up in the towel, grab your clothes and get dressed in the bedroom. But don't forget your hair."

"I won't, Mama." Raymond grinned.

Laura was appalled at the appearance of Raymond's teeth. They were coated with what looked like a thick, gluey yellowish substance. With a shudder, concealed by a smile, she opened the medicine cabinet and pulled out her toothbrush and a tube of Ipana toothpaste. "I want you to brush your teeth, too. How often are you guys brushing at the Stinnetts?"

Raymond glanced down. "Uh, we've been out of toothpaste for a while. We're supposed to use our finger and some baking soda." He grimaced and looked at Laura. "That stuff tastes awful."

"Okay. Brush real good when you get out of the tub while the water's draining out. You'll all have to share the brush, so rinse it real good when you're done. I'll send this brush and paste back with you. Maybe put it in your coat pocket so you won't forget it."

Laura left the room fuming. How in the world could those people get away with not even taking care of her boys' most basic hygiene needs?

Monday she'd have to get hold of Mr. Cooper and see what could be done. She'd also have to purchase a supply of new toothbrushes and toothpaste for the children and herself. Raymond was right. Baking soda and water on a finger didn't do much good and tasted awful, but would have to do until she could get to the store Monday after work.

Laura left a message for the lawyer on Monday, but didn't hear from him until Tuesday afternoon. "I don't understand," she told him, twirling the phone cord in her fingers as she paced her living room. "Everything I do is under the microscope, but my children come here filthy, in clothes that don't fit, and don't even have toothbrushes or toothpaste. How is that okay? Why can't the Children's Bureau do something about the way the Stinnetts treat them?"

"You can complain, and it's certainly your right. But they could also decide you're just a trouble-making parent. Would you prefer that they remove the boys from the Stinnetts and place them in three different homes? If that happens, you can forget about the kids seeing each other because making visitation schedules with multiple families would be too difficult. If you remember, it took weeks—and you rearranging your work schedule in order to have one Saturday a month off—before it was possible for the whole family to be together at all. You might win against the Stinnetts, but end up losing with the children."

Laura dropped to the sofa. "What can I do? It's not fair for them to live like this." She paused a minute and rubbed her forehead with the fingers of her left hand, while pressing the phone to the right side of her face. "If I buy them clothes and personal supplies, can the Stinnetts take them away?"

"I can't imagine they'd care. They're paid to provide for the children. If you purchase things for the kids and give them the stuff during visitations, that just means more money they can keep for themselves." Laura could hear him shuffling papers on the desk. "Be sure to show Mrs. Penneyworth what you've given them each time, so she is aware of the items being sent to the Stinnetts. That keeps the Bureau in the loop, and you safe from claims that you're trying to have the children smuggle things into the foster home."

Chapter Twenty

Attack On Pearl Harbor

Nine months later,
Saturday, December 20, 1941

It was after two in the afternoon. Laura and the children were scattered around the living room, stomachs full of their shared holiday meal, warmed by the crackling fire in the small fireplace. The wind roared around the building, while stinging rain clawed against the windows and raked the shivering, naked tree branches outside.

"Mama, everybody at school has been talking about the Japs attacking Pearl Harbor and saying that we're at war now. Will they come here?" June's voice was soft, but there was fear in the question.

Laura and June sat together on the sofa, watching the three boys play with cars and trucks on the floor in front of the hearth.

"June, please don't ever use that word. You know I don't like mean nicknames for groups of people," Laura said, remembering the cruel taunts of "half-breed" that had been hurled at her as a child. "The attack on Pearl Harbor was horrible, killing over two thousand people. And yes, as a result, America has declared war on Japan, as well as Germany and her allies. Nobody knows what will happen now, but I think we're safe here."

"But are you sure? We've been talking about the Civil War in History class, and it was terrible." At thirteen, June had become very serious about her studies.

"Papa fought in a war, didn't he?" Raymond chimed in. He sat up and focused his attention on his mom.

Jimmy looked up, eyes wide, toys forgotten. "Will they make Papa go again?"

"Your papa did fight in the last war, Jimmy, but no, he won't go again."

"Of course not. Crazy people can't be soldiers, and that's why Papa's locked up in the nut hospital." Raymond's answer was quick and full of scorn.

Jimmy doubled his fists and scowled. "Stop calling him crazy. He's in a hospital 'cause he's sick."

"Yeah, sick in the head," Raymond muttered.

It hurt to hear Raymond's judgmental comments. It was hard to guide him when he was under the influence of the Stinnetts for all but one day a month.

Laura sighed, but didn't respond. In some ways, she barely recognized her oldest son. At eleven he was rangier than ever, long arms and legs, with stringy muscles wrapping around a skinny torso. He was still protective of his brothers, but less tolerant of ideas or opinions that differed from his.

"Will we have to go fight?" Jimmy said, with a side-ways glance at Raymond.

"No, honey, you're too young to join the Army," she said. "You just turned ten and you have to be eighteen to go. This war will be over long before then." Laura's thoughts turned to her nephews, Elliot and Aaron, as well as Ruben, Isaac and Willa's son. They were all old enough to join or even be drafted. Please, dear God, don't let anything happen to them, she prayed, knowing that every mother on both sides of the war was uttering the exact same prayer.

The alarm clock, which had been moved to the kitchen counter when the children arrived, startled everyone with its loud ring. June jumped up and turned it off. "Guess we have to pack everything up."

"I want to play some more," David said.

"Quit whining." Raymond nudged David with his foot. "You're four years old, so stop acting like a spoiled baby."

"You can have five more minutes, David, then you have to start sorting your stuff and getting it ready to go," Laura said. "And Raymond, don't boss your brother. I'm the mother here, so I make the rules and decisions." She ignored both David's grin and Raymond's dirty look.

The kids were used to the routine. Both June and the boys decided what things they'd like to keep at Laura's apartment for next time and stored them in the bedroom. Each child had claimed a drawer in the long bureau beneath the window.

The boys left all their toys and books, since they'd learned the hard way that the Stinnetts viewed confiscating gifts from Laura as great punishments and never gave them back to the children. They packed clean clothes, some new from the thrift store Laura frequented, into sacks to take back to the Stinnetts. They also included bars of soap, toothpaste, new toothbrushes, and a comb and hairbrush, since they were allowed to keep those items.

Leave-taking had become routine. The kids watched through the front window for Mrs. Penneyworth's car to arrive, then hugged and kissed their mom before heading outside. Mrs. Penneyworth didn't even get out of the car anymore, just waited for the children to settle into their seats before pulling away. Laura always waved until the car was out of sight, missing her brood with intense, visceral pain from the moment they disappeared from view.

"They're growing up without me," she whispered, leaning against the front door, all alone again. "The divorce was final two months ago, and I've done every single thing the Children's Bureau staff has asked of me. But nothing is moving forward as far as getting my children back. And now with the war? Nobody seems to be paying attention to anything but that. I wonder if I'll ever have my children with me again?"

At work the next day, Laura learned that two young interns had left to enlist in the Army. The staff tried to remain upbeat and keep from sharing war news around the patients, but newspapers, magazines, and radio shows all seemed to feature stories about Pearl Harbor and the burgeoning war effort. All of which were deemed unhealthy and unsuitable for the patients, since stress was so harmful for their recovery.

Soon the war news permeated not only the hospital, but most phases of everyday life. Patriotic fervor infected men throughout the country, and many left their families, their careers, and their classes behind to fight for their country.

Chapter Twenty-One

Happy Birthday

Five months later,
Saturday, May 16, 1942

Laura stepped back from the kitchen table and gazed at the thick chocolate icing that covered the three-layer birthday cake. The green letters on top spelled out "Happy Birthday, June and David" with fourteen pink candles edging the top curve and four blue ones on the bottom curve. "That looks pretty good, if I do say so myself." Satisfied with how it had turned out, she carried the cake into her bedroom and placed it on the dresser. "Don't want them to see it until after lunch."

Laura turned on the radio, then checked the fragrant roast that was resting in the oven.

"Hi Mama," June said, bursting through the door. "Uummm, that smells so good." She joined Laura at the stove, but had her hand pushed aside when she started to open the oven door.

"Yes, it does, but I want it to stay warm until we're ready for it." Laura hugged June hard, inhaling the sweet, vanilla scent of her shampoo. "So, tell me what's going on at school."

The words bubbled out, almost faster than Laura could keep up with them. June prattled on about her classes, what her teachers had said, what she and her friends had been doing in their free time. "Wait a minute, Mama, where are the boys? It's almost eleven o'clock?"

Laura pursed her lips. "I'll bet they missed the first bus again." She made her way across the front room and peered out the window. "Now that they have to use a voucher for the bus, if the Stinnetts don't let them leave on time or if they dawdle on the walk to the bus station, they'll be late."

"Shoot," June said. "That means they'll be tired and crabby, too. It's not fair."

"I agree, but with gas rationing it's hard on everybody, since the Bureau issued bus vouchers rather than reimburse workers to chauffeur kids like you guys to and from visitations. And they don't care how far the kids have to walk."

June huffed, then spotted the boys turning around the corner and jumped up. "They're almost here," she said, opening the door.

Laura greeted the boys with a hug, but only Jimmy smiled back at her. David's eyes shone with unshed tears, and Raymond's face was sullen and unresponsive when she pulled him in close.

"Sorry we're late, Mama," Jimmy said, "but David couldn't walk very fast today."

Raymond stared at David and muttered, "Spoiled baby," under his breath. "If you couldn't walk by yourself, you should have stayed at the ranch."

Laura shot Raymond a warning glance, then knelt. "What's wrong, David?"

"He fell down yesterday," Jimmy said. "He's been complaining that his ankle hurts. Raymond said we should just leave him behind because he's too big to carry."

"Let's go take a look." Laura led David into the bathroom. "Pull your britches off, then sit on the edge of the tub." Laura tossed David's filthy pants toward the hamper. "Now take off your shoes and socks so I can check out the ankle."

Laura held her temper, but it wasn't easy. David's right knee and calf were covered with scratches and the ankle was swollen. Both his legs were grimy, and the bottom of his feet were almost black with ground-in dirt. It wasn't easy to check for bruises or to see if the scratches were infected, since the skin was so dirty. "Guess what, kiddo, you get the first bath today. Let's see if soaking in nice hot soapy water helps your legs feel better. And when you're done, I'll wrap that ankle."

Once David was settled in the tub with a washcloth and fresh towel on the rack near him, Laura rejoined the other children. June and Jimmy had dumped a jigsaw puzzle out on the coffee table and were searching for the edge pieces. Raymond watched them, still frowning, with his arms crossed around his torso.

Laura sat next to her oldest son. "David's ankle is swollen, and there are some nasty scratches on his leg. No wonder it was hard for him to walk." She waited in vain for Raymond to respond. "I'll wrap the ankle nice and snug to make it easier."

"Better or not, he has to walk by himself. We can't carry him all the way from the bus to the ranch. Everybody has to carry their own weight." Raymond's voice was soft, but still adamant.

"Honey, when someone is hurt, we have to help them. You were always such a great big brother. I can't imagine you not helping him now when he needs you."

Raymond just hunched his head lower, without another word.

Laura's shoulders drooped as she stood and headed for the kitchen to set the table. They wouldn't eat until the boys were clean and dressed in fresh clothes, but only David tended to dawdle and play in the tub. Once he was done, the others wouldn't take a lot of time.

"I'm done, Mama," a towel-wrapped David, legs still wet and dripping, called out from the hallway door. "I pulled the plug to let the dirty water out."

"I'm next." Raymond stood and marched toward David with Laura. "You fix him, Mama. I'll clean the tub before I fill it." His voice was softer, without any growl to it.

Laura nodded and thanked him, understanding that the words were his apology.

∼⸙∼

Laura removed what was left of the poor, ravaged roast from the middle of the table, then headed for her bedroom. The kids paid her no attention as they sat, glassy-eyed and content, on their chairs, pushing the last bits of food and gravy around on their plates.

"Happy Early Birthday to you, Happy Early Birthday to you, Happy Early Birthday dear David and June," Laura sang her way to the table, holding the cake with burning candles on top. "Happy Early Birthday to you."

David clapped and bounced in his chair, while June grinned from ear to ear. Raymond and Jimmy, who moments ago had proclaimed themselves too stuffed to eat another bite, started clamoring for big pieces with lots of frosting. June and David blew the candles out, then Laura dished out generous pieces all around. While the children attacked their sweet treat, she brought out the birthday presents.

David opened his two first, ripping the paper away and pulling almost new boots out of their box. "Thanks, Mama, these are really nice," he said. Then his eyes widened and his voice fell. "But I guess they'd better stay here. They'll get all messed up if I wear them at the ranch."

"Honey, those are work-boots. They're designed to protect your feet while handling all kinds of dirty jobs. The high tops should help support your ankles too. Now open the other package." Laura watched his smile reappear, hating that she couldn't do more for him.

The second present was a collection of colorful workbooks with games and puzzles. David wasted no time in collecting crayons from the bedroom and stretching out on the floor.

A soft gasp pulled Laura's attention to her daughter, whose first gift was open at last.

"Oh, Mama, thank you." June stroked the pink and green fabric cover on a small book. The pages were gilt-edged, and a slender band with a key lock stretched around the middle. June opened the front cover and caressed the first page. "Look, the first page has a place for my name and the date." Next came a small section for addresses and notes, then blank pages just waiting for her thoughts. "I've always wanted one of these."

Laura grinned and said, "Your very first journal. Perfect for your age. If you keep it up, you'll treasure it in years to come." She pointed to the second package. "Now open that one."

June didn't take nearly as long this time, pulling the paper and ribbon off almost as fast as David had. "So pretty," she said, then jumped up to hug Laura. "And the flowers on the stationery set match the colors on my journal."

"I'm glad you like them, Junebug. There's a supply of stamps too, so you can start sending letters." Laura cleared her throat and pointed to the journal. "I wrote down Helga's address. I know she'd love to hear from you."

Way too soon, the alarm clock went off, the signal for the children to get ready and head for the bus stop. Laura opened the door for them, wondering if she should say something about David needing help on the long walk from the bus to the ranch.

"Hey David," Raymond said, "since we're celebrating your birthday early, Jimmy and I are taking turns giving you piggyback rides today so you don't mess up the new boots."

David cheered, and Jimmy's eyes widened as he looked at his big brother. Laura hugged them all goodbye and kissed Raymond's cheek. Her vision blurred and she blinked away tears while she watched them walk away—David bouncing on Raymond's back, with June and Jimmy close on either side.

Chapter Twenty-Two

Open Up, Police

Thursday, May 21, 1942

Laura ran the iron up the length of her work skirt, sliding the tip almost to the waistband. "Lordy, it would sure be nice if someday, some smart inventor could figure out a way for clothes to not need ironing."

She turned the iron off and set it on its heel to cool, then pulled the skirt off the ironing board. She put it on a wire hanger and hung it over a kitchen cabinet knob next to a freshly pressed blouse. "Wish I could afford one of those new irons that use steam."

Just as she started to collapse the ironing board, someone banged on the front door. "Open up, police."

Heart racing in panic, Laura ran to the door and opened it. Two men in uniform stood on the tiny porch.

"What's going on?"

"Are you Mrs. Webber?" The officer, short and round, held a sheaf of papers attached to a clipboard. He stepped over the threshold when Laura nodded. "I'm Officer Nelson and this is my partner, Officer Stinson. Is your son Raymond here?"

"Raymond? No, of course not. What's happened?"

Officer Stinson, tall and thin with grey hair and mustache, tried to follow the other policeman into the room. "We need to look around and make sure he's not here."

"Wait a minute." Laura stood in the opening of the door, blocking their way. "Please tell me what's going on."

Officer Nelson sighed, then waved the paperwork at her. "Your son assaulted Mr. Stinnett, then ran away. He needs to come with us back to the station, so if he's here, tell us now. And if you know where he is, you'd better come clean or you'll be in a heap of trouble too."

Laura moved away, then dropped on the couch, unable to stand, like a puppet whose strings were cut. Her body felt limp with shock and disbelief.

"Oh my god, poor Raymond."

She took a deep breath, then all at once felt strength and determination surge throughout her body. She stood and faced Officer Nelson with her arms crossed, while watching Officer

Stinson look into the bedrooms and bathroom, opening the closets and cabinets.

Shaking her head, she said, "I do not believe that he assaulted Mr. Stinnett, certainly not without some major provocation. I cannot imagine Raymond doing something like that unless he was trying to protect his younger brothers."

"Believe what you want," Officer Nelson said. "We're here to find him, so if he's here, save yourself a lot of trouble and call him out."

"I haven't seen him since Saturday, the sixteenth. And no, I haven't heard from him, either."

Officer Nelson leaned into Laura's face and shook his finger at her. "Well, Mrs Webber, I hope you're telling us the truth. Because if you're lying and covering up for your boy, you'll be joining him at the station."

Laura uncrossed her arms and planted her fists on her hips. "I'm not a liar. Your partner has checked all the rooms, so you know he's not here. Is there anything else?"

Officer Stinson double-checked the broom closet, pantry, and the cabinet under the kitchen sink. "He's not here. But if we hear that you helped him get away, trust me, you'll regret it."

Laura followed the men to the door and locked it behind them. She heard them poking around the shrubs next to the building before they gave up and returned to their squad car.

When the sound of their car engine faded away, her entire body started shaking with anger and fear. Raymond had run away before, but had always managed to let her know so she wouldn't worry. Double-checking the lock, she ran into the children's bedroom and sat on the end of the bed. She wanted, no, she needed, to feel close to Raymond.

Laura closed her eyes and opened her mind, searching for a sense of her son, but didn't feel anything except her own anxiety. She stood, then dropped to the floor in front of the dresser where his things were stored, and opened his drawer. Nothing—but how could that be? She pulled it all the way out, but only found a pair of holey wool socks. She whirled around and opened the armoire, but all of Raymond's things were gone.

Oh my goodness, he had been here. He had to have come while Laura was working, but how did he get in? And what had he taken with him?

She sat back down on the bed, closed her eyes, and visualized all the items Raymond had accumulated in the room. A canvas duffel bag for carrying clothes back and forth from the Stinnett's place, a pair of second-hand, but almost new sneakers that Raymond loved to wear, a full set of clothes he'd worn on his last visit from the Stinnetts that Laura had washed, mended, and pressed, plus two full sets of clean clothes she'd bought him from the thrift shop. She jumped up and ran into the bathroom. Sure enough, Raymond's toothbrush was missing, along with a towel and washcloth, a bar of soap, a partial tube of toothpaste and a comb. Laura sat on the edge of the tub, sick with the knowledge that Raymond had packed everything he had.

"But where are you going?" Laura whispered. "You managed to break in, probably through a window, but I can't believe you left without a word." Sure she was right, Laura stood and started moving around the apartment, trying to figure out where Raymond might have left her a note. Then it hit her.

She ran back into the bedroom and opened the armoire. On the shelf above the hanging bar was a collection of board games and puzzles. She grabbed the box for Sorry! and pulled it down. She opened it, pulled the folded game board out, dumped out the cards and playing pieces, then lifted out the cardboard insert—and there it was, a folded piece of paper with the word "Mama" in Raymond's handwriting. Breathing hard, Laura opened the page and read.

Mama,
    Please don't be mad at me. I had to leave because old man Stinnett made David cry, then yelled at Jimmy for not

punching David to make him stop. It was awful. I jumped in front of them and told Stinnett to hit me if he wanted to, but to leave them alone. He got real mad, then hit me hard on the side of my head. I couldn't take anymore. I swung as hard as I could into his gut, then on his chin when he doubled over.

He screamed at me to get out, that he'd have the law on me and send me to jail. I think the boys will be safer with me gone. He really wanted to get my goat by messing with them.

Don't worry about me. I have some friends that are a lot older than me, that have traveled around hopping trains. They're good guys, and offered to take me with them to California. There's lots of work there, and I'm not afraid of hard work. I'll tell them I'm older, but my friends said nobody would care. When I get settled in one place, I'll send a letter so you won't worry.

I hope you won't be mad, but I took $60 out of the jar in the kitchen. I know it's stealing, but I need to have some money for food and to pay my way until I find a job. I promise I'll send it back to you as soon as I can.

I love you, Mama, and I'll try to make you proud of me.

Raymond

Laura read the letter again. "Oh, my baby boy, I'm always proud of you." She stroked the words on the page, then held it against her chest. "And I'm not mad. You could have taken all the jar money if it would keep you safe." She read the words one more time, then folded the paper. She pressed it to her lips, whispered "Stay safe, sweetheart," and hid it in the Sorry! game box where she'd found it.

Laura smoothed the bedspread and fluffed the pillows, then left the bedroom and closed the door. She curled up in the chair closest to the fireplace with her feet tucked under her and stared at the dancing flames. She relaxed her body from head to toe, closed her eyes, and laid her head back against the top of the chair. The sensation of heat warming her face and neck, and the arrhythmic crackling sound of the fire devouring the fresh logs enveloped her, pushing all thoughts away.

The faint sounds of youthful male voices slipped into her mind. She didn't have the energy to open her eyes, but within her mind saw flames flickering within a circle of rocks. Three pairs of young, strong-looking hands took turns adding twigs and small pieces of wood to the fire.

"You've gotta nurse a fire real slow out here, 'cause you don't want it to spread too much or for nosy people to see it." The young man's face, adorned with patchy bits of hair that might turn into a beard in the future, was lit by the flames. His hair needed a trim, but the smile looked sincere.

"I know. When I was pretty little, my papa used to make fires for cooking and to keep us warm when we were traveling from place to place." Raymond's voice was strong and confident.

Laura could see his face as he watched his friends build the fire. She wanted to reach out and touch him, but knew visions didn't work that way. She watched the boys dump a can of stew into a cast-iron skillet, stir and cook until the fragrant juices bubbled, then dish it out into four tin bowls. It was clear that Raymond's friends knew what they were doing and seemed to enjoy teaching him the ropes of living outside.

Laura woke up in the chair, legs asleep from their awkward position. The room was chilly and dark since the fire had gone out, but her heart felt light. She knew Raymond was warm and safe with his friends, and that he would be okay. She headed for bed, saying a prayer on the way for Jimmy and David to hold fast to one another.

Chapter Twenty-Three

Hug Everybody

Friday, May 22, 1942

After she got off work the next day, Laura left a
message for her attorney about the police
showing up and searching for Raymond. She
didn't tell him anything about the note she'd
found or about her reassuring vision, but
wanted him to know the story from her, rather
than through the Children's Bureau. Her biggest
concern was that the Stinnetts might take things
out on Jimmy and David, or try to mess up their
visitation schedule.

As the weeks and months went by, neither
Mrs. Penneyworth or her successor, Miss
Quincy, ever said anything about Raymond.
Laura figured that Mr. Stinnett might have been
embarrassed to admit he was bested by a boy,
and dropped his complaint after the officers
came up empty-handed when they searched for
Raymond. Or, Stinnett might have been afraid

that Jimmy or David would say something that wouldn't sound good for him, and stayed quiet after Raymond left.

❧

Why in the heck had she thought washing the windows was a good idea? It was already hot and sticky, and the sun was still low on the horizon. Laura wiped her damp forearm across her dripping face, then rubbed the wet windowpane with a fresh piece of newspaper, turning the paper and scrubbing until it squeaked against the clean glass.

"Good morning, Mrs. Webber, that's quite a job for an August morning." The mailman was almost right behind her, on the sidewalk, heading for the mailbox mounted against the porch column.

Laura jumped, threw her hands in the air, and dropped the paper. "Oh my goodness, you startled me."

"I'm sorry," the carrier said, handing her a small stack of envelopes and flyers. "You might want to be a little careful with one of these. The person didn't put a return address on the envelope, not even a name, so you don't know if it's legitimate or some kind of spy." He pulled one battered-looking envelope out of the stack and placed it on top. "You never know these days, what with war all around us."

Laura wiped her sweaty hands on her wrinkled skirt, then took the mail from him. Her heart stopped, then sped up at the sight of Raymond's handwriting on the paper. "You're right for sure, I'd better check this out right away." She nodded and smiled at the mailman, then hurried inside to open the envelope.

Hi Mama,

I'm sorry that it took so long for me to write, but things have been pretty crazy. Everybody is asleep now, but there is enough light from the moon to write before I go to bed. My friends—Ted, Allen, and Jonah—helped me jump into a boxcar just outside of the railyard in town. We switched trains a bunch of times before ending up in California.. We moved around a lot, working on different farms picking fruit. You wouldn't believe the huge amount of food that grows out here! We picked grapes and strawberries mostly. For the last five weeks we've been picking cotton near Bakersfield. It's really hard, dirty work. But there is so much cotton here that we will have steady work for a long time. I've heard tell that there are machines that can pick it now, but there aren't enough machines to handle these big fields.

I'm doing okay, and sure hope you, Jimmy, David, and June are okay too. I miss you all something awful, but don't dare come back. I never want to see the Stinnetts again, and sure don't want to go to jail for hitting him and running away.

I wish you could write to me, but I move around too much to get mail. I never know when we'll get a little time off and can hitch a ride into town, so have no idea of how long it will be before I can drop this into a mailbox. Oh well, at least I can think of you guys a lot. You'll probably think I'm nuts, but sometimes it feels like you're right next to me, especially at night. And I dream of you too, mainly about all the fun times we had when Papa was with us.

Hug everybody for me, and let them know I love them.

Your son,
Raymond

Tears dripped down onto Laura's hands, but she didn't care. She wiped them away and readjusted the letter to keep it safe and dry, then read it again.

"Thank God, he's all right." Laura folded the paper and put it back into the envelope. The timing was perfect, since the kids would be there tomorrow. June and Jimmy would be relieved and happy to hear how well Raymond was doing. She'd have to tell them in private though, to protect David from Mr. Stinnett's relentless and routine grilling after their visits.

The next day, June and the boys arrived at the same time, but what a difference in attitude. The boys were quiet, with David staying within arms-length of Jimmy at all times. June was exuberant. Her smile lit up her face and she bounced with each step.

"Mama, I've got a penpal. He's so nice, and even the timing was perfect since I'd hardly used any of my stationery." June didn't wait for a reaction before turning to her brothers. "I write him about everything. I even told Jack about my three brothers."

"Jack?" Jimmy tilted his head and pulled his eyebrows down. "We don't know any kids named Jack."

"A boy? Your penpal is a boy?" Laura's voice rose. "Where did you find out about him? I'm not sure I like you writing to a boy instead of a girlfriend, especially now with the world the way it is. How old is this guy?"

June went into the kitchen and filled a glass from the sink faucet. "Jack's a very nice boy, and has been nothing but polite in his letters." June downed the water, put the glass in the sink, and turned to face her mom. "He's not some stranger, either. His Aunt Mae works in the school kitchen where I help out on most weekends. She told me about him and gave me his address."

Jimmy's head swiveled back and forth between Laura and June, listening to every word. David watched them speak, but kept looking back at Jimmy, checking on his reactions to what they were hearing.

"I'd expect a woman to describe her nephew as a good guy, but how old is he and where does he live? Is he in school?" Laura tried to keep her voice nonjudgmental, but could hear a little more intensity than normal.

June crossed her arms and frowned. "Mama, I wouldn't be writing to him if he wasn't a good guy, and the school knows about our letters. If they aren't worried, you shouldn't be either." June paused and stared at Laura. "Okay, I should have asked you first, but didn't imagine you'd have a problem with me writing to him. And to answer your questions, he lives with his parents, is almost three years older than me, and is still in High School." June took a deep breath, then blew it out. "Just like I told you, a nice, normal boy who enjoys writing and receiving letters."

There was nothing more for Laura to say. To her surprise, Jimmy and David were more interested in Jack than asking her about Raymond.

Chapter Twenty-Four

Life Seemed So Unfair

Six Months Later, Monday, November 16, 1942

Laura stashed her coat and purse in her locker, fastened the padlock, then grabbed her card from the rack next to the timeclock. She was surprised to find a note paperclipped to it, asking her to report to Mr. Jeffries' office first thing.

"Uh oh, I wonder what he wants?" she mumbled under her breath.

Heading down the hallway toward the Housekeeping Supervisor's office, she remembered her two previous meetings with him. The first was a mild reprimand for infringing on the nurse's duties by doing too much for patients. The second was to work out a fixed Saturday off for her children's monthly visitations. What in the heck could he want now.

Laura knocked twice on Mr. Jeffries' door and waited for him to answer. Just like the first time, she found him with her personnel folder open on his desk. His chin was cupped in his hands, providing her with a view of thinning dark hair above an ever-expanding pale forehead.

"Come in and sit down, Mrs. Webber." Mr. Jeffries closed the folder and straightened in his chair. "You've been with us quite awhile now and have had nothing but good reports since that first couple of weeks."

Laura smiled, wondering what was coming.

"Lots of changes since then, what with the war and all," he said. "It seems like we lose good people every week. Not that I'm complaining, understand, the military needs our best for the war effort, but it does make it tough keeping up our staffing levels."

Nodding, Laura thought about the rumors that had been circulating among the staff about Mr. Jeffries' failed efforts to enlist. He was forty-five, but since all men between eighteen and sixty-four had to register with Selective Service, he'd thought the Army would take him. But he'd been turned down because of his age and health.

"And that brings me to the purpose of this meeting," he said. "How would you feel about training as a nurse's aide?"

Laura sucked in a quick breath. "I'd love that. I worked more with patients before and really enjoyed it," she said. Then her smile slipped. "But no matter what, I can't risk any changes with my scheduled day off for my kids."

"I understand. I'll let the Human Resources Director know, and we'll start setting things up. You'll still work here in Housekeeping part of the time, at least until the training is over." Mr. Jeffries picked up Laura's folder and placed it in the top tray at the corner of his desk. "Thanks for coming in. I'll keep you posted on all the details. And when you finish training, you'll not only have much greater responsibilities but a raise as well."

Laura's smile lit up her face. "Thank you, Mr. Jeffries. I really appreciate the opportunity. And I promise I won't let you down." She stood and left the office, her step much lighter than when she'd arrived.

※

When Laura checked out that evening, there was a sealed envelope clipped to her timecard. She slipped it into her coat pocket, not wanting to open it in front of the other people waiting for their turn to punch out. She ended up standing on the crowded bus, so couldn't satisfy her curiosity until she got home. By the time she opened her front door, mail in one hand and key in the other, she couldn't wait to kick her shoes off.

"Oh, my aching feet." Laura hung her coat on the rack next to the door, then headed for the sofa. "What I wouldn't give for a good foot massage." She pulled her feet up on the middle cushion and rubbed her throbbing insteps. When the pain diminished, she stretched her legs out, leaned back against the arm and reached for the office envelope and the mail she'd tossed next to her purse on the coffee table.

Wiggling her toes and ankles to work out the kinks, Laura opened the envelope—which only had her name on it. "Wow, I start training Monday afternoon. That's pretty fast." She continued reading, then chuckled. "I'll be in training half-days for three months, then switch to the new position full-time. A raise too, but not until I finish training."

Laura put the note on the table, then riffled through the mail. Two advertisements, a bill, and a thick envelope from Willa. Goosebumps broke out all over her body when she touched Willa's letter, eliminating the warm feeling about her new position. Laura decided she needed to chase away the chill in the air and headed for the fireplace. She lit the kindling that rested on the grate, then added two medium-sized pieces of wood. Only when the fire was steady did she return to the couch.

Dear Laura,

I hope this letter finds you and the children well. I can only imagine how hard it must be to only see them once a month, but I have faith that you will always make the most of every minute together. I know the war devours everyone's attention and slows down practically everything, but in spite of all your family has gone through, nothing can pull you apart or damage the love you have for each other.

Thank you for your prayers for Ruben since he enlisted after Pearl Harbor. I guess all our prayers have made a difference because he's alive while so many of our boys in the military have died, but he's been very badly wounded. I couldn't tell you before, since we didn't get all the information right away, but now we finally have the whole story.

Ruben ended up on the USS Yorktown and went through several sea battles without a scratch. But then, after just two days of repairs in Hawaii (they'd been told the repairs would take at least two weeks), his ship ended up fighting in the battle of Midway. Now they say that our valiant Navy boys fought hard enough to turn the tide against the Japanese fleet. I'm proud of that, but Ruben paid a very high price. He was injured and almost died when the Yorktown was hit by torpedoes and ended up sinking. Thank God he, together with hundreds of others from his ship, was plucked out of the water by the crew of the USS Benham.

Ruben is lucky to be alive, but lost both of his legs just above the knees. He was first operated on in Hawaii, but then was sent to the Bob Wilson Naval Hospital in San Diego. He will need more surgeries and has a long recovery ahead of him. Isaac and I have talked to the Navy Chaplain at the hospital, and he says that the physical wounds are the easiest and fastest to heal. He told us that Ruben's depression and emotional shock will be much tougher. His staff members have been very kind and helpful, and have promised to keep us posted on how he's doing.

San Diego is a great hospital, and at least it's in California, but *it's still a long, long way from Stockton. We're working with the Chaplain to figure out the best time to go stay with Ruben. Isaac let his clients know what's happened, and they've all been understanding about our need to go be with our son.*

Oh Laura, I'm so selfish and wish with all my heart that I had you here to hug and help me through all this. I know that's impossible, so please write when you can. Your letters help me keep going more than you know.

Please hug the kids for me and let them know we love them. I wish there was a way to send our love to Glen too, but wherever his mind and heart are, I'm sure he knows.

God bless always,
Willa

Tears poured down Laura's face when she finished reading the letter, and a big one splashed on the paper, blotching Willa's signature. Ruben was such a sweet, kind, and gentle boy when the families had met, and had stayed just as sweet as a young man. She hurt for poor Isaac and Willa. They'd lost one baby to miscarriage, and then a daughter died at only a few months old. Now to have their only son fighting for his life seemed so unfair.

She tucked the paper back into the envelope, took a deep breath, and sat up straight with her feet planted on the floor in front of her. "Willa needs comfort and support," Laura said out loud, wiping her eyes. "Mama, are you around? I need your help." She remembered so many times when her mother's presence had brought her strength. And so many other times when Laura had slipped close to Glen or hospital patients in visions and saw what had happened to them. The question was whether or not she could do it by herself, at will.

Feeling self-conscious, Laura added another log on the fire. Next, she headed to the kitchen and drank a tall glass of water before returning to the living room and settling in the corner of the couch. She cleared her throat, then picked up Willa's letter and placed it on her thighs with her hands resting on top, her fingers caressing the paper. "Mama, please help me do this."

Laura closed her eyes and slowed her breathing. She pulled an image of Willa into her mind, remembering her with a lovely smile and sparkling eyes. She felt warmth enveloping her body and heard the faintest echo of her ma's voice encouraging her. The vision of Willa changed. No smile now. Willa stood in front of her kitchen sink, both hands gripping the edge of the countertop. Waves of despair wafted off her slight body as she stood with her eyes closed.

Laura moved closer and wrapped her arms around Willa, holding her at the waist. She moved her face next to Willa's cheek and whispered into her ear. "Be strong, sweetheart. You aren't facing this alone. So many people love Ruben, and are here for him, and for you and Isaac."

Willa's breathing slowed and evened out, and the sobs stopped. Willa raised her apron and wiped her eyes, then turned and glanced around the room as if searching for an unseen presence. Her lips turned up, just a tiny bit, and she said, "Don't be a wimp, Willa. Isaac and Ruben need you, and you have to be strong. Your son is alive by God's grace, so stop whining and be grateful."

With an abrupt shift, Laura was back in her apartment. She looked around at the room lit only by the fireplace. "Thanks, Mama. I did it. I really did it," she whispered. "And this time it was on purpose instead of being caught up in a vision with no control."

Laura stroked the envelope on her lap, then put it on the table with the rest of the mail. She went for another drink of water, parched all of a sudden, even though she'd had a full glass just minutes ago. "I can't believe I did that."

"Why not?" Laura felt her mother's soft words and gentle chuckle. "You can do whatever you believe is possible. You are an amazing woman with very special gifts. Just believe in yourself and learn to use them wisely."

Before Laura could respond, she was alone once again.

Chapter Twenty-Five

Comforting Mental Messages

Friday, March 12, 1943

When Laura started working fulltime as a nurse's aide, her energy level doubled. Each time she punched in at the timecard machine, she almost skipped on her way toward the wards. She loved her new position, and enjoyed working with the nurses on her shift. She even had a smile for her new supervisor, Miss Easton, every time she saw her marching around the wards.

"Speak of the devil," Laura said to herself when she spotted Miss Easton as soon as she entered Ward 1B. She couldn't help grinning as Miss Easton, dark hair in a chignon with escapee strands waving around her temples and a figure that resembled a rotund snowman, bounced from bed to bed, greeting each patient with a happy smile.

"Mrs. Webber," Miss Easton called out when she spotted Laura, "you're just who I want to see." She motioned for Laura to join her across the room, then fast-walked to meet in the middle between the rows of beds.

"Good morning, Miss Easton," Laura said, after glancing around the room to make sure none of the patients' call-buttons were lit.

"Good morning to you too," Miss Easton said. She patted Laura on her arm. "I've been hearing good things about you from the nurses, and from the patients too."

Laura was surprised at the compliment, since personal comments were rare in front of patients. "Thank you. I'm happy to hear that."

"You're welcome." Miss Easton turned and pointed toward the hallway. "I need to steal you for a minute so we can talk in private."

Laura nodded and followed her into the corridor, then to a small conference room.

"We can talk in here. My office is too far and we only need a minute." Miss Easton led the way inside and plopped into a chair next to a big round table. "It feels good to sit down for a bit."

Laura joined her at the table, trying to keep the nervous, fluttery feeling in her belly from showing on her face. She wondered—no, worried—about what they needed to discuss, since private discussions with supervisors were scary.

"Mrs. Webber, you were top in your class, and the nurses tell me they almost never have to give you directions twice. I love hearing that, believe me." Miss Easton tilted her head and leaned toward Laura. "You have everybody puzzled about one thing, though."

Laura raised her eyebrows and clenched her fists, waiting for whatever was coming.

"You seem to have an amazing talent for calming patients down. In fact, the nurses have told me that sometimes when a patient is afraid, angry, or crying and they're too busy to figure out what's wrong, calling you to sit with that patient seems to work better than giving them a sedative. Nobody has seen you do or say anything unusual, but for some reason the patients seem to respond to you and relax in minutes." Miss Easton stopped speaking, but kept eye contact with Laura. "Believe me, that skill is appreciated, but if you could tell us how you do it, perhaps others could learn how, too."

Laura shrugged and smiled. Nobody would believe her if she tried to explain. And she doubted they'd understand that when she touched a patient—or sometimes just sat near them—she started feeling their emotions and seeing visions of their life. Once that happened, she was able to respond by sending them comforting mental messages. And very often, those mental communications contained specific personal information about their families and friends that helped bring them peace.

"I don't know, Miss Easton. I just try to be calm with them and maybe send them soothing thoughts. Sort of like what I used to do when my children were fussy as babies. It always seemed like they wouldn't stop and relax unless I could make myself relax first."

"Well, maybe that's your secret then, being able to relax and stay calm when everybody around you is going nuts." Miss Easton sighed and shook her head. "Wish I could master that. But you're the best, and I need your help. We have a new admission that is almost in a hysterical state, but her doctor says she doesn't handle barbiturates or narcotics well. They're all we have in the way of chemical sedatives, and physical restraints would only make things worse. I'd like you to take some time to sit with her and see if your presence makes a difference. I'll let the nurses know that I've taken you off this floor for a while. "

"Of course," Laura said. "I don't know if it will help, but I'll try."

⚊⚊

Miss Easton led Laura inside a curtained-off area. A young woman lay under a sheet that had slipped down to her waist. Her neck muscles stood out in stark relief against blotchy reddened skin, and the tension continued down her shoulders and arms. Her face was wet with tears and sweat, gluing strands of blond hair to her forehead and temples. Two nurses sat with her, one on each side, holding her hands and stroking her arms.

Miss Easton nodded to the nurses, then said, "Thank you both. You can go back to the floor. Mrs. Webber and I will take over now."

The nurses glanced at each other, then stood and slipped outside of the curtain. The patient grabbed the bed side-rails and started to pull herself upright.

Laura and Miss Easton each touched one of her shoulders to hold her in place.

"Ssshhh, now, it's important that you breathe easy and stay still," Laura whispered, leaning close to the woman's ear. "I'm Laura. Can you tell me your name?"

"Laura?" The voice was weak and raspy. "Laura, I need help. I can't stay here. Please help me."

"I know you need help, honey, you're running a nasty fever and your lungs are full of fluid." Laura patted her shoulder. "If you'll stay still a minute, I'll get a cool cloth and wipe your face. Gotta say you're a bit of a mess." Laura reached out for the wet cloth that Miss Easton handed her. "What should I call you?" Laura smoothed the damp cloth over the hot skin on the lady's forehead, then down her cheeks and chin.

"Lorraine... just call me Lorraine. Please, listen..." A deep, nasty cough ripped past

Lorraine's lips, propelling thick, pink-tinged mucous down the curve of her chin. Miss Easton grabbed some gauze from the table next to the bed and wiped the viscous fluid away.

"Easy Lorraine, I want to listen, and I will." Laura's voice was soft and soothing. "I'm not going anywhere, and I promise I'll pay attention to every single word as soon as you can speak a little easier."

Lorraine squeezed her eyes shut and brought her hand up to touch Laura's where it rested on her shoulder. Laura smoothed Lorraine's forehead with her other hand, a gentle massage that was soon matched by the rhythm of Lorraine's breathing. Miss Easton stood and eased away from the edge of the bed, nodded to Laura and slipped out of the curtained enclosure.

Once the two women were alone, Laura closed her eyes and was transported to what looked like a hotel or restaurant kitchen. Lorraine was smiling and humming along with the radio while she chopped vegetables to add to a succulent leg of lamb sizzling in a roasting pan. A wiry young man with a basin full of dirty dishes backed through a swinging door and limped toward the sinks. "Ummmm, that smells good. I may have to stay after work to sneak some for dinner."

"I heard that, Virgil," a booming voice preceded the entrance of a very tall woman from a pantry door. "No food for you until all our guests have eaten their fill."

"Ah Gloria, you know I was just kidding." Virgil winked at Lorraine as he took an empty basin from a shelf next to the sink and headed back out of the kitchen.

Lorraine giggled, then started coughing. She put the knife on the prep table, then turned away and covered her mouth with her hands. She tried clearing her throat to stop, but choked and began struggling to breathe.

Gloria watched Lorraine fight for air. "Girl, that cough is getting worse every day, and you're getting thinner and thinner." She crossed her arms and waited for the storm to pass. "Something is wrong, and you've got to find out what it is."

"I'm fine. Really, I am." Lorraine tried to smile. "Well, as well as I can be with a ten-year-old to raise alone while her daddy is off in Europe with the Army. My folks help a lot since we've been living with them, but it seems like all I do is worry and work. It's no wonder I'm wearing down."

"I know that, and I'm not trying to make things harder for you, but I don't want you to come in again after your shift tonight until you've been checked out by a doctor." Gloria raised her hand, palm out, to stop Lorraine from speaking. "I mean it, go see a doctor tomorrow."

Laura felt the fear that squeezed Lorraine's heart. Then the scene dissolved and changed into a small office. A white-coated doctor sat behind a cherry-wood desk, flipping through a stack of papers in a manila folder. With a sigh, he closed the folder and raised his eyes to look at Lorraine, who was seated in an armless wooden chair across from the desk. "I've reviewed your test results, and the fluoroscopy of your lungs leaves no doubt in my mind that you have tuberculosis. Treatment needs to start without delay, so I've arranged for you to go straight to the Ozark Rivers Sanitarium."

Lorraine jumped up, knocking the chair back. "No way." She shook her head hard. "I have a daughter at home and elderly parents who aren't in the best shape. I can't leave them this way." She turned to the side and stepped around the chair. "At least let me go home first and tell them what's..." The first cough caught her off guard, the ones that followed dropped her back in the chair as she fought to inhale. She grabbed a tissue off the doctor's desk and jammed it against her mouth. When the struggle eased, she wiped her lips—and gasped in shock at the bright red droplets that stained the white paper.

The doctor's office disappeared and Laura opened her eyes. Lorraine's eyes were still closed, but her breathing was loud and rapid.

Her hand was hot and damp under Laura's fingers. Laura closed her eyes again.

She watched Lorraine cry and argue with the ambulance crew that transported her to the sanitarium, and then with the doctor and nurses who insisted she change into a gown and get into bed.

Knowing how much Lorraine needed serenity, Laura thought about the incredible feeling she always got when her mother came to her, how she was surrounded and filled with the greatest tranquility she'd ever felt. She focused on sending that feeling to Lorraine. She visualized sending a peaceful cloud of white light to Lorraine until she was encompassed in the light and breathing it in with every inhale.

"Oh honey, I understand," Laura whispered. "But you're dangerous for your daughter and your parents. The very air you breathe around them puts them at risk, and you don't want that. The only way for you to heal is to stay in bed. There isn't any other cure. Your body has to rest, and your mind has to stay as calm as possible. I'll ask Miss Easton to make sure that your family is told what's happening and explain what services the hospital can offer." The words were not spoken out loud, but were clear in Laura's mind and she knew they penetrated Lorraine's mind, too.

Tears leaked from under Lorraine's eyelids, but her breathing slowed and synced with Laura's. "That's right. Let your body drift and relax. Your lungs and heart need the rest. I promise we'll see that your family knows. I can see your minister as well, and I'm sure he and your church family will help your parents and daughter." Laura kept the soothing thoughts flowing until Lorraine's mind quieted and she fell asleep.

Laura patted Lorraine's hand one last time, then tiptoed out of the curtained area. Miss Easton stood three feet away, arms crossed, and a puzzled look on her face.

"She's sleeping now, and I think she'll be much better when she wakes up," Laura whispered.

"I can hear that, but how did you make it happen?"

Laura felt her own heart-rate increase as she tried to find an acceptable answer. "I think she was just worn out. I whispered the same old things, that in order to heal she had to calm herself and rest. She'd been yelling about her parents and daughter, so I also whispered that we'd see what could be done to help them cope."

Miss Easton's eyes narrowed. "You were in there for quite a while, and I couldn't hear any whispering at all. It's hard to believe that just by repeating the same information the nurses have been telling her for hours, she quit fighting when she heard it from you."

Laura shrugged her shoulders. "I don't understand it either. Maybe by talking in such a low voice it forced her to quiet down in order to hear me."

She hoped Miss Easton would drop the subject because she sure couldn't explain about the visions or how to surround someone in a bubble of calm white light. Thank goodness it was Friday, so if she could stay out of sight for the rest of the day, perhaps Miss Easton would find something else to think about come Monday.

Chapter Twenty-Six

War Is Serious Business

Saturday, March 13, 1943

The next day, Laura jumped out of bed the alarm went off. She raced through her morning chores and was ready well before the children were due to arrive.

At long last, the children were staying with her all weekend. Not only that, but her attorney had gotten the new caseworker, Miss Quincy, to agree to two Saturdays a month. "If it weren't for those danged Stinnetts and their love of money and free labor, Mr. Cooper said I'd very likely have the kids back all the time. It would be fabulous to have the family all together again, if only something could be done about those horrible people." Laura talked out loud, like she always did when she was alone in the apartment. "I've done every single thing the darn Children's Bureau has asked of me and I'm making more money. David's in school now too, so there's no reason I can't have them except for the Stinnetts status in town." She stopped to take a moment to calm down. One day at a time, she'd just have to keep going forward one day at a time.

Jimmy and David arrived before June for the first time ever. They hugged Laura, then ran into their bedroom. "I get this side by the window," Jimmy said, stretching out on top of the quilt.

"I get to be close to the door," David sang out, taking his place.

"That's fine, but both of you need to get bathed and changed pretty quick." As usual, both boys were dressed in dirty, ragged clothes and looked like they hadn't bathed or washed their hair in at least a week. "Don't forget to wash your hair and brush your teeth."

The front door slammed. "I'm here." June's voice rang out as she headed for Laura's room.

Laura left the boys to get started and joined June in the other bedroom. "Hi Junebug. This is the first time the boys beat you here."

"Well, I had to carry my suitcase and that slowed me down." June slung the small case on top of the bed.

Laura sensed something just a little off, but didn't ask. She knew June would tell her what was happening when she was ready. "What all did you bring?"

"A couple of dresses, a nightgown, slippers, and a second pair of shoes. Plus my diary, of course."

"Good thinking. Listen, I'm taking you guys somewhere special after we eat, so I want you to change into something fresh."

In spite of their entreaties, Laura didn't tell the kids where they were going until they left the house and headed for the bus stop. Once the bus reached the middle of town, she stood and pulled the cord. "The next stop is where we get off."

Wide-eyed, the children followed her down the steps. The bus door hissed closed behind them and pulled away from the curb.

"Okay, can you figure out where we're going?" Laura opened her arms wide, directing her children's attention to the buildings around them.

They stared at stores, offices, and a cafe. Then Jimmy pointed two doors down from where they stood and said. "The movie theater? Are we going to see a picture show?"

"We sure are. Great guess Jimmy."

David started jumping and throwing his arms up and down. "Yeah, a movie."

"We have movies at school all the time," June said. But hurried to add, "but I've never been to an actual movie theater before."

"Then let's get going," Laura said, leading the way. "And you can each have popcorn and a soda."

A tall sign with the word *Palace* in neon script was perpendicular to the theater building wall, so everyone could see it from all directions. Lightbulbs lined the edges of the sign, but weren't lit since it was daytime. The triangular marquee below was also lined with lightbulbs, and bore the words "Double Feature" in giant letters on both sides, with *Yankee Doodle Dandy* on the next line, and below in somewhat smaller letters, *Bambi*.

When they reached the front of the line, Laura paid one dollar and eight cents for their tickets, then led the children toward the door where she handed the tickets to a man who nodded, tore them in half, and gave Laura four one-half tickets back.

"Why did he tear the tickets? You just paid for them?" Jimmy whispered.

"I'll explain later," Laura said, pushing the children through the lobby door. All conversation ceased as the children stared in wonder at the fabric-covered walls with huge glass frames that held posters announcing up-coming features: *Holiday Inn, Casablanca, Kings Row,* and *Flying Tigers.* After a stop at the concession stand, Laura and each child had their own popcorn and soda, while Laura's wallet was eighty cents lighter.

"Let's go find our seats." She led the way through a door into the dim theater. "Be careful. Watch your step, it's steep in here," she whispered.

Despite David and Jimmy's pleas to sit in the middle of the very front row, Laura settled everyone on the right side about six rows back, promising them they wouldn't miss a thing. She sat on the aisle, with the boys between her and June. They sat without saying a word, staring at a huge red velvet curtain. The boys wiggled, giggled, and poked each other until the room went dark and the enormous curtain began to lift and separate, revealing a vast blank screen.

Laura peeked at the children as the curtain rose. June and Jimmy had their legs stretched out, their attention focused on the screen. David was leaning forward, mouth agape, while his hands gripped the seat arms so tight that his fingernails pressed into the fabric. Newsreels and previews played first, with Jimmy whispering, "I want to see that one" after each preview.

Then the antics of Tom and Jerry in the first cartoon had David laughing out loud. And when Woody Woodpecker followed, Jimmy and June both laughed with—or at?—David each time he burst out with the giggles.

Laura stopped watching the children's reactions when *Yankee Doodle Dandy* got underway because she could hear them clapping, laughing, and humming along with the songs. It was over half-way through before David patted her arm and stood up. "I gotta go," he said. "I gotta go real bad."

"Jimmy, can you take your brother to the bathroom?" she whispered. Jimmy's shocked look as he tore his gaze from the screen changed her mind. "Never mind, I'll take him."

David was as excited coming out of the bathroom as he had been entering the theater. "Mama, you should have come in to see. There were so many toilets in tiny little rooms all by themselves. But the men peed in funny-looking sinks. A whole row of them against a long wall. And lots of sinks with soap that smells real pretty."

"Wow, you'll have to tell Jimmy all about that when the movie is over." Laura grinned, loving his enthusiasm.

"I'll show him. He'll think it's cool, too." David's excitement carried them back to their seats, where he whispered in Jimmy's ear about all the amazing features of the men's bathroom.

When the movie ended and the screen went blank, Laura explained about intermission. David and Jimmy darted out of their seats to go to the bathroom, while June headed to the concession stand to buy some candy to hold them through the second feature. Bambi kept them riveted until the end, and had them chattering all the way to the bus stop, then during the ride to the apartment.

"It was so sad when Bambi's mom died." June was a softy at heart.

"There were lots of other scary parts too," Jimmy said. "The forest fire and when the wolves attacked Faline."

"Yeah, but there were funny parts too," David spoke up. "Bambi made me laugh when he kept slipping on the ice."

Laura lit a cozy fire and curled up on the sofa with the children. The movie conversation died down, leaving them content to soak up the warmth of the room and each other.

"I'm so glad we get to stay tonight," Jimmy said. "I've missed sleeping in a comfy bed with a soft pillow."

Laura leaned across David's body and kissed the top of Jimmy's head. She hated the thought of sending him back to the Stinnetts tomorrow, but what a joy to have them together now. She sent a silent prayer to Raymond, asking God to watch out for him and let him know how much he was loved and missed.

Once the boys went to bed, they fell asleep in minutes. Laura and June slipped under the covers in the other bedroom and continued whispering. After a while, Laura finally said,

"Sweetheart, you seem distracted. Can you tell me what's bothering you?"

"Oh Mom, I'm so worried." Two fat tears slid free and coursed down June's cheeks. She took a deep breath, and then with a tremor in her voice said, "Jack joined the Navy. He's not old enough yet, but he lied and they took him."

Laura hugged June close and stroked her back. "Sweetheart, it seems like all able-bodied men are enlisting. This war is serious business, and they feel like joining is their duty."

"I know, but look what happened to Ruben. Some people say the Navy is safer than the Army, but sailors get killed and hurt all the time."

"Yes, they do. But most come home okay. You just have to keep sending him letters—they'll mean even more now—and pray for his safe return."

Laura kept rubbing June's back until she finally fell asleep. It just didn't seem possible for her baby girl to be old enough to worry about a friend going to war.

Chapter Twenty-Seven

The Germans Surrendered

Thursday, May 10, 1945

"Good morning, everybody," the driver sang out when he opened the bus doors.

Laura climbed up the stairs into the bus, surprised by the driver's huge smile and jubilant greeting. She said "Good morning" back, but wondered what was up.

When she started down the aisle, she noticed that every single face wore a big smile. Confused, she sat down next to an elderly woman holding a bright red bag of knitting on her lap.

"Haven't you heard the news, dear?" the woman said with a grin. "It's official. The Germans have surrendered. And this isn't a false alarm like what we heard last month. President Truman announced that Karl Donitz—that guy who took over when Hitler killed himself—surrendered to General

Eisenhower and ordered all the German troops to stop fighting."

Laura gasped, "It's true this time? Is the war in Europe over?"

"That's the news on the radio and in the newspaper." The woman nodded and patted Laura's hand. "Of course, our guys are still fighting the Japs in the Pacific, but at least now one enemy has given up."

Laura cringed at the use of the ugly term for the Japanese, but was elated at the news. Her thoughts turned to her nephews, Elliot and Aaron, who'd shipped to Europe right after they finished training in the Army. Her sister Ruth had cried on the phone when the boys enlisted right after the attack on Pearl Harbor, and the two sisters had shared a lot of tears since that day. Never knowing where the boys were had kept Ruth in a constant state of anxiety. Elliot and Aaron's letters hadn't helped because they were all censored—Ruth had told Laura that sometimes there were more blacked-out sections than readable words. Maybe now the boys would be safer, even if they couldn't come home right away.

When Laura arrived at work, the same euphoric mood permeated the sanitarium too, with all the staff faces wreathed in smiles. The feeling of hope was fresh and exhilarating, and for once no one worried about the patients getting overexcited. Laura turned down an offer to celebrate after work with other nurses aides, but decided she and the children deserved a celebration of their own on Saturday.

＊＊＊

"Clear the table, kids," Laura said, heading for her bedroom. "I've got some brand new jigsaw puzzles for you."

"I hope no pieces are missing this time. The last two puzzles you got weren't all there," David grumbled.

"I said new puzzles, kiddo." Laura carried three boxes to the table. "These didn't come from the thrift store, so you don't have to worry about that."

Jimmy reached for the puzzles. "That's neat. Wow, the boxes are still sealed up."

Laura swung the puzzles away from Jimmy's grasping hands. "And they won't be opened until the table is cleared off and dry, and the kitchen is clean. You guys get busy while I find some music for us to listen to."

Less than fifteen minutes later, David called out, "Let's do the Popeye one first."

"Then the USS Wasp one next." June held the box with the picture of an aircraft carrier on the front, then put it and the Donald Duck puzzle out of the way on the counter.

David broke the seal on the puzzle box and dumped the pieces in the middle of the table. June propped the lid of the box in the bottom half so they could all see the picture, as her brothers dove into the pile to separate the pieces. Laura settled on the couch, humming and rocking her ankles to *Don't Fence Me In* and *AcCentTchuAte the Positive*, then swayed her shoulders to *Sentimental Journey*. When the telephone rang, startling her, she jumped up and grabbed the receiver off the end table before the kids could reach it.

"Hello," Laura answered, "I'm just fine, Mrs. Bailey, how are you?"

June's face whipped around to face Laura when she heard the name of her school's vice principal. "Hush, I want to hear," she said when Jimmy asked her who was on the phone.

Laura turned her back on the children and kept the receiver next to her mouth so she could keep her voice low. When she hung up and turned around, three intent faces were focused on her.

"What did Mrs. Bailey want?" June said. "And why did she call on a Saturday?"

"Well, her call was quite a surprise, but a nice one." Laura put her hand on her chest, fingers spread wide apart, and took a deep breath. "The school has decided that since so few children were planning to stay on campus this summer, and considering staffing and rationing problems, the school will shut down at the end of this term. All teachers and students will go home until time to return in the fall." A huge smile lit Laura's face as she reached out and squeezed June's shoulder. "The school, together with our caseworker, Miss Quincy, has given permission for you to stay with me all summer. Isn't that wonderful?"

June shot upright, hands extended as if pushing the words away. "No! My friends and I have plans for the summer. We have all kinds of cool ideas, and now they're ruined. Why didn't anyone ask us what we wanted?"

Laura jerked her head back as if she'd been slapped.

"You spoiled brat." Jimmy slammed his hands on the table. "Complaining about not having good times with your friends? David and I would love to stay here all summer instead of working our tails off every single day like a couple of slaves."

"Why can't Jimmy and I stay here too?" David begged. "Can't you call Miss Quincy and tell her that's what we want?"

June huffed, crossed her arms, and sat back down. "You can take my place. I want to stay at school with my friends."

Jimmy leaned closer to June and flicked her ear. "What's the matter? Don't these work? The school said you have to leave, dummy. You're acting like a stupid baby."

June leaped up and punched Jimmy's shoulder.

"Stop it, both of you," Laura yelled. "June, the decision was made for us, so you'll just have to live with it. Somehow you'll have to suffer through living with me all summer." Laura was horrified to feel the sting of tears.

Jimmy glared at June, then rubbed David's arm. "We'd give anything to stay here. The idea of a soft, clean bed every night, getting to take baths and have clean clothes, and not being teased all the time about being dirty and stinky, would be like heaven. You make me sick."

And that sent June off again. The bickering raged on and off all evening between June and Jimmy. And poor David kept begging Laura to let him come stay with her, promising to be good and do anything she asked, if she'd just say yes.

When the kids fell asleep much later than usual, Laura was too exhausted and confused to join June in bed. She leaned against the doorframe and stared at her sleeping daughter. June was curled up in the middle of the bed they'd shared all the other nights the kids had stayed over. The distance between them felt like a huge chasm spewing icy winds of rejection.

What had happened? Laura thought June would be thrilled to spend the summer with her, since they had so little time together during the school year. It was great that, for the first time, June had several good friends, but to choose them over her mama hurt like a stab in the heart.

And her poor boys. David's sad resignation when he accepted the fact that he had to stay at the awful ranch. His heartbroken expression was almost harder to take than Jimmy's rage about the horrible way the Stinnetts treated them. The whole family felt broken beyond repair, and she was helpless to fix it.

Laura's legs shook with the strain of holding her upright, so she made her way to the couch and collapsed in the corner. She'd tried to do what was best for her children, but she must have missed something or done something wrong.

"You didn't do anything wrong, honey, but your children are growing up." The words filled Laura's mind, and the familiar warmth of her ma's presence enveloped and permeated every part of her body. "Your children are all teenagers now, except for David. It's natural for them to pull away from you and from each other as they stretch their wings and approach adulthood. They aren't rejecting you, they're trying to figure out things for themselves."

Laura started to interrupt, but was told to just listen.

"Your children are all alive, healthy, and strong spirited, thanks to you. You're all together except for Raymond, and he did what he had to do. You haven't lost him either, since he writes when he can." The sensation of a soft chuckle filled Laura and the space around her. "It's hard being the parent of three teenagers—hard for them too—but you'll survive and so will they."

Laura chuckled and relaxed into the cushions. "Thanks, Ma." She wanted to say more, but knew her ma was gone.

Chapter Twenty-Eight

He'll Never Be The Same

Three and one-half months later, Sunday, August 26, 1945

Laura woke up to the smell of coffee and bacon. She peeked at her alarm clock, turned it off thirty minutes early, and headed for the kitchen.

"This is the last day I can fix you breakfast, so I hope you don't mind finishing off the bacon." June filled two plates with fried potatoes, powdered scrambled eggs and bacon.

"Don't mind a bit." Laura filled two cups with coffee, then added a lot of milk to June's. "I'm going to miss you, Junebug. I've loved having you with me, even if you were pining for your girlfriends."

"It was fun. I liked working at Woolworth's too, but I sure don't want to be a waitress for the rest of my life."

"Don't blame you. What do you want to do?"

June cocked her head to the side. "I haven't given that much thought. Guess I just figured I'd get married and have some kids." June sipped her pale coffee, grimacing a little at the bitter taste. "I'll sure be glad when the rationing is over so I can have sugar in my coffee."

"We'll all be happy when the war is over, but it'll take time to get back to normal."

"Everybody says Japan will have to give up after being hit by the atom bombs. Then no more war."

"That's what we all hope, but until their leaders surrender, we don't know what's going to happen." Laura looked at the clock. "Better get a move on, the taxi is picking us up in twenty minutes."

Laura planned on helping June unpack her things at school, but changed her mind when four other girls surrounded June as soon as they arrived. One last hug and a whispered "I love you," and Laura left. In no hurry, she caught the bus home, missing her daughter's company already.

It would sure be nice to have enough money to buy a car again, Laura mused. The long walk home from the bus stop was hot and sticky. Thank goodness most of the sidewalk was shady. Her pace sped up when she caught sight of her building—wait a minute.

Why was a man sitting on her porch? He was on the top step, knees bent and feet on the ground, elbows resting on his thighs. Laura sprinted from the sidewalk toward her door. She couldn't see his face because it was resting on his hands. Who in the heck was he?

The man dropped his hands, raised his head, and clambered to his feet. "Hi, Aunt Laura."

"Oh my goodness." Laura gasped, staring. "Elliot? Is that really you?" She opened her arms wide and wrapped them around her nephew's waist. "I can't believe you're here." She leaned back, still holding him tight. "You look just like your father."

"Thanks. Papa's a good-looking man." Elliot gave Laura a final squeeze, then dropped his arms to his sides. "Could I bother you for some water? It's awful hot out here."

"Of course. I'm so sorry." Once inside, Laura told Elliot to put his duffel bag in the boys' bedroom, then sent him to the couch with a tall glass of cold water. "Are you hungry?"

"Well, I could eat, if it's not too much trouble." He joined Laura in the kitchen and sat at the table. He drank half of the water, then held the glass in both hands, rubbing the smooth surface with his thumbs.

Laura fixed a couple of meatloaf sandwiches from the last of the leftovers in the refrigerator, refilled the water glass, and watched Elliot eat. She didn't try to engage him in conversation, just smiled when he looked up.

Ruth had sent a lot of pictures through the years, but the young man across from her barely resembled them. He was thin, almost gaunt, with knife-blade cheekbones supporting deep circles beneath haunted brown eyes.

"Thanks. I didn't know I was that hungry." Elliot finished his water. "That sandwich was a lot better than Army chow."

"You're welcome." Laura waited, but Elliot just stared at his fingers without a word. "Ruth is going to be so excited to see you. Does she know you're on the way?"

"Not yet." Elliot leaned forward. "Please don't tell her, Aunt Laura. Mama would just worry. I want to see her but I need a little time."

Laura was surprised at the vehemence of his tone. "I won't if you don't want me to."

Elliot tipped his head back and closed his eyes. "Thank you."

Laura thought he was falling asleep in the chair. "You look exhausted. Why don't you lie down and take a nap?

"I can't sleep." He blinked his eyes and shook his head as if escaping cobwebs in his mind. "I need to know about Uncle Glen. Can you tell me what happened to him? Did he lose his mind from fighting in the first war?" Elliot cleared his throat. "Is it true that he'll never be normal again?"

"Oh honey, I can see you're hurting, but you aren't Glen. His original breakdown was from an experience in the war, but that isn't why he's the way he is now."

"Please, Aunt Laura, just tell me the truth." Elliot's quivery voice was almost a whisper.

"Okay." Laura rubbed her hands together and began the story.

She told Elliot about Glen's younger brother, Bobbie, enlisting in the Army and their mother's fear of losing him. She described Glen's promise to his mother to protect Bobbie and bring him back to her, and how he joined the Army so he could stay with his brother and look after him. It hurt to explain the awful battle scene where Bobbie was killed as the two brothers ran next to one another, and how Glen was forced to leave Bobbie's body behind. She told him about the incredible guilt Glen felt when he went home to his mother, only to watch her die from cancer.

"But wasn't he okay for a long time after that? You guys met and got married, then had your kids. He was alright then. Why is he locked away now?"

"He was fine most of the time. The memories came through in horrible nightmares sometimes. They never went away, nor did the feelings of guilt and failure at not keeping the promise to his mother. It was tough, but Glen lived in spite of them ."

Laura got herself a glass of water, drinking half of it at the sink. She turned around and leaned her back against the counter to continue.

"Glen broke down when a young man died in a cave-in where his crew was working on a bridge. The man was buried when the side of the hill collapsed. Glen dug like a madman to get him out, then kept trying to revive him. I was told they had to pull him off, and that he was screaming Bobbie's name and crying the whole time."

"That's awful." Elliot rubbed his face. "And he never came out of it?"

"Actually, he did. About four months after he was committed to the mental hospital in Springfield, he woke up one day and was back to his normal self. He panicked, scared to death about me and the children, but they wouldn't release him. He begged and begged, but they wanted to do lots of tests and make sure he wouldn't relapse again." Laura joined Elliot at the table. "Your Uncle Glen was never a violent man, but he attacked a guard—hurt him real bad—in order to escape. All he wanted was to come home and take care of his family." Laura stopped and took a deep breath.

"Guards on horseback tracked him with dogs. They said he fought them, but I don't think that's true. I do know that the guards set the dogs on him because his legs and back were badly bitten. I also know that the guards beat him into submission with chains. One of the doctors told me he'll always have chain scars on the back of his head, and that the blows caused severe brain damage. They said he'll never be the same because of the beating, but they reasoned it away by saying it was Glen's fault for escaping. He was transferred to a hospital for the criminally insane because of his violent attack on the guard. He'll have to stay there until doctors and judges agree that he's safe to release. When I asked how and when that might happen, I got nowhere."

"I'm so sorry. It sounds like everything would have been okay if they'd only let him come home." Elliot stood, walked around the table, and wrapped his arms around Laura's shoulders. "Thank you for telling me."

It wasn't hard for Laura to persuade Elliot to stay the night. They kept conversation light and played gin rummy. After losing five games in a row, Laura threw her cards down. "You should have told me you're a card shark. I have to go to work in the morning, so no more games for me."

Elliot grinned and gathered the cards in a pile. "Aaron and I used to play with Mom before we enlisted. Maggie played with us sometimes, too. Mom won most of the time, but I think I can beat her now."

"Oh boy, Ruth always hated to lose at games. Wish I could be there to watch your first gin rummy victory." Laura put their glasses in the sink and dumped the left-over popcorn kernels out of a big bowl they'd shared. "I'm going to take a bath and head for bed. Help yourself to whatever you want. The bed has fresh linens, so you can climb in whenever you feel like it. I'll try not to wake you in the morning."

Elliot kissed her on the cheek. "Thanks for everything."

Laura startled awake in the dark. What was that sound? She waited in the quiet for it to come again and realized it was Elliot moaning.

Would he roll over and go back to sleep? No, he cried out louder this time, and she could hear him moving. She climbed out of bed and pulled on her robe, then made her way to the boys' open bedroom door. In the faint square of moonlight through the window, she could see Elliot sprawled out on the bed.

He twisted his head from side to side, mouth moving, his expression a twisted grimace of horror. Laura wanted to go to his side and

stroke his face to try to soothe him. But Elliot
was a grown man now, not one of her children.

She leaned against the doorframe and
closed her eyes, hoping she could touch his
mind and help that way. Laura tried to see what
he was dreaming, but everything was black.
Horrific screams filled her mind. Nothing was
visible, but the sound of those screams ripped at
every fiber of her being, invading the protective
bubble that enveloped her and sapping her
ability to hold on or to help Elliot.

Laura backed away, knowing she had to
separate their minds and try to wake him
somehow. She turned on the hallway light, then
headed for the bathroom where she flushed the
toilet—twice. Next, she went into the kitchen
and put the teakettle on to heat. The whistling
sound of the steam did the trick.

"Why in the heck are you making tea in
the middle of the night?" Elliot stood in the hall
doorway, his voice thick from sleep and his
disheveled hair sticking out at all angles.

"You woke me up moaning and crying
out, something about screams, so I figured
maybe we both needed to wake up and start
over. I'll never get back to sleep if we have
coffee, so I'm making tea." Laura smiled and
leaned back on the counter. "Besides, you
would've slept through the coffee perking."

"I'm sorry, Aunt Laura. I guess I should
have gotten a room somewhere instead of

risking waking you up." Elliot's shoulders slumped. "Won't tea keep us awake just like coffee?"

"Not chamomile. It helps you sleep." Laura filled a tea-strainer with leaves, popped it into a teapot, then filled it with boiling water. "Now you need to talk to me. Talking about his nightmares, sharing what he'd gone through, helped Glen. It was kind of like releasing the pressure on a boil by lancing it. I know it's hard, but talking should make it easier." She brought the steeping pot to the table, together with cups and spoons. "Milk? I'm sorry, but there isn't any sugar."

Elliot shook his head. "Do you really think talking will help? I don't like thinking about things, much less talking about what I saw and did."

"I don't see how it can hurt. It sounded like you were having a pretty awful nightmare. Isn't talking worth a try?"

"Makes sense." Elliot clasped his hands tight and took a deep breath. "General Eisenhower's plan was to cut Germany in half so they couldn't recover. I'm in the First Army under General Hodges, and our orders were to race across Germany as fast as we could to meet up with the Russian Army at the Elbe River." Elliot rubbed his face in his hands, then picked up the cup Laura had placed in front of him. He took a sip, then continued.

"It was late when we made camp on the riverbank. The Russians reached the other side a little after we did. Then, after the sun went down, the screaming began." Elliot's hands started trembling, shaking tea out of the cup into the saucer.

Laura wanted to comfort him, but didn't dare make a sound or reach out to touch him.

"I've never heard screams like that before, and hope to God I never will again. The sounds were pure agony, ripped from more throats than you could count or comprehend. When one scream stopped, dozens more started and kept going. It hurt to hear, but when we begged to go across the bridge and try to stop what was going on, the officers told us to stand down. They'd already contacted the generals and asked for permission to stop what sounded like torture, but were told that we must not cross the river because the dividing lines for the three primary Allies—Britain, France and the United States—and the Russians had been established in advance. If we moved forward, we risked creating some kind of international incident."

Tears poured down Laura's cheeks, and her belly hurt with the effort to keep from crying out loud. Elliot wiped away tears from his own eyes, but couldn't stop his body from shaking.

"All night, Aunt Laura, those horrible screams lasted all night. Those poor women—

we learned later the Russians raped all the women and girls they could find, over and over. There was no way for us to escape hearing the shrieks throughout the night. Hour after hour, knowing those people were suffering excruciating pain was torture. And knowing we were close enough to maybe stop what was happening, was indescribable." Burying his face in his hands, Elliot broke down and cried. Raw, wrenching sounds that ripped from his convulsing frame.

Laura moved behind Elliot and placed her hands on his shoulders. "It's okay, honey, just let it out, let it all out," she whispered over and over, massaging his shoulders and neck. When the shuddering sobs slowed, she brought him a damp towel to wipe his face, hoping the cool fabric would soothe his flushed skin.

"I'm sorry. You must think I'm some kind of useless crybaby," Elliot whispered, his face turned away.

"No, honey, I think you're a good, kind young man who experienced something unspeakable. Something you've kept buried inside that could only escape when you slept." She smoothed his hair and patted his back. "Why don't you finish your tea, then go back to bed? I'll bet you can sleep through this time, as long as you want."

Laura watched Elliot trudge back to bed. "Please Ma," she implored, "let him find a few hours of peace. I fear those awful nightmares will haunt him for years, but at least one night of sleep will help."

"Yes, he'll sleep the rest of the night. And in the future he'll remember what you did for him. You've given him something very special."

Laura sighed and closed her eyes, enveloped in the comforting warmth of her ma's presence. She turned out the kitchen light and made her way to her own bed. Pulling the cover up to her chin, she whispered, "Thank you, Ma," and slipped into a dreamless sleep.

Chapter Twenty-Nine

Spam Hash

Monday, August 27, 1945

A different Elliot greeted Laura when she got home from work the next day. The haunted look was gone, his face transformed by a wide smile. "Hi, Aunt Laura," he said as he pulled the door wide open before she could insert the key. "Thank you so much for last night. You're amazing. I had the best night's sleep ever—well, night and half the day's sleep."

"I'm glad to hear it." Laura hung her purse on the coatrack, then headed for the couch. She kicked off her shoes and tucked her legs under her on the cushion. "Half a day's sleep?"

"Yeah. I have an alarm clock in my duffel, but didn't set it. Couldn't believe that it was almost eleven when I woke up."

"You must have needed it." She patted the sofa next to her. "So tell me how your day went and what your plans are."

"When I got my lazy bones out of bed, I foraged in your refrigerator for something to eat." Elliot dropped onto the couch, then leaned back against the side arm to face Laura. "I hope you don't mind, but I finished off that casserole in the covered dish. It was really good. Maybe I could get the recipe for Mom?"

Laura giggled. "Glad you liked it, but that was an end-of-the-month casserole, never to be duplicated. When the ration coupons run low, I just throw whatever I have in a pot—together with lots of potatoes, since we always seem to have plenty of those—and call it good. I'm sure Ruth will have even tastier things for you when you get home, since she was always a much better cook than me."

"Speaking of Mom, I called her today. I put money on your dresser to cover the long distance call, since we were on the phone awhile." Elliot's voice lowered. "She's eager for me to come home, and maybe a little jealous that I stopped here first. I didn't try to explain that this is the first good day I've had in weeks, but I guess I'll have to tell her when I get there."

Laura leaned forward and patted his knee, wishing she could reassure him that the bad days and nights were over, but knew better. "I'm glad you two talked. Your mom and dad love you to death and will be supportive, even through the bad days. I hope you can spend a decent amount of time with them before you have to go back."

"No going back for me. I've been discharged. Operation Magic Carpet is demobilizing and sending soldiers back home as fast as they can. It feels pretty strange, but I'm a civilian again." He rubbed the leg of his fatigue pants. "Stuck in these clothes until I get home, though, and can get some civvies."

"That's great," Laura said. "Now Ruth will only need to worry about one son instead of two. I guess Aaron is still in the Pacific somewhere. And now that President Truman bombed those two Japanese cities, maybe it will be over soon."

"Yeah, let's just pray that Japan follows Germany's lead and surrenders before long."

Laura stood and picked up her shoes. "And on that hopeful note, let me change clothes and start dinner."

"Can I help? I hate to put you out, what with rations and all."

Laura's laughter rang out from the bedroom. "Don't worry about that. Our menu choices are pretty slim at the end of the month, but there'll be enough to fill us up. Hope you like Spam hash."

Laura turned on the radio to her favorite music channel and danced her way toward the kitchen to Johnny Mercer's *G.I. Jive*. Before she got there, Elliot reached for her hands and started dancing. When that song ended, Glen Miller's *Snafu Jump* followed, and the dance continued.

"Wow," Elliot said, a little breathless when the second fast song ended and Dinah Shore's sweet voice started singing about *Silver Wings.* "Mom said you used to be quite a dancer and musician in your day. Guess she wasn't kidding."

Laura's heart was pierced with longing for the days when music united her and Glen, before he was taken away and she lost her hearing on one side, but she kept her smile in place. She thanked him for being such a good dance partner, then suggested he would be a good kitchen partner, too.

"Here you go." She handed him a knife and four medium potatoes. "You start with those while I cut up the onion and the Spam, and start melting some meat drippings from the Crisco can."

In no time, the savory smell of Spam, potatoes, and onion crisping in black pepper and bacon fat filled the room. They took their time eating every scrap Laura had cooked, enjoying quiet conversation about family with the food. Elliot helped clean the kitchen. Then they played dominos and talked until Laura started yawning.

"I'm sorry. I forgot you have to go to work tomorrow. And you didn't sleep half the day away like I did," Elliot said.

"No problem. I can manage. It's wonderful having you here to talk to and dance with." Laura placed a double-five domino on the table, increasing her already substantial lead.

"Doggone, we should have played gin rummy again." Elliot shook his head, then had to draw a domino from the boneyard. "It's been great. And I feel so much better after sleeping last night for the first time since I mustered out. I don't think I could have taken many more sleepless nights without losing my mind."

Laura reached out and pressed her hand on top of Elliot's. "I'm glad, but honey, there may be times when the nightmares come back. When you get home, promise me you'll find somebody to talk to. Maybe someone at your church, or an older veteran—even your Papa. I know Paul will listen when you need him. It's so important that you don't bottle stuff up inside again."

When the game ended, Elliot hugged Laura hard. "I think I'll go to the bus station tomorrow and see about getting a ticket home."

"I think you should." Laura couldn't help the sting of tears as she thought about him leaving. "Your parents and your sister will be so happy to see you. I'm selfish enough to hope you'll be here for one more night, but if you have to leave tomorrow, be sure to leave me a note with all the details."

※

The next day crawled by. Laura's thoughts kept turning to Elliot, as she wondered whether he'd still be at the apartment when she got home. She wanted at least a little more time with him, but could only imagine how anxious Ruth and Paul were for their son to return. It seemed like a week before she closed the sanitarium door behind her and began marching toward the bus stop.

"I hate not knowing," Laura whispered to herself. "I wish there was some magic way he could push a button and tell me what's happening from across town."

She smiled, thinking that they already had telephones. What more could she ask for? Maybe phones they could carry around with them? Sure, with cords that plugged into their ears from phones they carried on their backs. She chuckled, then told herself to not be so silly and impatient.

Chapter Thirty

It's Over

Monday, September 3, 1945

Laura slammed the door closed and dove for the phone. "Hello."

"You sound out of breath. Have you been screaming and cheering all day like the rest of us?"

Recognizing her sister Ruth's voice, Laura dropped onto the couch, and tossed her purse on the coffee table. "You know I have. But I'm out of breath from racing to catch the phone before it stopped ringing. I can't believe it's over, really and truly over."

"I don't think I'll believe it until I see Aaron walking through the door. Of course, Paul keeps reminding me that a certain number of soldiers and sailors will have to stay deployed to keep the peace. I know he's right, but at least I'll know that nobody's shooting at him anymore."

Excited, but aware of the high cost of long-distance calls, the sisters raced through news about their family members, then said goodbye. Laura turned on the radio, then changed clothes while listening to an enthusiastic newscaster describe victory celebrations all over the country. She carried a basket of clothes into the kitchen, set up the ironing board, and turned on the iron. The phone rang just as she lifted the first piece of clothing and shook it out.

"Hello."

"Hi Mom." June's exuberance bubbled over. "Isn't the news wonderful? Everybody here is singing and dancing, we're so happy."

"You should be," Laura said. "You'll remember today for the rest of your life."

June laughed, then whispered to someone in the room with her. "Sorry, but there's a bunch of people waiting for their turn on the phone. Got to go. Love you!"

Just like that, June was gone. In an instant, the celebration sounds on the radio sounded artificial and far away, with no connection to Laura. Wow, the entire country was one big party—and she was getting ready to iron? No. No, not doing it. She turned the iron off, ignoring the ironing board and basket of clothes. She darted to the radio and turned it off, not wanting to hear any more cheering.

That didn't work. The sounds of people shouting and laughing a few doors down seeped through the window, emphasizing Laura's solitary status. This was crazy. She had friends, lots of friends, and could join them right now if she wanted to. But did she?

She realized that what she wanted was family. Talking to Ruth was wonderful, but now Ruth was home with her husband, Paul, and two of her kids, Elliot and Maggie. And her other sisters, Lizbeth and Becca, were right there in the same town with their families. It had been over twenty years since all the sisters had been together, and without any warning, the pain of missing them doubled Laura over.

Laura fell onto the couch, fists clenched on her knees. She hadn't gone to Ardmore, her hometown in Oklahoma, after Glen was taken away because she didn't want her children anywhere near her horrible pa or her awful brother, Ben. Her goal had been to protect her children, but that sure hadn't turned out very well. "Why didn't I listen when Ruth begged me to bring the children home? If I'd let the family help us out, the kids and I would never have been separated. I was so stupid, so full of pride and fear, and so sure I was right. All of this is my fault."

The tears started flowing in earnest. Not dainty little sparkly tears either, but a flood that stung her eyes and wet her blouse with big blotchy patches. Tears that filled her nose to overflowing, making it hard to breathe. She didn't even try to stay quiet, but sobbed in great, loud, gulping gasps, a dissonant counterpoint to the revelers outside. Laura cried until there were no more tears left, and her eyes were lined with dry, crusty debris.

She sat up, breathing through her mouth because her nose was stuffed. Her whole face felt hot and swollen. Laura trudged to the bathroom, filled her hands with cold water from the faucet and immersed her sticky, flushed skin. She pulled a washcloth from a shelf above the toilet and scrubbed the crusts and streaks from her eyes, nose and cheeks. The cool cloth soothed away the heat in her flesh, and eased the swelling. She looked into the mirror and gasped, squeezed her eyes tight and shook her head. Then opened them again and looked at her reflection. She leaned close to the glass, examined her image from both sides, and wondered how, for a few seconds, she could have seen a woman with long, loose black hair.

A chuckle, along with the warm, loving essence of her mother, filled the room. "I thought showing myself would get your attention."

"How about almost gave me a heart attack?" Laura muttered. "Was that you in the mirror? I don't remember how you looked."

"You were only three years old when I passed. No way you'd remember. But yes, that was what I looked like. You favor me a lot."

Laura sat on the edge of the tub, away from the mirror, and wrapped her arms around her torso. "I'm so lonely, Ma. I miss Ruth and Lizbeth and Becca. When Elliot was here, it was delightful, but then he left and now the place feels so empty. It hurts to know that I'll never have Glen here to hold me again." She grabbed some toilet paper, wiped her eyes, and blew her nose. "And the children. They're growing up so fast, but I'm not a real part of their lives. I don't even know where Raymond is. I miss them—and I feel like I've failed them."

"Don't you dare start crying and feeling sorry for yourself again." Ma's voice was stern, but Laura could feel layers of love and warmth surrounding and enveloping her. "You had a good cry and let yourself wallow in all that misery until the tears dried up, but that's enough."

"It's hard, Ma."

"Hard never stopped you before."

Laura smiled, just a little one, but a smile nevertheless. "But did I make the right choices for the kids? I know I always had good reasons and tried to make the best decisions for them, but I'm not at all sure now."

"Honey, you love your children with every fiber of your being and always did what you thought was best for them at every turn. How could anyone do more than that?"

"But will they understand that? How can they know I love them when we're all split up?"

"They probably don't understand right now, and there'll be lots of times when they'll have doubts about your choices. But your children, like all of us, have their own lives to live. Just keep on listening to your heart and doing the best you can. Nobody could expect more than that of you. Of anyone." And with those words, she was gone.

Chapter Thirty-One

I Ain't No Snitch

Saturday, October 13, 1945

"Hi Mom, we're here," June shouted.

Laura answered, then heard scuffling noises and the sound of the front door slamming shut.

"Wow, how'd you get that shiner?" June's voice was loud and clear.

What the heck?

Laura rushed out of the bedroom to join her kids. "June, what did you say about a shiner?"

"Look at David's face." June pointed at David, who turned his head away.

"Leave him alone." Jimmy shoved June's hand down. "It's none of your business."

Laura put her arm around David's shoulder and pulled him away from the others. "Look at me, David." She gulped at the sight of dark blue and green bruises surrounding his left eye, and the scab just below it. "Who did this? What happened?"

David shrugged her arm off and backed up. "Don't matter. It's over," he snarled. "Why are you asking, anyway? You can't do nothing about it."

"Did one of the Stinnetts do this?" Laura looked from David to Jimmy and back again.

Jimmy snickered. "Stinnetts are smarter than marking up his face. Even the dumb Children's Bureau caseworker might ask questions if a teacher said one of us got hit in the face at the ranch."

"Jimmy, that's enough." Laura turned back to David and took hold of both his shoulders. She knelt to look him in the eye. "I want to know what happened. Tell me the truth, all of it, right now."

David sniffed, glanced at Jimmy, then back at Laura. "At school, there's a bunch of kids that tease me all the time, and call me names. At recess, they got all around me so the teachers couldn't see what was happening, and chanted 'dirty David dogsbody, Stinnett's stinky slave' over and over. I got sick of it and shoved that nasty Evan Wilson down. He jumped up and punched me in the face a couple of times. Then the bell rang and everybody ran to class."

"And then what?"

"Then nothing."

"Nobody at school noticed? Didn't you talk to your teacher or the nurse?"

"I ain't no snitch. Telling on them would only make it worse." David scowled. "I just told the teacher I slipped and fell."

"What about when the Stinnetts saw your face? What did they do?"

Jimmy started laughing. It wasn't a funny or happy sound. Laura glared at him, then turned back to David. "I asked you a question," she said. "What did the Stinnetts do about your being hit at school?"

"He said I should have finished off the guy who hit me. That he'd only stop picking on me if I hurt him bad enough." David touched the swollen eye, then reached around to the back of his head. "Then he hit me in the back of the head. His ring made a big goose egg that hurts more than my eye."

"Mama, don't even think about it," Jimmy said.

"Think about what?" Laura snapped. "This isn't right. You two have put up with way too much from those people, and maybe it's time the caseworker started thinking about your welfare like she's supposed to."

Jimmy shoved David and hissed, "I told you to make something up. Now you've gone and done it for sure."

"I ain't lying to Mama." David pushed Jimmy right back, then turned to Laura. "You can't say anything to anyone. You can't! Stinnett told us over and over that if we ever said a thing to get them in trouble, he'd find a way to hurt us real bad and make us sorry. Promise, Mama, promise you won't tell, please."

Laura studied her sons' faces, then sat down and buried her face in her hands. "Go get cleaned up. We'll talk about this later."

The mood stayed stiff and somber for the rest of the day. The boys listened to serial shows on the radio after dinner, and in between programs played an almost endless game of war with Laura's deck of cards. Then they went to bed after lackluster hugs and mumbled "goodnights" and closed the bedroom door behind them.

Laura stared at the door, hurt that for the first time ever, it hadn't remained open. She'd always been close to her sons, but now she had no idea of how to reach them or how to make things better.

June scooted close to Laura's side on the sofa. "Mom, now that the boys have gone to bed, can we talk?"

"Sure, Junebug. I'm sorry, seems like we haven't spoken ten words today." Laura took a deep breath and focused her attention on her daughter.

"Well, now that the war is over, Jack's ship, the USS Willmarth, is being overhauled at

Norfolk, Virginia. He's on liberty, and he wants to come meet me in person."

"Wait a minute. Traveling from Virginia to Missouri is quite a trip just to meet a penpal."

"His Aunt Mae works in the kitchen at the school, and he's coming to see her." June rolled her eyes. "Remember, I told you she's the one who gave me his address in the first place. We've been writing to each other for over two years."

Laura looked at her daughter. With shock, she realized that her baby girl was an almost grown up seventeen-year-old. Somehow, in her heart and mind, June would always be that sweet toddler she and Glen had adored. "Uh, if he comes, I want to meet him. But I don't want you spending time with him alone."

June laughed. "I knew you'd say something like that. Don't worry, the school has very strict rules about boys visiting. I'd like to have him come here to meet you and the boys."

"I think that's a good idea. Could he come on our next family day?" Laura jumped up to look at the calendar on the kitchen wall. "Why don't you ask him to come on Saturday, the 27th?"

"He can come with me from school. He should arrive next week and will be staying with his aunt, so that would be easy."

Laura looked at June's wide-eyed expression, the one she always wore when she thought she was getting away with something. "Not a bad idea. Just make sure he knows the way to the bus-stop for when he leaves in the evening. It wouldn't be proper for him to stay here overnight."

"Of course."

June's grin was familiar too, the same one she always wore when she got caught at something.

Laura was exhausted when the children left Sunday afternoon. June had chattered all day about the plan for Jack to come with her next time. She expected her brothers to be excited about meeting him, but was surprised and disappointed by their responses. Jimmy and David mocked her, mincing around the apartment and making kissing noises, then laughed when she got mad.

This time Laura was grateful for the empty rooms, a welcome relief from two days of sullen silence interspersed with arguing and pleas for her to referee. And nothing she said—or suggested, or demanded—made a difference. Had her children been damaged beyond repair by all they'd gone through, or were they behaving like any other normal kids? Maybe she was just a terrible mother whose awful decisions had turned her children into bratty monsters.

Chapter Thirty-Two

We Want To Get Married

Saturday, October 27, 1945

"Mama, this is my friend, Jack Archer," June said as she closed the door behind them.

The young man whipped his white dixie cup hat off with his left hand and tucked it into his belt, freeing a mass of brown curls above his high-forehead. "Pleasure to meet you, Mrs. Webber."

Laura smiled and nodded. "Come on in, you two." She watched June introduce Jack to her brothers, who were engrossed in playing War at the kitchen table. Judging by the stacks of cards, a delighted David was winning.

Penpal, huh? The way June kept sneaking glances at Jack and touching his arm when they were close together didn't look at all like they were just penpals. And something about June's appearance was different, too. Her hairstyle. Deep, soft waves framed her face—waves that only rollers could have produced. And she was wearing makeup too, for heaven's sake. Not a lot, but it was there on her eyes and lips. Laura had never seen June wear makeup before, nor had she seen evidence of rollers before, either.

"June, can you help me with something?" Laura looked back over her shoulder and headed toward her bedroom.

"Okay," June said. "What do you need?"

Laura closed the door behind June, then crossed her arms. "What I need are some answers, young lady. You told me that Jack is just a penpal, but you've curled your hair and are wearing makeup. Girls don't get all dolled up for a penpal." Laura tilted her head and raised June's chin with her fingers. "And where did you get the makeup? I've never seen you wear it before. Are you using it at school? I thought they had some pretty stiff rules about stuff like that."

June pulled her face away. "Oh Mom, I'm seventeen years old. There's nothing wrong with me wanting to look pretty for Jack. I like fixing my hair nice, and all the girls are wearing makeup on the weekends. We can't wear it during classes, but on free time we can do what we want. I'm not a little kid anymore."

Laura realized that she and June were staring eye-to-eye. In fact, June was a little bit taller. "I know you're not a little kid anymore, but you aren't an adult yet either." Laura sighed and sank down on the edge of the bed. "It hurts to find out things like this out of the blue. You could have talked to me about hairstyles. I'm not an old lady, you know. And I would have appreciated being consulted when you started thinking about makeup. Those are things that mothers and daughters should share."

"I guess you're right," June said. "But I only see you two times a month. And we almost never have time alone for girl talk. I see Mae almost every single day, so I guess I've just gotten in the habit of talking to her about things."

"Mae? You call Jack's aunt by her first name? You know better than that."

"Everybody calls her Mae. She likes it that way. And all the girls talk to her, not just me. She's young and pretty, and she stays up with the latest fashion news." June turned toward the door. "Can I go now?"

Laura nodded, but stayed seated. She knew the boys didn't open up to her about everything that happened during their time with the Stinnetts, but had always thought she and June were closer. What else had she missed? And was it because June was seventeen or because she lived at the school? Or some combination of the two? Would their relationship be that much different if they lived together?

No magic answers or words of wisdom popped into her head, so Laura went back into the living room, where she could keep an eye on everybody.

At dusk, Jack thanked Laura for dinner and for letting him visit, then shook hands with Jimmy and David. "It was a real pleasure, but I have to get going to catch the bus."

"I'll walk you to the corner." June pulled on a sweater. "And no, you can't go with us," she said to David, motioning him back down on the floor next to the coffee table where he had a domino tower under construction.

Laura was just starting to worry when June returned, hung her sweater on the coatrack and sat down next to her mom.

"Jack liked you and the boys a lot."

"That's good. He seems like a nice young man," Laura said, waiting for more.

June rubbed her palms together, then pressed her hands on her thighs. "He's more than nice. He's smart and funny, and he treats me like I'm the most special person in the world." June looked up, took a deep breath, then blurted out. "Mama, we want to get married. I know we're young, but we love each other and want to be together."

"Married? You and your penpal want to get married? That's quite a leap, don't you think?"

"We've been writing a long time now, and thought we were just good friends. But Mama, we've seen each other every single day for over a week. We don't ever want to be apart again," June said.

Laura bit her lip, then took June's hands in hers. "Honey, he's still in the Navy and you haven't finished high school. You two have plenty of time."

"I know all that. We've talked about everything, but want your consent to get married when we can. He has to get permission from the Navy anyway, but we want to start the process. It's our future, and we love each other so much."

"Why didn't Jack ask me? That would have been the proper way to do things." Laura tried hard to keep her voice and expression calm, in spite of her racing pulse. More than anything, she wanted to take her daughter in her arms—to hug her, but also to shake some sense into her. At the same time, she feared that the wrong move or words would just push June away.

"I wouldn't let him," June said. "I'm not somebody's possession to be given away. It's my life and my future, so it's up to me to tell you."

Tell me? Interesting choice of words. Laura saw the tension in June's body and sensed the seeds of defiance bubbling below the surface. "I won't tell you no, because it's your decision and your life. But I hope you two give yourselves time to get to know each other better, and think long and hard about what getting married entails."

June squealed and leaped into Laura's arms. "Oh, thank you. You're the best mom in the world. I love you." Then she jumped up and whirled around the room, singing "I'm getting married, I'm getting married to the best guy in the world!"

The rest of the evening seemed to pass in seconds. When the house was still, with only the soft sounds of sleep in the darkness, Laura's mind wouldn't slow down. She kept seeing herself when she accepted Glen's proposal. She hadn't been in love with him then, but knew he loved her. They were close friends who shared a love of music and dreams of having a family. She'd shut down her doubts, refusing to listen to her internal concerns about committing herself to him, instead vowing to be the loving wife he deserved.

She'd fallen in love with Glen after they'd gotten married, but they'd been lucky. Jack and June were babies, with no real world knowledge or experience. How in the world could they make it together?

Chapter Thirty-Three

Another Huge Mess

Sunday, October 28, 1945

Laura blinked, rolled over, and was surprised to see an empty pillow next to hers. That was strange. June usually stayed in bed as long as possible on Sunday mornings. After a quick bathroom stop, Laura headed toward the kitchen—then stopped dead in her tracks.

Where was June? She wasn't in the living room or the kitchen. Laura turned around on the slim chance that she was in the boys' bedroom or the bathroom. Both room doors were open, but there was no sign of her. Might she have gone outside?

Laura ran to the front door and threw it open, then leaned out and looked both ways. Scared now, she slammed the door and headed back to her room to get dressed.

Then she saw it. A note, leaning against the dresser mirror.

Dear Mom,

Please don't be mad, but I've gone with Jack. He has to be back on his ship on Tuesday because it's leaving for Florida. We're going to find someone to marry us today, then I'll stay with another sailor's wife until Jack gets discharged. There's a lot of jobs available all over the state, too, so both of us should be able to find work pretty easy.

I know you wanted me to stay and finish school, but I can't bear the thought of Jack and I being apart for so long. And if the caseworker found out about our plans, she might try to interfere. I love Jack, and I know what I'm doing. You don't need to worry because I'm fine. In fact, I'm happier than I've ever been.

Please don't try to stop us. It might hurt Jack with the Navy. Besides, by the time you caught up with us, we'll be married and it will be too late to do anything.

Give my love to Jimmy and David.

I love you,

June

"No, no, no." Laura threw the note back on the dresser. "How could you be this stupid, June?" She opened the armoire, then the bottom right bureau drawer, hoping against hope June's things would still be there. No such luck. Everything was gone.

"You and Jack planned this. You had to, and that means you both lied to me yesterday. Bald-faced, straight-up lied." She slammed the drawer shut. Her face felt hot and sweaty, and her chest heaved with tight, shallow breaths.

"What the heck is going on?" Jimmy looked confused from where he stood in the doorway. "Why are you yelling and slamming things?"

"Sorry, but I'm so mad I need to scream. I'd like to slap your sister right now, but I can't reach her. She ran away with Jack to get married."

"June ran off?" Jimmy looked wide awake now, with his eyebrows raised almost into his hairline.

"That's right. But we're not supposed to worry because she knows what she's doing."

David, rubbing his eyes, joined Jimmy in the doorway. "Are you guys fighting? Why are you so loud? You woke me up."

"No, we're not fighting. The only one I'm mad at right now is June." Laura took a deep breath and patted David's shoulder. "I'll fix you guys breakfast in a few minutes, but right now I need to get dressed and try to figure out what to do."

Once calmed down, several ideas chased through Laura's head. Call her attorney to find out what she should or should not do. Can't do that because it's Sunday. Call the caseworker to report June as a runaway? Same problem, it's Sunday. Besides, who knows what trouble she might stir up. It was always better to talk to Mr.

Cooper before calling the Bureau. The only call she had to make was to the school since June wouldn't be returning—but with only the main switchboard number to call, it might not be answered on Sunday either.

Laura didn't even know if she could find out what bus June and Jack took, or where they were headed. She knew the ship was in Norfolk, but June said she was going to Florida.

Laura's thoughts kept circling around and around while she cooked, right up until she started to pour bacon grease into the Crisco can full of drippings. The skillet slipped out of her hands, knocked over the can, then crashed to the floor. Grease spattered everywhere.

"Just what I need, another giant mess to clean up." Laura wiped her hands on her apron and stared at the thick, viscous pool on the stove top and the shiny rivulets running down the front of the stove and cabinets.

"Uh oh," David said, leaning closer to see better.

Laura's icy stare shut him down. "Stay out of my way or I'll make you clean it up." She looked past David to Jimmy. "Both of you do what you want, but don't talk to me or bother me until this is cleaned up."

Hours later, all traces of grease had disappeared from the stove, cabinets, and floor.

And the Crisco can, minus over half of the precious drippings, was back in place. Laura was sweaty and exhausted. She pulled off her filthy apron and glanced at the clock. "Oh my word. Boys, you've got less than thirty minutes before you have to leave for the bus."

"That's not fair," David whined. "Raymond and June both got away. Why do we have to go back to the Stinnetts? Can't you just say that we ran away too?"

Jimmy stared at his little brother. "That's dumb. You know the Stinnetts would send the cops here to get us and then we'd never get away from the ranch." He cuffed the side of David's head. "Heck, he's so mean, he'd probably try to put Mom in jail."

David pushed Jimmy away, then crossed his arms. "It's still not fair. I don't want to go there anymore. Why can't we run away to join Raymond or June? You'll go next and I'll be all alone. I'd do anything to get away." David turned and pointed to Laura. "It's our turn. You've gotta help us escape."

The argument continued until the boys marched out the front door. Jimmy kept explaining the facts to David, including the danger to Laura if the cops thought she'd helped the boys get away. Logic didn't sway David at all. He just wanted to escape and expected his mother to help him do it.

Laura closed the door behind her boys, then leaned back against it and closed her eyes. David was right, this whole situation was unfair. And as the mother, it was her responsibility to find a way to help them. Even June might be better off with Jack. At least she'd be out of the system and able to speak for herself. And after all, she'd be eighteen and a legal adult in just over five months, anyway.

The Children's Bureau was never going to give her kids back, because the Stinnetts had too much power. They wanted the money they got for keeping the boys, plus the free labor the kids provided. Raymond had escaped on his own and was doing okay. June might be making a huge mistake marrying Jack, but as a married woman, nobody could force her to go back to the school or to some other home if she didn't want to. Even if Jack wasn't the wonderful person she thought he was, at least he'd set her free.

Somehow, Laura had to get Jimmy and David away from the Stinnetts and send them out of the state to a safe place. And she had to do it without getting herself in trouble with the law.

Laura paced around the room, trying to devise a plan.

There was no way she could do this alone. All three of them would be caught, and they'd be even worse off. But who could help?

The loud sound of the ringing phone nearly sent her flying straight up in the air. Irritated at the interruption, she yanked the receiver up to her ear. "Hello, this is Mrs. Webber."

"Mom?" The voice sounded like it was coming through a tunnel. "Hi. This is Raymond."

"Oh my God, Raymond, is it really you?" Laura sat down and clutched the receiver to her ear with both hands. "Honey, I've missed your voice so much. You sound different."

"It's been three years, Mom. My voice has changed and I've grown up a lot." He coughed and cleared his throat. "Listen, I've been working in Wasco for weeks now, and can receive letters addressed to me through General Delivery, Wasco—W A S C O—California. And I have Sundays off, so can use the pay phone once in a while. Please write to me. I want to hear all about everybody and can't afford that on the phone. How are Jimmy and David doing? Where are they now?"

"Not that great. They're still at the Stinnetts and..."

Raymond interrupted her. "No, they can't still be there. That place is torture. You've got to get them away from those horrible people."

"You're absolutely right, and your timing is perfect." Laura squared her shoulders. "June ran away last night to get married to a sailor named Jack. Jimmy and David had a fit going back to the ranch today, insisting that it's their turn to escape. But if I try to take them and run, we'll all three end up worse off than we are now. Can you help?"

"Let me see what I can figure out. I'll call you in the next day or so, I may have to call collect, though."

"That's fine. Oh, Raymond, if you can help save your brothers, that'll be an answer to our prayers."

A metallic voice cut in. "Please deposit sixty-five cents."

"Gotta go, I love you."

"I love you, too, honey," Laura said to the dial tone. She put the handset back on the telephone base and whispered, "Thank you. Now we have a chance."

A throaty chuckle echoed in and around her. "You're welcome," her ma's familiar voice said.

Chapter Thirty-Four

Mrs. Jack Archer

Monday, October 29, 1945

"Good morning, Miss Eason." Laura could hear a slight tremor in her voice, but didn't try to control it. "I'm so sorry, but I can't come in this morning, maybe later though."

"What's wrong? Are you ill?"

"No. I wish it was that simple. My daughter ran away with her sailor boyfriend to get married." Laura twisted the phone cord in her fingers, hating the need to discuss personal matters with her supervisor. "I've got to go see my lawyer and find out what I can do."

"Oh no. If they got married, you're stuck. There's no minimum age for marriage in Missouri."

"I know, but since she's a ward of the Children's Bureau, this will be a big mess." To her horror, Laura felt tears welling up. "I don't have an appointment with the lawyer, so I'll have to go and sit until he can fit me in. I could come in after seeing him, if you need me."

"That's okay. You've never asked for time off before, so you're fine," Miss Eason said. "Just take care of things and we'll see you tomorrow."

Laura wished meeting with her lawyer was as easy as talking to her supervisor. She'd been sitting in the office lobby for almost an hour, staring at the walls. Hearing "Cooper and Goodwin, Attorney's office. How can I help you" umpteen times wasn't helping. She had changed her mind about what she wanted to accomplish with Mr. Cooper after talking to Raymond. The two wild cards were the caseworker and the Stinnetts.

After what seemed like days, Miss Watkins said, "Mrs. Webber, Mr. Cooper will see you now."

Laura nodded and sprang out of the chair, her mouth dry as cotton. Trying hard to swallow, she entered Mr. Cooper's office and sat down in the chair across from his desk.

Mr. Cooper steepled his hands on his desk and asked, "So, what's the emergency that's brought you into my office this morning? I thought everything was going pretty smooth for you and your children."

"It's June. She ran away Saturday night with a young man named Jack Archer. They've been writing to each other for a couple of years, but now they've decided they want to get married." Laura stopped to clear her throat. "In fact, in her note she said they were planning to find somebody to marry them as fast as possible."

"Oh boy." Mr. Cooper leaned back in his chair. "How old are they?"

"June's seventeen. She won't be eighteen until next June. Jack will turn twenty next month. He's in the Navy."

"Well, there's nothing you can do if they've gotten married. If Jack was twenty-one and she was under sixteen, it would be a different matter, but if they're legally married, that's it."

Laura nodded and tried to find the best words to broach the subject of her boys. "I was afraid of that. But what do I do about the Bureau and the school?"

"That's a different kettle of fish. I can contact them for you, if you'd like." He picked up a pen and made notes on the legal pad in the middle of his desk. "The big question on their minds will be whether you were part of her decision to run away."

"No way. Jack was staying with his aunt, who works at the school, and came to my house with June. He was supposed to meet me and the boys, have dinner and spend some time with us, then leave. I made it very clear that it would be inappropriate for him to stay over. They talked about being just penpals and great friends. Then after Jack left, June told me they were in love and wanted to get married. I assumed she meant sometime in the future." Laura paused to take a breath. "But when I woke up in the morning, June was gone. I found a note on my dresser telling me they were in love and were getting married. And that I shouldn't worry because they knew what they were doing."

Mr. Cooper snorted and shook his head. "Oh yes, at that age we all think we know everything." He raised his cup and took a sip. "I hate to be the bearer of bad tidings, but the truth is, there isn't anything you can do. The only issue might be some unpleasantness from the Bureau if they think you were negligent in some way. Perhaps that you weren't being attentive enough to what June was doing."

"It was a little difficult to know what she was doing, or planning, when I only see her twice a month. Maybe they should direct their ire toward the school."

Mr. Cooper grinned. "You have a very good point. So we're done here?"

Laura squeezed her hands tight together. "Not really. I'm worried about Jimmy and David. They were angry about June leaving. Not about her taking off, but mad because they want away from the Stinnetts so much. Raymond ran away from them, and is doing fine working on a farm in California. What would happen if his brothers ran away as well?"

Mr. Cooper crossed his arms and stared. "That depends on whether they were successful in getting away. But either way, it would be tough on you. Those folks are vindictive people with a lot of power in this little town. If the boys were caught and brought back, most likely the Stinnetts would try to say that your influence was the problem and do their best to stop you from seeing your sons at all. And if your boys actually escaped, the Stinnetts would be furious at the loss of income and free labor. I'd expect them to try to have you prosecuted for interfering in legal custody."

"They're horrible people, and the boys hate them." Laura rubbed her hands on her thighs and tried to calm her breathing. "I try hard to help my sons cope, but it isn't easy."

"I understand. My best advice is to make sure you don't encourage them." Mr. Cooper put both hands on his desk and tapped his fingers. "The most important part is that you cannot know anything about plans for running away, and can't help them in any way. I've no doubt the police would question you— interrogate you, in fact—and if you lied to them, it wouldn't go well. I'm also sure that the Stinnetts could drum up witnesses to accuse you, so you'd have to be able to prove where you were when the boys ran off."

"Of course."

Mr. Cooper's eyes seemed to bore into her and read all her thoughts.

"But I'd never do something that was against the law. My only concern is for the welfare of my children."

"Good." Mr. Cooper stood and stepped out from behind his desk. "Remember, all our conversations are covered by attorney-client privilege, but take care. I wish you and your sons the best."

In spite of Laura's constant stares at the telephone, Raymond's call didn't come until Thursday evening. Laura pounced on the phone before the end of the first ring. "Hello."

"This is the operator. Will you accept a collect call from Raymond Webber?"

"Yes, ma'am." Laura licked her dry lips. She heard the operator click something, then Raymond's voice.

"Hi, Mom. Sorry to call collect, but I don't want to get cut off in the middle."

"No problem. It's so good to hear your voice."

"You, too. So, is my big sister a married woman yet? What's her married name?"

Laura sat down on the couch and relaxed her grip on the handset. "Yes, she called to let me know she's okay. And that she's now Mrs.

Jack Archer. Jack married her, then they boarded separate busses. He went back to his ship in Norfolk, Virginia, while she traveled to Jacksonville to stay with the wife of a friend of his in an apartment near the shipyard. Her plan was to look for a job so she could work until Jack gets out of the Navy."

"Wow, it's hard to get my mind around the idea of June married," Raymond said. "But I do have good news for you. I've figured out how to get Jimmy and David out here. Then they can stay with me. Jimmy will have to work in the fields just like I did, but there is a school for farm worker kids where David can go."

"That's wonderful. Thank you so much. How do we get them to you?"

"Mom, I can't give you the details. There's a whole network of people—hobos—who will make it happen. They made me promise not to give you any details because that might put you and some of them in danger. You only need to know it will happen, and that Jimmy and David will be well taken care of."

Laura thought a minute, hating the idea of not knowing anything. Then she remembered her conversation with Mr. Cooper, and realized Raymond was right. "Okay, I understand. But what do we do?"

"What is the next day they'll come to you, and when do they leave?"

"They come on Saturday, the tenth, and will leave the next afternoon."

"Okay. You can't say a thing to those two. I'll call on Sunday morning and you can say I want to talk to them. I'll tell them they can't say anything to you about our plans. They've got to think it's all a secret, just in case some rail-yard bulls catch them somewhere." Laura's sharp intake of air stopped him a minute. "Don't worry. I don't think it will happen, but we'd be stupid not to make plans for every possibility. If the boys are positive you don't know anything, they can't accidentally spill the beans."

"But how can I help them? Wouldn't it be better if I could go over the plans with them?"

"No way. You'll be the first person the cops would suspect. In fact, you'll need to be a pretty good actress on that Sunday. After talking to me, Jimmy and David are going to insist that they have to leave your place at noon, which is about three hours earlier than normal. You have to fuss a lot when they blame the Stinnetts, but not try to stop them. And after they leave, you need to go to a neighbor and borrow something so you have a chance to complain. That will provide you with proof that you weren't with the boys when they left, and that you were mad about them leaving early."

"I can do that," Laura said. "But are you sure they'll get the directions right without my help?"

Raymond laughed. "Don't sell those kids short. David is young, but he trusts Jimmy and will do what he says. And Jimmy is about the same age I was when I took off. They'll be fine. They'll want to protect you, so don't blow it for them."

"Okay, but what will they need to take with them? I should make sure whatever they need is here for them."

"Stop it, Mom. You aren't supposed to know anything, so why would a bunch of new stuff just happen to be around? Stop worrying and trust me. I love you, and I won't let anything happen to my brothers."

When Raymond hung up, Laura replaced the handset. "Stop worrying. Everything will be fine," she whispered, then looked around to make sure no one heard. Easier said than done. Raymond sounded so sure of himself, so grown up. She just had to believe and trust him.

Chapter Thirty-Five

It's Really Happening

Saturday, November 10, 1945

Laura's thoughts kept returning to the conversation with Raymond, just as they had every single day since the phone conversation. Act normal today, act as if she knew nothing about any plans. Sure. Nothing different about today, the last full, normal day she'd have with her sons for who knew how long.

Jimmy shoved the door open, right on time. "Hi, Mom. Do I smell pancakes?"

"Yes, you do. Plus bacon and scrambled eggs," Laura said from the kitchen.

"My favorites." David walked straight to her side, then reached one grimy hand toward a plate of crispy bacon slices.

Laura slapped his hand away. "Go wash up first. There's plenty."

The boys ate until they were stuffed, then asked a million questions about June. Laura told them all she knew, then ignored their disgruntled complaints about how they wished they could take a bus to Florida too—or anyplace else, for that matter.

Before the mood could deteriorate into jealousy and whining, she suggested a game marathon. Jimmy pulled Monopoly, Sorry!, Life, and checkers out of the bedroom armoire and piled them on the table. Laura grabbed the deck of cards and box of dominos.

"I get first game pick." David grabbed the Life box. "And I choose the green car." He opened the box and pulled out the game board, spinner, and his favorite car. "I'm the youngest, so I'm first."

Laura ruffled David's hair, Jimmy reached for the red car, and they were soon engrossed. The games progressed at a slow pace, with a lot of pauses for silly conversation and laughter, but time seemed to race by for Laura. She kept tamping down thoughts about how long it would be before she would see her sons again, but the questions would pop right back.

~⧫~

Laura couldn't sleep. She'd get into bed, then climb back out and pad on bare feet to the boys' bedroom. Not wanting to wake them, she leaned against the doorframe and watched them sleep. Jimmy still sprawled out on his back, and David curled up on his side facing the edge of the bed. They slept hard, seldom moving, but snored in soft, sibilant whispers. She needed to touch them, smooth their hair, fix the covers, but didn't want to disturb their sleep. With a sigh, she hugged her torso to resist the urge, then headed back to her room. She repeated the same pattern throughout the night, then gave up at dawn.

After getting dressed, Laura tossed the boys' dirty clothes into a laundry basket. Heading for the washing machine would be her reason to leave while they talked to Raymond. She parked the basket near the door, then started fixing breakfast. She wanted Jimmy and David to have a solid meal before they left—and their last meal with her should be a memorable one.

"Morning." Jimmy scratched his head and shuffled into the kitchen. "Wow," he said, peering at the skillets on the stove. "Pancakes yesterday and thick ham slices today? And you know David and I love fried eggs and hashbrowns. We never ate like this on food rations."

"No, it would have been impossible," Laura said, thinking about how she had planned and scrimped for this last weekend's meals. "It's almost ready. Would you wake David?"

"I'm awake." David sniffed the air, then sat in his place at the table. "Hope you made a lot. I'm hungry."

Both boys ate like they hadn't had a decent meal in weeks. They helped clear the table, then headed back to their bedroom to dress for the day. Laura started washing dishes, and was arm-deep in suds when the telephone rang. She grabbed a dishtowel, wiped the soap off, and ran to answer the phone. Her heart pounded and she almost couldn't answer when the operator asked her to accept the collect call.

"Yes" Oh my God, it's really happening.

"Hi, Mom, everything is ready to go. Are you okay?"

"Yes, I'm fine." Laura's hands shook. Her legs threatened to collapse, so she sat down. "They just finished eating a huge breakfast and are getting dressed now."

"You haven't said anything? They're not suspicious?"

"No, just think it's great that rationing is over."

"Good. Now tell them I want to talk. If you could, go outside or something so I can have them repeat the instructions until I know they've got them memorized."

"I've got a basket of laundry ready to take to the washers," Laura said, taking a deep breath, then yelled, "Jimmy, David, come talk to Raymond. He's on the phone and wants to talk to you."

Laura placed each article of clothing in the washers, one by one, sorting the whites and colors. She took her time adding detergent and setting the cycles. Since she was alone in the small, windowless room with the door shut tight, she crumpled onto the one chair and let the pain take over. Her sobs were silent, her insides ached. She pressed the heels of her hands tight against her eyes to stem the tide of tears that fought to flow. When the sound of water filling the washers stopped and the agitators started, she stood and pulled a tissue from her pocket.

"No more of this. I can't go back looking a wreck or they'll ask questions." She dried her face, blew her nose, and threw her shoulders back. "I can do this. I have to do this." She picked up the empty basket and marched back to her apartment.

"Did you guys have a nice talk with Raymond?" Laura said, closing the door behind her.

Both boys startled at her voice and jumped apart. "Yeah, it was great," Jimmy said. "He sounded really good."

"We just remembered that we have to leave early today," David said, prompting a scowl from his brother.

"What do you mean you just remembered? And why do you have to leave early? This is our day together," Laura said. Her words and tone sounded artificial to her ears.

"Uh, Stinnett said he has a bunch of work for us that has to get done today. So we have to leave by noon." Jimmy scowled at David and tapped his hand on his little brother's chest. "He didn't care that it was our family day, but said we have to leave at noon or else." One final glare at David. "We want to stay, but you don't want Stinnett to get mad and punish us, do you?"

"Of course not. But it's so unfair. I'll call the caseworker tomorrow for sure." Laura flounced into her room and slammed the door. She hoped her act had convinced them. Her anger at the Stinnetts was real. In fact, years of buried rage against their cruelty and thoughtlessness threatened to boil over.

"Mama, don't be mad at us." David's voice sounded miserable through the door. "We didn't mean to hurt your feelings. Maybe we could stay a few minutes later than noon."

Laura heard what sounded like a punch and a cry, then whispers back and forth. She opened the door and said, "I'm not mad at you guys, just sorry that we won't have more time. I know it isn't your fault."

She reached out and hugged them both, surprised at how hard and long they both hugged her back. When they released the embrace, she said, "Noon isn't very far away. Why don't you guys pack your bags so they'll be ready, then we can play cards or something until it's time."

Laura curled up on the sofa and pretended to read a magazine while the boys filled their suitcases. She could only imagine their discussions about what to take and what to leave behind, but was sure that Raymond had instructed them on what they'd need. The boys moved from the bedroom into the bathroom where she figured they were gathering their personal stuff and maybe a washcloth and towel. She pretended not to hear and kept her eyes on the pages in case they checked on her.

"We're all ready," David said, holding a case that looked much rounder than usual. He looked at Jimmy, who placed both cases by the door.

"Okay, I'll deal the cards for War, and whoever has the most cards when it's time for us to go is the winner," Jimmy said.

To Laura, it seemed like only minutes before David was declared the winner and the boys grabbed their bags and were out the door.

She followed them outside. "Hey, you two, if you have to leave early, I should at least get an extra hug."

And then they were gone, and she was inside, alone, leaning against the closed door. She waited until enough time had passed for them to get past the corner, then finished the last act in the play she and Raymond had devised.

Laura marched to the neighbor's apartment and knocked on the door. "Hello, Mrs. French," she said to the tiny, grey-haired woman who answered. "I hate to bother you, but I'm planning on baking cookies this afternoon and ran short on eggs. May I borrow two from you? I'll return them in the next couple of days, if that's all right."

"Of course, dear. Hang on a minute while I get them for you." She turned and moved away from her open screen door.

Laura watched Mrs. French's painful steps, and the way the hump on her back pressed her upper body forward and down. She made a little promise to be kinder to her elderly neighbor in the future.

"Here you are." Mrs. French handed three eggs over to Laura. "There's an extra just in case."

"Thank you so much. I'll bring you some cookies tomorrow, if you'd like."

"I'd like that."

"Great. I need to hang some laundry, then I'll start on the cookies. Take care."

Laura put the eggs away, grabbed the laundry basket and her bag of clothespins, then headed for the washroom. She lugged the heavy wet clothes to clotheslines in the fenced area behind the apartments, pleased to find another neighbor taking her dry clothes down. Laura nodded at her, sure that she'd remember seeing her. How strange to meet people and think of them in terms of an alibi.

Chapter Thirty-Six

Stop Lying And Step Back

They came that night at half-past eleven, well after her normal bedtime. Fists slammed against the door while loud, commanding voices rang out, "Police, open the door!"

Raymond was right, Laura thought. Thank goodness the boys left three hours early to give them a head-start. She took her time walking to the door, glad she didn't know any specific details and could answer all the questions that would be thrown at her with the truth.

Laura opened the door just enough to talk through. "Yes? What do you want?"

"I'm Officer Stinson, with Officer Nelson. Open the door, Mrs. Webber, and let us in. We're looking for your sons, Jimmy and David. You got away with helping one of your boys run off before, but that's not happening again," Officer Stinson said, pushing against the door.

"What are you talking about? Jimmy and David left at noon today. They went early because Mr. Stinnett had extra work for them and insisted on taking over some of our family time. And you can be sure I'll be calling my attorney tomorrow to complain about that." Laura kept her foot wedged against the base of the door, while her body resisted the pressure of the policeman's hand.

The tall, thin one, Officer Nelson, laughed. "Oh, you're good. Make it easy on yourself and open the door. We're coming in, so you might as well stop lying and step back before we have to force our way in."

"I don't understand. Are you saying something has happened to Jimmy and David?"

"Yeah," Officer Stinson said. "Something happened, all right. They never made it to the Stinnetts' place. I suppose you don't know anything about where they might have gone?"

"Oh, my God." It was easy for Laura to act scared, because she was terrified of saying something wrong. "Somebody needs to look for them. Please, they might have been in an accident, or hurt, or something." Tears welled up, and they were real.

Officer Stinson looked at his clipboard. "We've already had officers check, and your boys didn't get on the bus. There were no accidents or reported incidents between here and the bus stop, so they had to have gone somewhere else."

"But they didn't get on their regular bus. I told you, they left at noon, three hours early.

They said they had to go then, so somebody needs to check on the earlier bus."

Officer Nelson shook his head. "Well, we're not sure of that at all. We can radio in and have that checked, but in the meantime you need to let us in so we can eliminate you as a suspect in helping runaways—children who are wards of the court." He leaned forward, hands on his belt. "If you don't want to let us in, we'll just arrest you right now and take you downtown. You can answer all our questions there, and if the sergeant is satisfied, he might let you go."

"Fine, come in." Laura stepped out of the way and let them through the door. "I have nothing to hide. You need to find out where my children are. I can't imagine what's happened to them." She trudged to the sofa and sat down.

"I'll bet," Officer Nelson said. "I'm going to search your place. Are you going to give us any trouble?"

Laura shook her head, hating the smug expression on the man's face.

"Mrs. Webber, I need to know everything that happened today from the time your kids woke up until you claim they left at noon." Officer Stinson sat on the other end of the sofa, opened his notepad and held his pen at the ready.

"I said they left at noon because they did." Laura rubbed her face, then dropped her hands into her lap. Then she went through all the day's activities.

Officer Stinson finished his notes, then tucked his pen into his pocket. "Mrs. Webber, I find it hard to believe that you just sent your sons off early without demanding more information. And I don't believe that they ran off without saying anything to you. That makes no sense at all. You need to tell us all you know and stop hiding information."

"Officer Stinson, when my son Raymond ran away from the Stinnett's ranch, you came here to accuse me of having something to do with it. You were sure he'd come here, and that I'd helped him. Now you're accusing me of masterminding some big escape for my other sons. I watched them leave, then went next door to borrow some eggs for baking. After that I hung wet laundry on the lines. I've been here all afternoon.

You were wrong to accuse me of helping Raymond, and you're wrong now. My boys all hate the Stinnetts because of the horrible way they were treated. Perhaps you should investigate them and find out why all three of my sons were so desperate to get away from them."

"Don't get smart with me, Mrs. Webber. And I promise you, if we find any evidence at all that you had something to do with their running away, we will arrest you for violating custody laws."

"I've got something." Officer Nelson came out of Laura's bedroom holding a piece of paper in his hand. "I found a note signed by Jimmy tucked under your pillow."

"Oh my God, please, read it out loud. I need to know what he said," Laura begged. Inside, she prayed that Jimmy's words wouldn't reveal anything about Raymond's plan.

Officer Nelson handed the note to his partner, sneered at Laura, then folded his arms.

Officer Stinson cleared his throat and read.

Dear Mom,

I'm so sorry, but David and I just can't take any more from the Stinnetts. We lied to you about having to leave early, but needed a head-start before anyone would come searching for us. I can't tell you where we're going. We're not sure, but it will be as far away from this town as we can get. We're kind of thinking about joining June in Florida, but don't know for sure.

We haven't told you half of the things that the Stinnetts have done to us, and now that both Raymond and June have escaped, it's not fair that we have to stay another day. Last time he slammed David to the floor, I almost hit him. He keeps hurting David, and I can't take it. But if I fight back, he'll hurt both of us. So we have to leave.

We love you and are really sorry to hurt you. Please don't worry, we'll be okay.

Your son,
Jimmy

Laura couldn't prevent the tears from flowing. Her son's words, combined with the callous attitudes and expressions after the police officers read the note, were more than she could bear. She wanted to scream and hit something—someone—but couldn't do a thing. She buried her face in her hands and prayed that they'd just leave. "Please leave my son's note. It's all I have from him."

"That's evidence," Officer Nelson said.

"Please," Laura looked at Officer Stinson and stretched out her hands. "I don't know where my boys are or when I'll see them. It's been years since I've seen my oldest son, who also left to escape the Stinnetts. Please copy the note if you must, but leave it with me."

"Okay, I can do that."

Officer Nelson's disgust was obvious from the way he shook his head and the noises he made.

"But this investigation is not over," Officer Stinson said. "If we uncover a shred of evidence that suggests you helped those boys run away, you will be arrested. I promise you that. And if we catch them, they'll be detained until the Children's Bureau decides what to do with them."

Laura took the note after Officer Stinson finished copying it and stroked it as if it had a direct connection to Jimmy. She stayed seated until after she heard the door close behind the two policemen, then lowered her head to the table and cried.

Chapter Thirty-Seven

We'll Stay Together Now

Wednesday, November 28, 1945

The days after Jimmy and David left passed in a daze, with Laura's mind trapped in an emotional fog. She alternated between fear for the boys' safety, and anger at the police who continued to question her and everyone who knew her.

June had called her on Thanksgiving. She was feeling a little blue since Jack was stuck on the ship, which was now moored at the Jacksonville shipyard. They were physically closer, but still didn't have much time together. June had prattled on about her job, file clerk at a furniture company, which was just as boring as being a Woolworth waitress. The big excitement for June was their plan to go out for a fancy dinner on Jack's next liberty to celebrate his twentieth birthday.

Laura was almost relieved when June hung up. She didn't want to celebrate anything until she knew the boys were safe and was depressed about missing Jimmy's fourteenth birthday. It reminded her of all the birthdays and holidays she'd missed with Raymond.

Steps slow and measured despite the rain and wind, Laura walked inside her apartment and hung her wet coat on the rack. Work had been one problem after another, and the horrible storm outside hadn't helped. She had one rainboot off when the phone rang. She yanked the other one off, and padded to the sofa. "Hello."

"Will you accept..."

"YES!" Laura shouted, cutting the operator off mid-sentence. "Raymond, is that you?"

"Yes, Mom, it's me. And before you shatter my eardrums by yelling again, Jimmy and David arrived just after three o'clock this morning. They didn't get to bed until almost six, so they're still asleep. They were so tuckered out they'll probably sleep right on through until I wake them in the morning."

How can you laugh and cry at the same time? Laura didn't know, but the tears poured down her face, right past a huge smile. "Oh, Raymond, thank you so much. Are they okay? Why did the trip take so long?"

"It's a long way from Nixa, Missouri to Wasco, California. And traveling by freight car is a lot different from riding a passenger train. Lots of zigzagging all over the map, depending on who was with them, how many times they had to jump off and on, and where they were headed after each stop."

"I don't understand. I thought you'd arranged for someone to go with them all the way."

"Oh no, there was a whole network, like I told you. I don't want to give you details on the phone, but after a month or so when things calm down and the police aren't bothering you anymore, I'll send a letter and tell you all about their trip."

"I understand," Laura said. "But they are okay? And can you still care for them like you said?"

"Mom, don't worry. All three of us are together now, and we'll stay together. None of us are afraid of hard work, so we'll be fine."

"I miss you so much," Laura said. "I wish I'd never left you, but I didn't know what else to do."

"Don't start, Mama, please. I didn't understand at the time, none of us did, but I do now. And don't cry, please. I'll write as soon as I can."

"Okay. I love you. Please tell your brothers that I love them too."

"They know, but I'll tell them for you."

Laura heard the dial tone come on after Raymond hung up, but held on through the recorded message asking if she wanted to make a call. She put the handset back in place after the loud off-hook tone interrupted her reverie. Somehow she'd felt connected to Raymond as long as she was touching the phone receiver.

She stayed on the couch, replaying the conversation in her head, over and over. The room felt cold and damp, so she lit a single log in the fireplace. She sat on the hearth and stared at the flames while listening to the rain pepper the window. When her muscles cramped from holding the same position, Laura adjusted the fireplace screen, then stood and walked to her bedroom. She changed into her nightgown and slippers and started to pull the bedspread back, then stopped and left the room. Minutes later, she curled up in the middle of her sons' bed and fell asleep.

Chapter Thirty-Eight

Live A Life Of Your Own

Four years later,
Friday, August 12, 1949

Laura stood in the doorway of what once was the boys' bedroom. She'd better do a final check to make sure she hadn't missed anything in the room. She opened all the drawers and the armoire to make sure nothing had been left behind. The empty shelf above the hanging bar looked strange, since it had been full of games and puzzles. They hadn't been touched in the four years the boys had been gone, and they'd probably sit somewhere in June's and Jack's house at least that long before Sharon and Mike were old enough to play with them.

Laura left the room, closing the door behind her. Thinking about her grandchildren—imagine that, her a grandmother—always brought a smile to her face. Sharon wasn't quite two, and Mike was just five months old, but they were the most beautiful, most perfect children ever. Well, maybe she was a little bit prejudiced.

"Am I really doing the right thing, leaving everything and everyone behind to go to California?" Laura wondered aloud. She'd mulled over her decision for months, but had she made the right choice?

Jack and June did argue a lot. And June still needed help with taking care of her house and the children, and would have to improve a lot before she could call herself a good cook.

"Stop it," she told herself. "Jack was lucky to get on with Coca-Cola right after he got out of the Navy. They moved to Hollister, still in Missouri, and less than an hour's drive away. He makes good money, too, enough to buy their first house and a car." Laura left the bedroom and closed the door behind her. She stepped across the hallway into the bathroom.

She opened the medicine cabinet, then the cupboard below the sink. Both empty and clean. She bobbed her head, then continued her dialogue about June and Jack. "They take good care of their babies, and are saving money for the future. They have lots of friends their own age, plus a built-in babysitter in his Aunt Mae. And we can stay in touch by letter and phone once I'm settled in California."

Laura took a deep breath and headed into her own bedroom to continue with the inspection. "Stop debating. You're only forty-six years old today, much too young to give up on living a life of your own."

Bedroom done, she double-checked the kitchen, dining room, and living room—all clean and stripped of her things. Laura picked up her purse and walked out the front door for the last time.

Her shiny, dark blue, 1939 Studebaker Commander sedan was parked in front of the apartment, its trunk and back seat packed with neatly taped and labeled boxes that contained all her earthly possessions. One suitcase and a make-up train case sat in front of the passenger seat, holding the items she thought she might need during the trip. The passenger seat held a stack of state maps for Missouri, Oklahoma, Texas, New Mexico, Arizona, and California. All were marked with the routes she planned to take on her trip.

She climbed into the driver's seat and put the key into the ignition. "Okay, Bertha, let's get started. Tonight we'll stay with June, Jack and the babies, but starting tomorrow morning, it's just you and me, girl. I'm depending on you."

In less than an hour, Laura pulled into the graveled driveway behind Jack's pickup truck with the Coca-Cola logo on the door. Their family car was next to the truck. Jack hurried down the steps from the porch. "You made it. June's been antsy, about ready to send out a posse to look for you." He opened Laura's door. "How's Bertha doing?"

"Perfect. You found me a real gem with this car. Thanks so much. She may be ten years old, but she thinks she's brand new and purrs like a kitten."

"Good. What do you need to take in for tonight?"

"Just the two cases here in front." Laura dragged her purse off the seat, while Jack picked up the two items Laura indicated.

When they reached the porch, the screen door burst open. June and a pale-skinned little girl with bright red curls rushed out the door. "Grammaw," Sharon yelled, arms outstretched.

Laura bent down and scooped up her granddaughter, whose little arms wrapped tight around her neck. "Love you, sweet pea. Where's Mikey?"

"Sleeping. Play wif me?"

"Grandma can play with you a little later, Sharon. Let her get settled," June said, taking her rambunctious daughter and putting her down. "You'll have to sleep on the couch, Mom, but it's pretty comfortable."

"It'll be fine. I want to start early tomorrow, anyway."

The afternoon was chaotic, but Laura loved every minute. Sharon brought out her favorite dolls for Laura to inspect and stayed close to her grandma's side whenever she wasn't perched on her lap. Mikey woke up within minutes of Laura's arrival, and refused to fall back to sleep. He'd been a fussy baby from birth, totally different from his sister. At long last, when the children had settled for the night, the adults were able to relax and talk.

June checked on the baby, then plopped down in the rocking chair. "Do you have your maps all marked? How far do you plan to go tomorrow?"

"I'll head to Springfield to catch the Will Rogers Highway and stay on it all the way to Tulsa. Local roads will take me from there to Ardmore, where I'll stay a couple of days to visit with Ruth. That part of the trip will probably take two days or so. I'm in no hurry, and plan to stop whenever I feel like it."

"I just wish you weren't traveling alone. It isn't safe. What if something happens with the car?" June shifted in her chair and looked at Jack for support.

"I'll be on the best highway in the country. And I'm not worried about the car." Laura grinned at Jack. "The car is in great shape, and Jack has given me plenty of lessons about what to do with it. I know how to change a tire and have a brand new spare as well as a patch kit. I'll get the oil and tire air-pressure checked each time I stop for gas. And I'll start looking for a gas station to fill up whenever I get a quarter tank low. I have plenty of travelers checks with me hidden in the car, plus a small amount of cash. See? I've thought of everything. Quit being a worrywart."

"Okay, but don't forget your promise to call me when you stop each night."

Laura nodded. She knew June didn't want her to go, but that discussion was over. "If you guys don't mind, I'd like to take a quick bath and get to bed. I worked hard today, and want to be well rested to start tomorrow. If I'm gone when you wake up, don't worry. That way there'll be no fuss with the children."

When Laura finished her bath, the couch was all made up for her. She hugged everyone goodnight, said goodbye just in case she missed them in the morning, and fell asleep when her head hit the pillow.

The sound of Mikey's wails pierced through Laura's sleep, then soft fingers trying to pry her eyelids open woke her the rest of the way. Sharon giggled with delight when Laura grabbed her and started tickling. Hand in hand, they found June changing her soaked son, who was only interested in being fed.

"Morning, Junebug. Shall I fix breakfast for us all while you take care of the little guy?"

"I ate with Jack before he left for work, but if you want to fix something for you and Sharon, that would be great. She usually has cereal, either Cheerios or oatmeal. There's still enough coffee in the pot for you to have a couple of cups before you go."

By the time breakfast was over and Laura had taken her two cases to the car, Sharon figured out that grandma was leaving. A lot of hugs and tears later, Laura was able to climb into Bertha and pull out of the driveway. She watched in the rearview mirror as her family disappeared behind the screen door. She missed them already, but was also filled with excitement at the thought of the road ahead.

Chapter Thirty-Nine

Sisters Together Again

Sunday, August 14, 1949

"Bertha girl," Laura said, used to talking to her car after two days of driving. "We're halfway across Oklahoma, and almost there. Another thirty minutes or so and we'll hit Ardmore. I can't wait to see Ruth. It's been way, way too long." She reached into a small bag on the passenger seat and pulled out an apple. "When we talked on the phone last night I estimated our arrival time at about three this afternoon, and that still looks about right." She bit into the crunchy Granny Smith, and smiled at the thought of seeing her sister and the rest of her family.

Laura parked Bertha next to the curb in front of Carpenter Mercantile. She turned the motor off, reached down to pick up her purse from the passenger leg space, then heard a high-pitched squeal next to the car. She turned to face the sound, and was pulled out of the door into her sister's arms.

"Oh, my word, is it really you?" Ruth leaned back and cupped Laura's face in her hands.

"It's me," Laura said. "And you look exactly the same as I remember."

Ruth burst out laughing. "Sure I do. I don't know how you managed to find us with eyesight that bad." She stepped back and tugged on Laura's hand. "Come on, let's go upstairs. Paul or one of the boys can come get your stuff later."

Ruth led the way to a side door that opened into a tiny foyer with benches along each wall and an elevator in the middle. She punched the button and they stepped inside.

"This is new. Nothing like the creaky, little old one you used to have," Laura said.

Ruth laughed. "No kidding." Her smile disappeared. "When Martha got cancer, Jake replaced the old elevator so she could get up and down in a wheelchair. It made a huge difference for her. And later, after she passed, Jake just seemed to fade away. He ended up in a chair too, then confined to his bed for his last few months. He just didn't have any will to live without her."

"That's so sad. Your in-laws were two of the sweetest, most generous people I've ever known. Losing them must have been devastating for Paul."

Ruth nodded as the doors opened. "Yes, for all of us, but no more sad talk now." Ruth led Laura through an entryway into a living room full of people. "Laura's here, everybody. She finally made it."

Family surrounded Laura, patting and hugging her from all sides. She hadn't seen her three sisters, Ruth, Lizbeth and Becca, for years. Laura had never met Becca's family members before, but they were circled around Becca. Elliott and Aaron, Ruth's sons, both favored their father, Paul. Their baby sister, Maggie, looked just like their mom. Laura could see even more faces she didn't recognize, but knew there would be time to meet them all.

Hours of conversation and laughter later, only Ruth and Laura still sat in the kitchen, steaming cups of tea in front of them. Ruth took a sip, then said, "Is this tea going to keep you from sleeping? I can get you lemonade or water."

"Are you kidding? I don't think there's anything on earth that can keep me from sleeping tonight. I'm going on pure adrenaline." Laura held the cup to her lips and inhaled the sweet fragrance. "The last time I saw your boys together, Elliott and Aaron were toddlers. and now they're handsome young men. And Maggie wasn't even born yet. She's lovely—and appears to be head-over-heels for Cliff."

"She is. Nobody is supposed to know yet, but they're planning to get married. He's in his third year of medical school in the University of Oklahoma in Norman, so they have a long, tough road ahead of them." Ruth tilted her head. "What did you think of Jocelyn?"

Laura giggled. "Aaron's wife? She's quite a little firecracker. I never saw her sit down—or even slow down. She just sparkles. And their children are cute as can be, what with their soft black curls and French accents. I'm sorry, but I can't remember their names."

"Nadine and Tristan," Ruth said. "Jocelyn is amazing, and captures the heart of everyone who meets her. She was so shy when Aaron brought her home from France. We were not expecting him to bring back a wife, but couldn't help falling in love with her. The children are precious, and Aaron is very supportive of raising them as bilingual."

"It's wonderful to see you, Lizbeth, and Becca—all us sisters together again after so many years," Laura said, reaching out to pat Ruth's arm. "Sometimes I wish I'd let you talk me into bringing the children here to live, surrounded by family. But I just couldn't do it. Thinking about Pa and Ben being within mere miles of the kids was more than I could take." Laura shook her head and grimaced at the thought of their brother Ben, who had become just as mean and vicious a man as their pa. "Besides, you all had your own troubles to deal with, too."

"True, but that's all water under the bridge. Pa died a long, hard death from facial cancer, and was horrible to everyone the whole time. I sort of hoped that Ben might change after Pa passed. And he did, but not for the better. He's even meaner to his wife and children than Pa was. He lives in Norman, but we never see him."

Laura finished her tea and put the cup in the sink. "We could talk all night, but I'm about to fall asleep standing here. If you'll point me to the bedroom, I'd better call it a day."

⸺

Right after breakfast the next morning, Ruth and Laura set out to explore the city. Laura relished being a passenger for a change. "I can't believe this is the same town," she said. "So much has changed through the years. It's twice the size, and has more businesses than I could have imagined." After circling the downtown area, Ruth took Laura to visit Lizbeth for a couple of hours, then headed to Becca's, where they chatted over lunch.

"Thank you so much," Laura said when they got back in the car. "Last night was wonderful, but getting to spend time with Lizbeth and Becca at their homes was amazing."

Ruth agreed, then said, "I think we should make one more spot before heading home. How do you feel about going to the cemetery and taking some flowers to Ma and Bonnie's graves?"

"Perfect. In fact, I was going to ask if you'd mind taking me there."

After stopping for bouquets, Ruth drove to what she said was now called "the old cemetery" since a new one had been consecrated. She parked as close to the back as she could, then they got out and walked toward two graves marked with wooden crosses.

"This place has changed so much," Laura said. "I don't see any empty spaces at all."

"True. The church maintains the grounds, but it's been full for years."

The crosses were weathered and rough, and the carved words were nearly impossible to read. Laura and Ruth placed the flowers in small vases at the base of the upright wooden monuments, then sat on the grass in front of them.

"Do you remember when you brought me here just after my eighth birthday?" Laura turned to Ruth. "We made flower chains and draped them over Ma's cross."

"I sure do. It was your very first trip into town with me, just the two of us." Ruth chuckled. "We went into the Carpenter's old store and your eyes were big as saucers when you walked up and down the aisles."

"I loved every second of that trip," Laura said. "Well, almost. I was crushed when Paul offered me a free piece of hard candy and you wouldn't let me have it."

"Oh yes, I do remember that. I told Paul 'we don't take charity' because I was afraid you'd mention something when we got home, and we'd both get a beating."

"I know it sounds awful to say, but I'm glad Pa's dead. He was a horrible, mean man who made our lives a living hell. And then Ben took after him and ended up killing Bonnie. It still makes me sick to think of what he did to her—and got away with it."

"I know. And I'm ashamed to say I got mad at Ma many times because she wouldn't speak up to Pa. It wasn't until after she died that I realized she let him humiliate and beat her to protect us." Ruth reached for Laura's hand. "And when you told me what Ben did to Bonnie, I didn't want to believe you. I never did tell anyone. Nobody would have accepted your story of seeing what happened in a vision. They'd have thought we were both crazy."

"It's okay," Laura said. She pointed at the faint words on their mother's cross. "I wish I could afford to buy new, proper tombstones for both Ma and Bonnie. Pretty soon no one will be able to read these."

"I know," Ruth said. "It doesn't seem right that nobody will know who's buried here."

"That's true."

Laura heard a familiar voice in her head. "You know better than that, Laura. Bonnie and I are not tied to these graves. We can go anywhere in the universe we please."

Ruth tapped Laura's shoulder. "What just happened?"

"What? I don't know what you mean."

"Don't give me that, Laura. I know when you're hiding something," Ruth said. "Just a minute ago you tilted your head a little like you were listening to something. Then you nodded and smiled. I must have missed something. What was it?"

Taking a chance, Laura said, "I heard Ma's voice say 'You know better than that, Laura. Bonnie and I are not tied to these graves. We can go anywhere in the universe we please.' I smiled because I know she was reminding me so I wouldn't be sad about the fading words."

"You heard Ma's voice?" Ruth shook her head. "I remember you telling me that she talked and sang to you when you were a little girl." Ruth paused and stared. "But Ma's dead."

"Ma's body died, Ruth, but our souls never die."

"Do you really, truly believe that?"

"I not only believe it," Laura said, clasping Ruth's hands in hers. "I know it in every fiber of my being."

Tears spilled from Ruth's eyes. "Please tell Ma how much I love her, and that I'm sorry."

Laura wrapped her arms around her sister and pressed their cheeks together.

"I love you with all my heart, and always will." The familiar voice was sweet and full of love.

Ruth said, "Thank you, Laura."

Laura pulled back, a huge smile on her face. "Honey, I didn't say anything."

"But I heard...You mean?"

Laura nodded. "That's right. I didn't say anything, but I heard Ma's voice, too."

Ruth's tears became a torrent, but she laughed at the same time. "Oh my God, Oh my God. Thank you so much. I know I can't tell anybody because they won't believe me, but I'll never, ever forget this.

Chapter Forty

You're A Brave Woman

Friday, August 19, 1949

"Needles, California," Laura read the sign and pulled off the road. "Bertha, we made it to California." She parked in front of the 66 Motel. "This place looks perfect. Small, but with a little restaurant next door for me and a filling station next to that for you. We both need fuel and a good rest."

"Can I help you?" The man behind the cramped counter was short and bald, but had a great smile marred only by a missing upper front incisor.

"You sure can," Laura said. "I'd like to book a room for one night. Do you have a laundry facility here?"

"Yes, ma'am," he said. "There's a laundry with a nice washing machine in the back of the building, and a clothesline outside right next to it. As hot as it is, your things will dry in no time." The man watched Laura fill in her name in the hotel register. "Where are you from? You don't sound like you're from around here."

"Missouri. But I'm moving to Stockton"

"That's a long trip. And all by yourself? You're a brave woman."

Laura just smiled, not wanting to invite further conversation. She took her key, and a sheet with the motel layout, and a map of the city showing where points of interest were located.

Laura moved Bertha to a parking spot in front of their room door, carried her bags inside, then turned on the air conditioning unit—an unexpected luxury. She unpacked, piled her soiled, sweaty clothes by the door, then put her personal items in the bathroom. "What I wouldn't give to take a cool bath, then plop down on the bed and take a long nap." Instead, she promised herself a long soak and early bedtime after the laundry was done and she had a decent meal.

It didn't take long before Laura was back in the room, content from a filling meal of chicken-fried steak, mashed potatoes, and corn. After eating, she'd taken Bertha to the gas station to fill the tank and check the radiator and tire pressure. She planned to leave in the wee hours, well before the station would open in the morning.

Laura checked her clothes, but they were still damp. Now she had time to kill before she could conk out for the night. She looked at the phone on the dresser and wished for the millionth time that she had a number for Raymond. She was closer to him and his brothers than she had been for years, but there was no way to reach him. Why didn't somebody invent a system where you could reach somebody no matter where they were? Oh well, maybe a kid in diapers somewhere would grow up and figure out a way.

Laura turned on the television and flipped from channel to channel. She recognized the words "Ripley's Believe It or Not" when they filled the screen and sat down to watch.

"I'll bet half those outlandish stories are just plain lies. But how in heck can you tell?"

When the show ended, the news came on. All the local stories and commercials dealt with places and people she didn't recognize. Then a panel of reporters and government people began talking about the Fourth Geneva Convention, which included humanitarian protections for civilians in a war zone. Laura's thoughts turned to what Elliott had told her about the Elbe River, and couldn't bear to watch.

"It doesn't matter what agreements they make, war is awful and nobody ever seems to care about the innocent people who are caught up in the fighting."

Just the tiniest hint of dawn cut through the darkness when Laura climbed into Bertha the next morning. She turned onto the road marked "Will Rogers Highway, US Route 66" and sped up.

"This is it, Bertha, our last stretch until we reach Los Angeles and turn north up the middle of California. Today should be quite an interesting day, since we're going to cross the Mojave Desert. I know we've seen lots and lots of desert in New Mexico and Arizona, but the Mojave is supposed to be something special— and super hot. By leaving this early in the morning, we should be through most of it before the worst of the heat." Laura patted the dashboard, appreciating Bertha's easy company.

With the end of the trip beckoning, Laura covered more territory than on any previous day of the trip. She stopped in Barstow, but only for a meal. Bertha purred all the way to Los Angeles, where they found a motel not far from the junction of the Will Rogers and Golden State Highways, otherwise known as 66 and 99. Once she'd carried her things inside, Laura collected a handful of change and settled inside the phone booth near the office.

A deep voice answered, "York residence, may I help you?"

"Isaac, is that you? This is Laura. I'm calling from Los Angeles."

"Hi Laura. No, this is Ruben. Dad has a client in his office, so I'll get mom for you."

Ruben's voice sounded wonderful on the phone. Laura hoped his spirit had healed, as well as his legs.

"Laura, how are you? Ruben said you're in Los Angeles." Willa's voice was warm and inviting, a perfect reflection of the woman's personality.

"I'm just fine. In fact, I'm better than fine. I'm staying at the Cozy Orange Inn tonight, and plan to travel all the way to your place tomorrow. If I get delayed, I'll call and let you know."

"Fantastic. We've been a little worried about you traveling all alone."

"I've actually enjoyed it. I talk to myself and to Bertha, my car, and sing along with the radio. Bertha never talks back or complains if I'm off-key."

Willa giggled. "I'm glad you're having a good time. We can't wait to see you. Stay safe and be careful."

"Always. Love you guys, and I'll see you tomorrow."

☙

It was dusk when Laura parked in front of Isaac and Willa's house. "Bertha the magnificent, you're the best driving companion anyone could ask for." Laura stroked the dashboard one last time, then got out and ran around to the passenger door. She hauled her suitcase and train case out on the sidewalk, and slipped her purse strap over her shoulder.

"Hold on, let me help you with those," Ruben said, wheeling toward her on the sidewalk. He grabbed her cases and piled them on his lap. "I saw you out the window when you pulled up, and figured you could use a hand."

"Thanks, I appreciate it." Laura followed him toward the door, saying a silent thanks for his easy manner and open smile. It was hard for her to ignore the lack of his lower legs, but his dexterity and control of the chair were both great signs.

Ruben propelled his chair down the hallway. "I'll put these in your room, just like before. Mom and Pop are in the kitchen."

"Laura," Willa said, as she wrapped an arm around her friend's waist, "we're so happy you're here. Come on in and help yourself. You must be hungry."

Isaac stood as Laura entered the kitchen, a huge welcoming smile on his face. He gestured toward the table where Willa had placed platters of meat, cheese, fresh bread, and fruit. In the middle of the platters was a tall pitcher of iced tea and four glasses.

"Help yourself and tell us all about your trip."

Laura's experience traveling across the country was much different than her friends'—their broken-down car had been pulled by a draft horse—but the scenery had been the same. Then Willa asked about June's children.

"They're so precious. I took lots of pictures before leaving. I'll drop them off at the drugstore tomorrow, then we can look at them together." Laura took a sip of her tea. "I'll miss them, but June and Jack are doing well on their own, and are even talking about maybe coming to California in the future. As soon as I get a job, I'll start saving money and vacation time so I can go see my boys. Now that I have a car, everything will be easier."

Willa gasped and raised her hand to her mouth. "Oh my goodness, I forgot. Raymond called this morning when he went into town to pick up some machinery parts. He said he'll try to call again soon, but wanted to let you know that Jimmy left yesterday to go join the Army. He bought a bus ticket to Bakersfield, since the Army has a recruiting office there. Raymond said Jimmy doesn't like farming and figured the G.I. Bill is his best bet for an education after he serves his time."

Laura's heart felt like it turned to stone. Who knew where the Army would send him? How many years would it be before she got to see Jimmy? And even if he stayed in the states,

how many hundreds or thousands of miles
would separate them?

Chapter Forty-One

I'm Going Out On A Date

Sunday, October 2, 1949

"Please be there, please be there," Laura whispered as she dialed the last digit of the phone number.

"Wilson's machine shop, this is Raymond."

"Hi Raymond. Happy Birthday, son." Laura clenched the phone so hard her knuckles were white. "Is it okay for you to talk since it's Sunday?"

"Hi Mom, it's perfect since I'm here alone. Hold on a sec." The sound of a radio in the background cut off. "Like I wrote you, I'm working whenever the machine shop needs help on the weekends, plus the farm during the week. Thanks for the birthday wish. How are you doing? It's been quite a while since we've been able to talk."

"I'm doing fine, sweetheart. I love working at the Stockton Hospital, especially now that I'm a Certified Nursing Assistant instead of in housekeeping. It almost feels like I've been there forever. And two weeks ago I moved into my two-bedroom furnished apartment. I wanted the extra room just in case you can ever get away and bring David up. And I have my new telephone number too, so you can call. It's San Joaquin 7-2256. I just sent you a letter today with all the new information."

"We still can't believe June's a mother, not the way she used to sass you all the time. Hey, thanks for the last letter with the pictures. David and I loved them."

"You're welcome." Laura's voice dropped. "How is David? I always think of him as a baby. Would he even recognize me now?"

"Of course he would, Mom." Raymond cleared his throat. "David is getting big, but he could never forget you. And you'd be so proud of him. He's the smartest kid in school. That boy'll accomplish something great when he grows up."

Laura wiped away an unwelcome tear. "Thank you, honey. I better go before this call costs a fortune. I love you" She placed the handset back in its cradle, stroking the plastic as her connection to her sons.

"Stop getting all weepy," Laura scolded herself. "Your kids are doing well, and so are you. Be happy for them."

"Well said. In fact, that's what I was going to tell you." Ma's voice and loving spirit filled Laura's mind and enveloped her body.

"Hi Ma. I've missed you. Just think, you're a great-grandma now. And who would have guessed you'd have a curly-haired, redheaded granddaughter?"

Ma's soft chuckle reverberated through Laura's body. "You've done well, and the future still holds some amazing things for you."

"Thanks. What things? Can you at least give me a hint?"

The chuckle tickled her from the inside again, then the warm spirit faded away.

※

Laura's life fell into an easy pattern, split between working at a job she loved, enjoying the company of friends, and frequent contact with her children by phone and letters. She was a favorite among both the staff and patients at the hospital, and had her favorites as well— especially a tall, slender, gray-haired man named George Wagner.

George was a bit of an enigma. One day, he wouldn't be able to get out of bed, but the next he'd be up and walking around with apparent ease. He never appeared to be in pain, but of course, in a mental hospital, that didn't mean much.

"Good morning, Mrs. Webber." Mrs. Franklin, Laura's supervisor, sang out from the hallway behind her. "You have a new patient this morning in 7B, Mr. Belden. He's schizophrenic, but went off his meds at home. Shouldn't take long to get him back on track."

"7B? Did Mr. Wagner get moved to another room?" Laura's surprise was clear in her voice.

"No, his doctor released him last night." Mrs. Franklin's tight, fire-engine red curls shook as she talked. "Word is, his driver is back from vacation and picked him up."

Laura tilted her head and squished her eyebrows together. "His driver? I don't understand."

Mrs. Franklin laughed and patted Laura's shoulder. "I don't either, dear. But Mr. Wagner checks himself in every now and then because he needs assistance on his down days."

"Down days?" Laura repeated. "I don't understand."

Mrs. Franklin shrugged. "Nobody else does, either. But for many years Mr. Wagner has alternated between his up days and his down days. On his up days, he is up and around like everyone else. But on his down days, he doesn't get out of bed at all—and nothing changes that schedule."

Laura shook her head. "But nobody knows why?"

"Nobody has ever learned the reason," Mrs. Franklin said. "When his driver is away, he has no one to help him, so his doctor sends him here. It's been going on for a few years, and Mr. Wagner always pays his bill. No one questions it."

Laura shrugged her shoulders. "Sounds strange. I'll miss him, though, George is a nice man."

"Yes, he is, and I'm sure we'll see him again." Mrs. Franklin gave Laura a tight little smile, then walked away.

※

Laura was finishing dishes when the phone rang. "Wonder who that is? It's too late to be Raymond or June." She dried her hands and lifted the handset. "Hello"

"Mrs. Webber?"

"Yes. And you are?"

"This is George Wagner. I met you in the hospital a couple of weeks ago. I'm not sure if you remember me."

Laura sat on the couch and leaned back. "Of course I remember you. We had some pretty good talks during our walks in the atrium." She smiled and stretched her legs out in front of her on the coffee table.

A husky chuckle came through the phone. "That we did. I've thought about you quite a lot since I came home."

Laura waited through a silent pause, not sure what to say.

"Would you consider letting me take you out to a nice dinner? We could take our time and get to know each other better, or maybe have dinner and then go to a movie."

"I'd love to go to dinner with you. We could continue talking about whatever comes to mind, and solve all the world's problems just like we did before."

"Wonderful. My driver and I can pick you up Friday at seven, if that works for you."

"Your driver?"

"Yes. Rudolph is my nephew, and he's been my driver for several years. He'll drop us off at the restaurant, then pick us up when we're ready to leave."

"Friday at seven will be fine. I'll be looking forward to seeing you."

After they said their goodbyes, Laura put the receiver back on the cradle. Then she raised her arms over her head and stretched. "Wow, I can't believe it. I'm going out on a date."

Chapter Forty-Two

His Watch Cost More Than My Car

Friday, October 28, 1949

Laura changed clothes three times before settling on her favorite of the four good dresses she owned. She tied the sash in front of the mirror, making sure the square knot was centered. The dark blue and light green pattern was simple and flattering for her dark hair and eyes, and the full, sweeping skirt that ended at mid-calf flattered her figure. The long sleeves had cuffs that matched the notched collar, which looked quite perky when she stood it up in the back.

"Looks pretty good." She told her mirror image. "If I do say so myself."

She turned side to side to make sure the dress hung right all around, then smiled at the difference in what she wore now and the stylish clothes that were fashionable when she used to go dancing with Glen back in her twenties.

"This dress feels good too, a lot different from wearing ones with a dropped waist down on my hips. I hated those darn bras that bound me flat just so I could look like I had the figure of a teen-age boy. Besides, my knees were never that pretty."

Laura headed for the sofa to wait, but didn't make it. Her heart sped up when she heard the knock on the door. She closed her eyes, took a deep, calming breath, then opened the door.

"Mr. Wagner, please come in."

Goodness, he looked elegant in his camel-colored suit, white shirt, and butter-yellow tie.

"Just George, please." George stepped inside. "Mrs. Webber, you look lovely. I knew you were a pretty woman, but those nurse's uniforms don't do you justice."

Laura giggled and blushed. "Thank you, but please call me Laura."

George helped Laura into her coat, then offered his arm to lead her to the car.

The first things Laura noticed were the way the streetlights hit the brilliant chrome front bumper and grill, the shiny word "Cadillac" on the side of the swooping front fender above the gleaming chrome strip, and the impeccable white sidewalls of the tires. The paint was a flawless forest green that glowed wherever the light hit it. A young man stepped out of the driver's door, then held it open for

Laura. She settled into the back seat as George walked around behind the car, entered on the passenger side and took his place next to her.

Laura stroked the soft beige leather seat. "This is a beautiful car."

"Thank you. Rudolph does a great job taking care of it."

Laura sank into the luxurious upholstery for the short trip to the El Rancho Inn. Rudolph parked at the front, then opened the door and stretched out his hand to help Laura out. She thanked him, then tucked her hand into George's elbow and turned her attention to the restaurant. The white clapboard building was large, but not impressive looking. There were two doors and four large windows at the front, a white picket fence separating the side yards from parking spaces, and a neon sign suspended from a metal frame perched on the roof. But when they walked inside, the aroma made Laura's mouth water.

"Sir and madam, follow me please." The maitre'd, whose embroidered name said Raul, gave a slight bow. He led them to a corner table where they had privacy, but could still watch the other people in the room. "Here are your menus for food and beverages. Rafael will be your server tonight. If you need anything special, just let one of us know." A final nod, and then he left them alone.

"This place is something," Laura said. "I've heard of it, but never been here before."

"It's one of my favorites, and the food is superb. Their specialty is a steak and lobster plate, but you'll want to get a doggie bag to take home. The portions are large, and the food is too good to waste."

"I've never had lobster before." Laura looked over the menu, trying hard not to show her shock at the prices.

"Then let's both order that. If you don't like it, you'll still have plenty of steak—but I'll bet you enjoy the lobster too."

George was right. She loved the lobster, and they both left with wrapped containers of food. The evening was not like any other Laura had ever spent. When George asked her if he could take her out the following Saturday night, she accepted.

Once she was alone in the apartment, Laura leaned back against the door. She was intrigued by George. He was different from any other man she'd ever met. Judging by his clothing, his car, his mannerisms and speech, he was wealthy. But his behavior was unlike the only other rich man—just past a boy, really—that she'd dated.

Laura had fallen in love with Bruce, a banker's son, when she was only nineteen, and thought his attention meant he was in love with her too. Then she learned he only wanted her for a mistress instead of a wife. She still remembered the painful sense of shock and betrayal.

But George was reserved and respectful, sort of old fashioned. Laura hung her coat on the rack and kicked off her shoes, then carried the leftovers to the refrigerator.

"Of course, he's different. He was born in San Francisco to parents who emigrated from Germany."

Laura chastised herself for her thoughts, glad no one could hear her talking out loud again. George had told her that his family owned entire blocks of commercial and residential property in San Francisco and around the Bay Area, and passed it on to him when they died.

"I'll bet his watch cost more than my car," she grumbled.

But he seemed so casual and down to earth. Instead of making a big deal about his money or bragging about his possessions, he was kind and easy to be around.

"Heck, I only learned what I did about him by asking nosy questions," Laura said, still surprised that he'd answered them.

*

The next date led to another and another, for six weeks. Then George asked Laura to spend a whole day with him so he could show her around San Francisco. She offered to drive, but George said nobody's first visit to The City should be behind the wheel, especially during December when the weather could make driving difficult.

"But why?" Laura told him she'd driven across country by herself and was a very good driver.

George just smiled. "You'll see. The City isn't like any other place in the country."

And she did see—trolley cars clanging by in the middle of the roads, streets on hills so steep her knuckles were white as she clutched the edge of the seat, and magnificent ocean waves that crashed into craggy cliffs before collapsing into the white-capped sea.

George and Laura's day in San Francisco was windy and wet, so they stayed in the car, but still managed to see Alcatraz peeking through the swirling fog, drive over the Golden Gate Bridge, and travel down the famous block of Lombard Street with its eight hairpin turns— where Laura was grateful not to be behind the wheel.

After a few months, though, Laura was maneuvering around the Bay Area with ease. She'd drive to George's house in Hayward, then park Bertha and switch to the Cadillac for their adventure of the day. It took her two hours to travel—a long day, but always a pleasure.

Laura rose right after dawn on Sunday to get ready for the drive to Hayward. She was dancing around the apartment to music on the radio, when the announcer broke in. "News Flash! Northern and Southern Koreans at war! Thousands of North Koreans poured over the 38th parallel into South Korea today. Fierce fighting has broken out as the South Koreans try to hold the line. The US pledges support for South Korea."

"What? What did you say?"

Laura dropped to her knees next to the end table where the radio sat and turned the volume up. The announcer, almost hysterical in his excitement, added a few facts, then repeated the story all over again.

"No, not again. Not war all over again." Laura's thoughts turned to Jimmy. "Oh God, please don't make Jimmy go there. He's only eighteen, just a boy. Please."

The news on the radio repeated several times, then the announcer promised to break into the regular programming with any new information. Music resumed, but the songs sounded alien and pointless.

"I wish I could call Jimmy. And would they take Elliot or Aaron back in?" Laura stood and paced around the room, wringing her hands. "I forgot about George. I'm supposed to be on the way to his house, but I can't do it right now." She ran for the phone, which rang before she reached it.

"Laura, I just heard the news." George's voice was soft and reassuring. "You don't need to be driving right now, not with Jimmy on your mind."

How did he know? Laura started to cry.

"I can't help it, George. All the deaths and pain—Glen's breakdown over his brother's death, Elliot in agony over what he went through, thousands of young men dead or damaged for the rest of their lives—and now Jimmy, just eighteen. I swear, I couldn't bear it if he goes and, and..."

"Honey, you don't need to face this alone. I'll be there as soon as Rudolph can get us there."

Chapter Forty-Three

Worth The Wait

Two Years later,
Friday, December 21, 1951

"Mrs. George Wagner," Laura whispered to herself in the bathroom, staring at the mirror lit only by a soft night-light.

She didn't appear any different with her new name. She looked at her left hand, moving it around so the light caught and flashed off the large square diamond and the small diamonds that surrounded it, covering the silvery band. George hadn't let her see the ring until he'd placed it on her finger during their ceremony at the Justice of the Peace office that afternoon.

Laura smiled, remembering what he'd said after he carried her over the threshold of his—now their—little house in Hayward. He'd cradled her chin, then kissed her with such tenderness. "I love you, my adorable wife. And one of the joys of being married will be giving you things, beautiful things that you deserve, just to see you smile."

She'd thanked him for everything, then said, "I like the white gold with the diamonds."

George had smiled and chuckled. "That's not white gold, sweetheart, it's platinum. Much harder to work with, but much tougher. It won't scratch or wear away through the years."

She tiptoed into her husband's bedroom that she'd left minutes ago, leaned down and kissed his forehead. He smiled, but dreamt on. Laura couldn't help contrasting her two wedding nights.

She'd been scared to death with Glen, who thought she was just a frightened virgin, and was as tender as his passion could manage. It was many years before she confessed her fear was from the horror of being raped by her violent father. George, on the other hand, treated her like a master violinist handled his most treasured instrument.

Laura made her way to her bedroom, turned on the light and sat down at the dressing table. She began her nightly ritual of brushing her hair one hundred strokes, her mind roaming through memories with each stroke. So much had happened since she'd met George. He'd been her rock when Jimmy was deployed to South Korea, helping her stay strong through the weeks and months since.

George cared for the rest of the kids as well. He'd talked on the phone with Raymond and David more than once, lamenting the fact that to drive down would require a two-night stay in town with the boys before they could come home.

Now that they were married, George promised Laura that they'd try to plan a trip to go see them. Both Raymond and David were doing well in a little town called Victorville. Raymond worked full-time as a mechanic and did weekend gigs as a musician in a country band. He also had a girlfriend and was talking about marriage. David insisted that he was going into the Navy as soon as he was old enough so he could travel all over the world. Since he was small, he had his sights set on submarine school.

Laura put the brush on the dresser, turned out the light, and climbed into bed. She knew she'd be happy in this house, and in her new life, but she missed June and her children. They should be moving to California in a few months, though. Jack had traveled to Sacramento with his Aunt Mae to look for work, so he could save enough to move the family. He'd been in Sacramento just over three months, leaving June, Sharon, Mikey, and the new baby boy, Patrick, in Hollister.

Laura was almost asleep when she jerked upright, startled. Had she set the alarm? Can't be late for work in the morning. It took her a few minutes to remember that she didn't work anymore, hadn't for a full week. She'd driven Bertha, loaded down with the last of her personal things, from Stockton yesterday. George had insisted she not wait until their wedding day to make the drive, but she refused to stay in the house with him—no, not even in what would be her bedroom—until after they were married.

She'd put all her things away in her new room yesterday, went out to dinner with George, then spent the night in a hotel.

Laura sighed and smiled, cuddling into her pillow. It had all been worth the wait.

Chapter Forty-Four

Thanksgiving In September

Almost Five Years later, Saturday, September 29, 1956

Laura was up before dawn, singing while she prepared a huge turkey for the oven. Today was the day, a true Thanksgiving in September.

"Wow, if that bird was any bigger, it wouldn't fit."

She laughed at herself for talking out loud, but didn't care. George had caught her at it once, but just chuckled, saying that at least she had an appreciative audience for her words. She looked around the kitchen. Everything was in order. She knew the house was spotless after a week of scrubbing.

Laura headed to the front porch and settled into one of the matching rockers, letting the motion sooth her, until a taxi stopped in front of the house. A dark-haired young man got out, then started up the walkway carrying a suitcase.

Laura jumped up, opened her arms and ran to meet him. "Oh, my goodness. Just look at you, Jimmy. You're all grown up and so handsome."

Strong arms lifted her off the ground and swung her around. "It's so good to see you, Mama." The deep voice quivered. "I love you so much." Jimmy set her down, but kept his arm around Laura's shoulder. "I hope you don't mind my arriving this early."

"Not at all. George is still sleeping, but I can fix you something to eat if you'd like." Laura couldn't stop staring at her son. He'd grown into such a handsome man—dark hair and eyes, chiseled jaw and chin.

"I'm fine," Jimmy said. He dropped into one of the rockers. "I kind of hoped we'd have some time to talk before the others arrived." He clasped his hands together and hunched his shoulders.

Laura sat next to him, and placed her hand on his knee. "Of course."

Jimmy nodded and took a deep breath, staring down at his hands. "Korea was hell on earth. So many people died on both sides, but we ended up in the same place we started, the bloody Thirty-Eighth parallel. The first year of the war was vicious fighting, mostly hand-to-hand, never more than a grenade throw apart. The front moved back and forth that whole year, until everybody knew there wouldn't be a military victory for either side." Jimmy paused, rubbing his face in his hands. "Then the top brass decided to try to take some hills to improve our bargaining power." He snorted and shook his head.

"Take your time." Laura kept one hand on his knee and rubbed his shoulder with her other hand. "I'm just so sorry you had to go through what you did."

Jimmy snorted. "Me? I'm the lucky one. No injuries, still alive, even got a field grade promotion. I'm lucky to be alive, all right, when thousands of others died or ended up crippled for life." He cleared his throat, and started again. "Three stupid hills, little ones, didn't even have proper names, just numbers—983, 940, and 773. I heard that once it was all over, the news reporters come up with a fancy name for the fight over those stupid hills, The Battle of Bloody Ridge. All I know is that my platoon, 3rd platoon, Company C, 9th Infantry Regiment Division, started out on the morning of September 3rd, 1951, with twelve men out of Company C's eighty-five men. At the end of the day, there were only thirty-five left in the whole company—and I was the only one left in my platoon." Jimmy started to shake, and his eyes glistened with unshed tears. "I spent the next two years asking God, why me, and begging him to let me die too. Why did the others, all good men, most better than me, many with families,

why did they all have to die? Every single day I'd
wake up and wonder why I wasn't dead like the
others. And a lot of those days—more than I
can count—wondering if I should take my own
life to join them."

"Oh Jimmy, I'm so sorry." The words
sounded inadequate and trite, but Laura didn't
know what else to say.

"It's okay, Mom, after so many months of
asking that question, I decided God must have
had a reason to save me. I didn't tell anyone in
the family, but I just graduated from the
Southeastern Baptist Theological Seminary in
North Carolina. I'm a credentialed pastor now,
and hope to have my own church soon. I'll
probably get teased a lot by Raymond and
David, but I wanted you to know the whole
story."

Laura leaned over and hugged her son.
"I'm proud of you, honey. She took his face in
her hands. "Just don't forget to keep an open
heart for other people's beliefs. Do you
remember that insufferable, judgmental
Reverend Lowell? He was the pastor at your Pa's
Aunt Gladys' church when we lived in South
Dakota. If you end up like him, I'll swear I'll box
your ears."

⌐╼

Raymond arrived next, joining George
and Jimmy on the porch. Laura ran from the

kitchen to hug him so hard he claimed she was crushing his ribs. As soon as she let go, June's family drove up in their station wagon.

June got out of the car with two-year-old Jerry in her arms, and rushed into a tight group hug with her brothers. Jack and the three older children joined the pack which surrounded George and Laura, while June and her two brothers hugged and cried.

The happy mob gathered in the front yard, since the porch was too small to hold them all. More hugs and laughter all around, until a voice called out, "Is this a private party or can a stranger join in?"

All eyes turned toward a young man on the sidewalk, dressed in a sailor uniform, with a duffel bag at his side.

"David!" Several voices rang out together, then he was pulled inside the group.

When the excitement calmed down, Laura looked around and said, "I can't believe it's happening. After so many years, we're all together again." She started to cry. "I love you so much. Can you ever forgive me for leaving you and causing all the suffering you went through?"

Jimmy and Raymond wrapped their arms around her from both sides. "Enough of that," Jimmy said. "Don't you dare say anymore. We know you did what you had to in order for all of us to survive."

"That's right, nothing to forgive."
Raymond kissed her cheek. "I'm hungry. How about that meal you've promised us?"

"Yeah, I need to get inside," David said. "Some teenage girls followed me here from the bus station." He pointed down the street, where three girls were leaning against a front fence. "They kept asking for my phone number and wouldn't believe that I'm married with a baby on the way."

"That's what you get for being short and having such a cute, baby face." Raymond laughed, and pulled David's dixie cup hat down over his face.

"Hey, this baby face just finished submarine school," David said. "Joining up on my eighteenth birthday was the smartest thing I've ever done. After liberty, I'll be joining the crew of the USS Nautilus, the first nuclear powered submarine in our fleet."

"Oh no, we've got a lifer in the family." Jimmy grabbed David in a headlock and pulled him inside the house.

The table was filled to capacity with food, but wasn't big enough to seat the family. Everyone filled their plates, then found places to sit in the living room or outside. The conversation and laughter lasted until dusk, when Raymond and June both got their last hugs and headed home. Jimmy and David were spending the night, so talked long after George and Laura went to bed.

Laura was exhausted, but couldn't seem to fall asleep. "Oh Glen, I wish you could see them. You would be so proud. June and Jack both have good state jobs, and are raising four wonderful children. Raymond took after you, both with his mechanical skills and musical talents. He's pretty rough around the edges, but a fine man. Great father, too. He couldn't bring his wife and the kids, five of them now, since it would have been too hard on the little ones, but he's a good man. And Jimmy—a preacher? Never expected that, but after what he went through, it makes sense. As long as he doesn't try to convert everybody in the family, we'll do fine. Who would have guessed our baby, and he still looks like a little boy, would end up a career Navy man on a submarine." As usual, she didn't feel any connecting spark with Glen, but wished him well anyway.

Chapter Forty-Five

Thanks For Trusting Me

Two Years later,
Saturday, November 22, 1958

Laura refilled George's coffee cup. "I can't believe that June is getting married today," she said. "I mean, Al seems like a wonderful man, but she's only been divorced for a year."

"I know what you mean. But I've got to tell you, there did seem to be some tension between June and Jack at the reunion. Nothing I could pinpoint, just a feeling." George took Laura's hand. "We just have to be here for her when she needs us."

"I know." Laura sighed and squeezed his fingers. "I felt it too. June called to talk a lot about their problems before she took the final step and filed the divorce papers. Sure hard on the kids, though."

George agreed, then looked at the kitchen clock. It was a silly thing that Laura loved—a black cat with the clock on its stomach, and a long tail that swung side to side in sync with the cat's eyeballs. "June and Al should be in Reno saying their vows about now."

"Yes, they'll stay through Tuesday, then drive home." Laura sipped from her cup, made a face, then warmed the coffee up from the pot. "Let's just hope the rest of the kid's marriages stay strong."

George laughed. "Judging from the number of kids they all have, I sure hope so."

"No kidding. When David's second gets here, we'll have a total of thirteen grandchildren."

<hr/>

Four months later, after smooth sailing on the family front, Laura woke in a panic. Her watch said one o'clock. It was pitch black outside since there was no moon. She grabbed her robe and ran to George's bedside. "George," she said, shaking him hard. "Get up and get dressed. We've got to get on the road right now."

"What's going on? It's the middle of the night."

"I know, but something terrible is going to happen. I don't know what it is, but we have to get to Raymond's house as fast as we can."

George sat up and swung his legs over the side of the bed. "Raymond's house? That's a six-hour drive. Are you sure? What did you see?"

"Just trust me. All I know is we must be there as early as possible. Please, George," she pleaded. I know it's crazy, but you've got to believe me."

George took her hands, then kissed her. "I trust you."

They were on the road within thirty minutes. They didn't want to stop, so had a hamper with a big thermos filled with water, cups, and a supply of bananas, apples, and cookies For some reason, at the last minute Laura felt compelled to run back inside to grab a stack of hand-towels.

The Cadillac, less than a year old, already had a full tank and sped down the highway as fast as Laura dared. It ate up the miles, purring its way through the night, passing the few cars and trucks they encountered on their way.

The sun crept up, illuminating the highway. "How are we doing?" George's voice was soft.

"I still feel the same urgency, so I think we should be okay." Laura glanced at George. "Thanks for trusting me. Nobody has ever believed in me like this. It means more than you could ever imagine."

George rested his hand on the back of her neck, stroking the tired muscles. "I love you more than you could ever imagine."

Another hour, then Laura had George open the map and guide her toward Raymond's place. They saw the house, sitting in what looked like a huge, barren field dotted with plants that could only survive in a high desert. They roared up into the driveway, shut off the engine, and ran to the front door. Laura wanted to rush in, but knocked instead, her heart racing.

Timothy, at seven years the oldest of the children, opened the door and burst into tears. "Grandma," he wailed, "Cindy is hurt real bad."

Glancing back at George, Laura knelt down, terrified to see large splotches of blood on Timothy's clothes. "It's going to be okay, honey. Take us to her."

Timothy ran into the house, leading the way to the sofa where his brothers and sisters were grouped around Cindy, only five. There was blood everywhere.

"I didn't mean to do it," Kevin cried, sobbing so hard Laura could just make out his words. "We found the gun in the trash heap and were just playing."

"George, bring those towels right now. Then have Kevin show you where the phone is and call 911. It may be faster for us to take her to the hospital since we're so far out. Find out where the hospital is, and what they want us to do."

As she gave instructions, Laura ran her hands over Cindy's unconscious body, grateful to see that she was breathing and had a thready heartbeat. She found an entry bullet wound just behind the little girl's left ear, and an exit wound on her right forehead. Both were bleeding, but there were no signs of any pulsing spray.

"Timothy, where are your parents?"

"Mama took Daddy to work. We went out to play right after they left. And then..." He started crying again. "We were all playing. Kevin didn't mean to hurt Cindy."

"I know, honey."

"Here are the towels. The hospital said their ambulances are tied up with a multiple car accident, so we should take her in. They gave me directions and are calling the police to let them know we're on the way and to give us an escort. I wrote the information down so we can leave it for Betty."

Laura wrapped Cindy's head in a towel, securing the ends. She wrapped her little body in a quilt from the back of the couch to keep her warm. "We have to take Cindy to the hospital right now." She looked around at the terrified little faces. "You did a great job caring for your sister before we got here. I need you all to be brave and strong while we get her the help she needs. When your mom arrives, tell her we're headed for the hospital with Cindy. Your Grandpa George wrote everything down, so she can call us there. We're counting on you guys, can you do it?"

Solemn nods and silent tears from the children, then Laura and George ran with Cindy to the car.

A police car, with full siren and lights, led the Cadillac for the second half of the trip to the hospital. Medical staff whipped the doors open and ran Cindy into the Emergency Room. A chaplain joined Laura and George in the surgical waiting room, holding their hands and praying with them. Two hours into their vigil, Raymond and Betty arrived.

"Have you heard anything?" Raymond was shaking so hard it was difficult for him to talk. "It's all my fault. I forgot that old gun was out in the shed trash heap. I didn't think it even worked, and never dreamed there was a bullet in the chamber." He sat down and buried his face in his hands.

"They took her straight into surgery," Laura said. "We haven't heard anything yet."

Betty sat next to Raymond, wringing her hands. "I should have packed them all into the car when I took Raymond to work, but the car's so crowded that way." She stopped mumbling, tilted her head, and looked at Laura and George. "We didn't know you guys were coming. You must have left home in the middle of the night to get here this early."

Before Laura could answer, a surgeon walked into the room. "The surgery isn't quite over, but Cindy is doing well. The bullet, for some reason, circled around the inside of her skull rather than plowing through her brain. She isn't out of the woods yet, and may have some neurological problems because of the injury, but we expect her to recover." The doctor paused, then turned toward Laura and George. "I don't know how you two managed to arrive at the house when you did, but that made all the difference. Thank you both."

Cheering replaced tears. Since no one could see Cindy until she was out of recovery and moved into an ICU bed, George and Laura left to find a hotel room near the hospital before they collapsed. George was sound asleep minutes after a hot shower. Laura took one too, but since they hadn't brought a change of clothes, she washed her bloody dress in the bathtub and hung it to dry.

Laura slept until noon, when the telephone rang. "Hello, Mom? Sorry if I woke you, but just wanted to let you know Cindy is doing fine." Raymond sounded hoarse. "And Mom, I don't know how you knew to come when you did, but you saved Cindy's life. Betty and I don't know how to thank you. If we'd lost our little girl..."

"Honey, don't even go there. I just knew we had to get here, so we did. Don't question it, just be grateful."

George stayed in bed all day. Laura spent most of the day resting with him. She visited the hospital in the afternoon and spent time with Raymond and Betty.

"Kiss the kids for me," she said when they left. We have that long drive tomorrow, but I want them to know we love them."

Chapter Forty-Six

He Killed Himself

Almost three years later.
Saturday, April 1, 1961

"Laura, Al's on the phone. June had a baby girl." George, with a huge grin, held the phone out to his wife.

"It's a girl?" Laura grinned back at George, prancing in place. "How are June and the baby? What did you name her?"

"They're both fine. June's asleep right now. We named her Lauri Ann."

Al answered a few more questions, then said goodbye.

"Another granddaughter. They named her Lauri Ann." Laura joined George on the couch. I remember the day June was born. Never dreamed she'd grow up and have five children."

George hugged Laura. "I'll bet you never dreamed you'd have so many grandchildren either." He kissed her and grinned. "I think you're still a pretty sexy grandmother, no matter how many there are."

June stayed in the hospital for three days, then called Laura when she and the baby went home. "Hi Mom, we're home and the baby is beautiful."

"Of course she is. She has a beautiful mother," Laura said. "How are you feeling? And what do the other kids think of little Lauri?"

"They love her and think she's adorable. Of course, she just got here. Wait until she keeps them awake during the night or when I ask them to help with diapers."

"That's pretty normal. Those jobs are for you."

"True," June agreed. "Listen, I've got a surprise for you. It looks like the adoptions will be final in May, then all the kids will have the same last names."

"Adoptions? You haven't told me anything about any adoptions." Laura didn't like the sound of what she was hearing.

"Oh, I thought I had. Before Jack left to move back to Missouri last year, I asked him if he'd let Al adopt the kids. He'll always be their dad, but this way, we'll all have the same last name. And Jack won't have to pay child support, since he would give up his parental rights."

"You and Jack may have had your problems, but he loves his children," Laura said.

"Asking a man to give up his parental rights is a very big deal. I can't believe he agreed to that."

June's voice hardened. "Well, he did. And I never told you half of what our problems involved. I know Jack loves the kids, but Al is a much more stable father for them. I thought you'd be happy about this, happy for all of us."

"I'm not trying to create problems, and I know Al is a good man. But June, I can see so many potential problems. I don't want to make you unhappy, but I sure hope you've thought through what you're doing."

June insisted she had and terminated the call with a quick goodbye.

"What's the matter? You looked so happy at the start of that call, but you don't now," George said.

Laura explained what was going on, and the potential problems she feared. She knew how persuasive and stubborn June could be, and was sure that Jack would regret giving his children up. In spite of June's desire for the perfect new family all sharing the same last name, that goal seemed pretty shallow compared to the pain it would cause Jack.

George said that if Jack had agreed, he must have been okay with the plan. Either that, or June had been persuasive enough to push him into agreeing.

May came and went, and Laura didn't say a single negative word about the adoptions when June called to say, "Now we're the Silva family, everybody with the same last name."

Laura wondered what the children thought of the change, but didn't ask June. Then, at the end of May, June called to catch up on family news and announced that Jack had invited Sharon to come stay with him for the summer.

Laura's body broke out in cold chills for no apparent reason. "Are you sure that's a good idea? That's a long way for her to go by herself."

"Don't start, Mom. I know what I'm doing. Sharon's really excited about going and I'm not going to take that away from her."

Laura didn't say anything further about the plan, but she couldn't escape the shivery feeling that something was very wrong. She didn't mention the trip in future conversations, but tried to connect with her fears and feelings and understand better. Each night before she went to sleep, she asked for guidance, but didn't receive any new images.

Then, during the first week in June, Laura got a call from June saying that she had changed her mind about letting Sharon go. Somehow, Laura's concerns must have connected. June had contacted Jack and told him that all four of the children could travel to Missouri, but Sharon wouldn't be allowed to go alone. Jack was livid, insisting that this was to be a special treat just for him and his daughter. When June wouldn't budge, Jack refused to take the boys and slammed down the phone.

Laura was relieved. but still unable to explain why. Of course, Sharon was hurt and angry, and refused to talk to her the next few times Laura called.

The summer passed with picnics, boating, and Sharon's first summer job babysitting for a neighbor. She had recovered from her disappointment and let go of her anger at her mother and grandma.

Then June called Laura on a Wednesday evening in October. Her voice sounded shaky and scared. "Mom, I just got a call from Missouri," she said. "Jack's dead. He killed himself, just like he threatened to do for years." June broke into heavy sobs, making her words almost incoherent. "Mom, the people that called me said he was angry and raving. He was on the phone, yelling about nobody loving him anymore, and that I'd taken his children away from him. Then he put the gun in his mouth and pulled the trigger."

Laura pressed her hand to her face, trying to shut out the image that filled her mind. "Oh my God. Oh my God. If Sharon had been there..."

"I know, Mom," June cried. "When they told me, I knew that if she'd been there, he would have killed her first to keep her from coming back to me."

Laura could only shake her head and listen to June bawl, knowing the truth of what she'd said. "Honey, just be grateful that you did the right thing. Sharon is all right, thanks to you. Does she know?"

"Yes, she overheard me when I took the call. And Mom, when I hung up and looked at her, she was white as a ghost and said, Daddy would have killed me to keep me there." I didn't say anything like that on the phone, but she knew. Deep inside, she knew."

When Laura got off the phone, she sent a silent prayer to Jack, wishing that there had been something that she could have done to ease his pain and despair. She knew June would work her way through, and that they would talk about what had happened as often as June needed. Her greatest concern, though, was for Sharon. She was certain that her granddaughter would stuff her pain down deep inside, unable to cope any other way.

Chapter Forty-Seven

Today Is The Right Day

Sunday, February 13, 1966

"George, are you ready? The stores in The City open at eleven, so we can shop for an hour or two, then have a late lunch. Then, if I haven't found the perfect dress and shoes—and a new shirt and tie for you—we can continue until we're finished."

George rolled his eyes at her. "Sharon's wedding isn't until another month. Tell me again why we have to do a marathon shopping trip to get everything today?"

"It's a woman thing. I don't like leaving things for the last minute, and just have a hunch that today is the right day. Besides, it isn't every day that our first granddaughter gets married."

"That's for sure," George said. "And since she's just eighteen, I'm pretty darn sure that June and Al would have preferred the date be postponed for about five years. At least until she finished at UC Davis. One semester for a straight-A student when they expected her to go on through vet school? No, I imagine you're about the only one in the family cheering this marriage on."

"That's just because the others don't see what I see." Laura giggled. "Besides, I am the one that got them together.

Laura reminded him that Jimmy and an Air Force family that had attended his church in Karachi, Pakistan, had both come to Sacramento at the same time. Jimmy had invited Laura to go to dinner with them, and she'd met their teenage son—who would soon be Sharon's husband.

George preferred spending his up days traveling, but had an excellent eye for shopping. Laura had had a difficult time changing a lifetime of checking price tags before making choices, but George insisted on her not peeking at prices until after she decided whether she liked a particular dress. When they arrived at the Stonestown Shopping Center, they strolled past the store windows, entering only if there was a display that they both liked.

When Laura shopped by herself, she worked her way through the racks until she found something interesting. But George would find a comfortable chair, then ask the first salesperson to approach for help. He'd point out the display item that had brought them in, then ask the salesperson to bring that dress and any others that looked like they would be flattering on Laura.

They had a wonderful time, and in spite of George, Laura kept to her plan and only bought the one perfect dress she'd been seeking. It was a soft, black and white paisley print silk that seemed to float around her body. They found a new suit, shirt and tie for George too, then shoes for both of them. They were both grateful and ready to go when the valet brought the car around.

"What a day," Laura said when they worked their way out of downtown San Francisco and headed home. "I told you this would be the perfect day for shopping. And I, for one, had a great time."

"Me too. Watching you carry on like a carefree kid is a treat. Let's stop at that new steakhouse and celebrate for dinner."

"Sounds good. What are we celebrating?"

"How about no more shopping? Or, since tomorrow is Valentine's day, we could celebrate that?"

Dinner was superb, the ideal end to their day. They carried the packages inside and locked up the car. George was wearing out, so opted for an early shower. He planned to watch television until it was time for bed.

Laura was wound up and decided to call her kids. David was out at sea, but she had a great conversation with his wife, Sheila. They discussed the kids, the farm, and David's Navy career. Laura had always liked Sheila, and knew David adored her. Next on the list was Jimmy, who was staying with his wife, Lenore's family, until they returned to Karachi. Jimmy was eager to go back, since Pakistan had become his home after serving there for over fifteen years.

Whenever Laura talked to Raymond, she always thought of Glen. Raymond not only favored his father in appearance and skills, but always preferred dressing like a rangy ranch-hand. He brought her up to date on Cindy's progress, which had been excellent so far. She only had a slight limp and weakness on one side, which was remarkable considering what she'd gone through.

Laura called June last, since she was so close to her daughter. The years since Jack had committed suicide had been smooth on the surface, but Laura worried. June assured her that everyone was fine, just nervous and a bit frazzled about the upcoming wedding.

"June, remind your mother that she's on long distance. That's expensive." Al's voice rang out in the background.

Laura laughed, and said, "Tell Al that it's only money. Family's much more important."

Very pleased with the conversations, Laura put the receiver back into the cradle and went to check on George. She found him asleep on the couch. "Wake up, sweetheart. You'll sleep better in bed." She got him up, walked him to his room, and kissed him goodnight.

"I think a bubblebath would be the perfect end to a perfect day." Laura poured crystals under the running faucet, then slid into the scented water. She soaked and drifted in and out of the most delicious feeling of utter contentment, at peace with the world.

After the delightful soak, Laura headed for her bedroom. She draped her robe over the back of the dressing-table chair, and brushed her hair before climbing into bed. I'm such a lucky woman, she thought. I have sisters I adore, and friends that have stayed with me and supported me through the years. I've been loved by two very special men, and have four children who have grown into wonderful people. My grandchildren have been such a treat—and someday I'll have great-grandchildren.

Laura snuggled down into the pillow and closed her eyes. She thought of the one thing that she missed, the one thing that would have made her life right now absolutely perfect. If only her Ma had lived to see her children and grandchildren. How she would have loved them.

"But I do know them and love them, honey, and am proud of each and every one."

Laura hadn't heard, or felt, her mother's voice for years, but the warmth and love that surrounded her was unmistakable. She opened her eyes and was stunned to see a lovely woman with long black hair standing by her bed. The face was familiar too, very similar to Laura's own when she was young. The woman seemed to be shimmering with a faint glow from within, rather than illuminated by the soft moonlight coming through the window.

"Ma? Is that really you?" Laura whispered and sat up. "I can't believe I can see you."

"Yes, sweetheart, it's me. But then, I've always been with you. I've watched over you every single day since I came to this side when you were only three years old."

"Oh Ma, I've missed you so much."

The beautiful woman smiled, her face radiating love and tenderness. "I'm here now. Your life has been filled with challenges, but you've done an amazing job."

Tears welled in Laura's eyes. "I couldn't have done it alone, Ma. Without your help and support, I'd have given up a hundred times."

"No, honey, you'd never have given up on your children." The woman smiled even wider. "And now it's time for you to come with me. It's more beautiful than you can even imagine on the other side—and we'll never be apart again."

Laura tilted her head. "I don't understand." Then her eyes widened, and she took a breath. "Wait a minute. Do you mean..."

The woman laughed, then lifted her hand and extended it, palm up.

With a joyous sigh, Laura reached out and took her mother's hand.

Acknowledgments

This book could not have been written without the help of my mother, June Azevedo. Her stories about growing up helped me create the emotional framework for the fictionalized characters and events. She told me about her mother's incredible strength, and how she stepped up when her father began losing touch with reality. Mom remembers the time they spent on a lovely farm. She remembers the awful day her father was taken away, never to return. Mom also told me how much it hurt to leave the farm when her mother, the real Laura, wasn't able to handle all the work alone.

I also have to thank many writers in the Sacramento community for their support, patience, and guidance. The superb critique group led by Gini Grossenbacher helped me every step of the way, including Carolyn Radmonovich—who also helped by serving as a wonderful beta reader—as well as Mary Ann Bernard, Sande Heaton, Emily Boyd, and Judith Vaughan. Other special people, both writers and beta readers, kept me going with their skills, humor, and kind words, including Michelle

Hamilton, Norma Jean Thornton, Judy Pierce, and Marlene Meincke.

Writing can play havoc on home life but I am blessed with a marvelous husband, Stan Darrow, daughter, Sheryl Wilson, and grandsons Christopher and Nicholas. They put up with my lack of attention while I agonized over the manuscript, and loved me anyway.

Thank you all.

About the Author

I've been passionate about three things my whole life: reading, flying, and animals.

I was one of those kids who walked down the halls holding an open book, glancing up to keep from running into people or walls. I no longer walk down the street holding an open book, but I do manage to read a few sentences on my Kindle at red lights. Reading is as important to me as breathing, and one of my greatest joys now as an author is getting to know other writers. What could be more awesome than reading a fantastic book and being friends with the writer?

Thanks to a marvelous husband who knows how much I love flying, I've been up in a hot air balloon, a two-man helicopter, a glider, and an open cockpit bi-plane. He even encouraged me to get my private pilot's license, and sympathized when I had to quit during the economy crash of 2008. Every minute in the air was amazing, and today I'd go up in anything, with anyone willing to take me, anytime, and anywhere. No wonder one of my writing idols is Richard Bach, pilot and author of *Jonathan Livingston Seagull* and my favorite book ever,

Illusions, The Adventures of a Reluctant Messiah.

My love of animals made me want to be a veterinarian, but I fell in love and married during my first year of college. In spite of dropping out, I still made a contribution to animal welfare by raising 514 bottle-fed kittens, working an all-volunteer cat spay and neuter clinic every month for 20 years, and writing books about animal rescue.

I believe that a supportive family is key to a happy life and am blessed with an understanding husband who has been my best friend and life partner for 55 years thus far.

Sacramento, California has been home for most of my life. Stan and I live next door to my parents, and share our home with our cats Gracie, Portia, Bonnie, Becca, and Ash. We now also have three chickens—Bernice Williams, Anna Banana, and Lady Cluck—that fertilize and cultivate our garden while taking care of insects throughout the yard.

My philosophy of life is simple. If you find harmony within, you can make a difference to the people around you. That in turn spreads out and makes a difference in the world. Life just gets better each year as long as you keep dreaming and loving.

One of the best things in life for a writer is hearing from readers. I'd love to hear your comments, questions, or suggestions. You can

find me on my website,
https://www.sharonsdarrow.com, on Facebook
at https://www.facebook.com/SamatiPress, or
you can email me at sharon@samatipress.com.

I hope you enjoyed *Her Triumph*, the last
book in the Laura's Dash series. If you'd like to
learn more about what happened before, here
are the first chapters from Book One, *She
Survives*, Book Two, *Strive and Protect*, and
Book Three, *Desperate Choices*.

SHE SURVIVES

CHAPTER ONE

Hardscrabble Birth

August 1903, Five miles outside of Ardmore, Oklahoma

"Look, Jon, ain't she pretty?"

"She? She? Another damn girl? What's the matter with you, woman. Five young'uns so far, and only one boy. And him the last a'fore this'n, so he's no use to me on the farm for years." Jon turned away from the bed with a disgusted expression and headed toward the open door. "Pretty? Hellfire, just another useless mouth to feed."

Vera watched her husband shove five-year-old Becca aside as he pushed past his four older children to get through the doorway. He went straight to the wagon, jumped up on the wooden bench, and grabbed the reins.

"Miz Dobbs, aint you 'bout ready to head home?" he yelled.

The youngsters, clustered around the open door in the sweltering August midday sun, stared at Vera and Miz Dobbs. They were careful to not look back at their father, hoping he wouldn't focus his attention on them. Ruth, the oldest, made sure Lizbeth and Becca stayed just outside the threshold where Miz Dobbs had told them to remain. She held Ben, just turned three, by the hand to keep him from rushing through the door.

Miz Dobbs patted Vera's arm and shook her head. "I got to go, Miss Vera. Mr. Cavanaugh sounds mighty impatient. You and the baby'll be just fine."

"I know. Thanks for your help. Can't imagine having to birth a baby without you." Vera squeezed the midwife's hand.

Miz Dobbs started to turn away, then looked back and whispered. "Miss Vera, you know your baby was born with a caul on her head. Ain't never seen part of the birth sack stuck to a baby's head like a hat before, but I've heard some folks believe that's a sign that the baby's born with the second sight. Least ways, that's what my gram told me. Do you want to keep the caul?"

"I'd love to keep it for Laura when she's grown, but Mr. Cavanaugh wouldn't like it. Would you keep it?"

"Yes, ma'am, I'll be proud to keep it for you." Miz Dobbs smiled, packed a collection of bottles, jars, and rags back into her battered leather bag, then hurried out the door.

As soon as she settled herself on the wagon bench, Jon slapped the horse's back hard with the reins. The horse lunged forward into the harness, jerking the wagon onto the rutted road.

Vera waited until the sound of hooves faded in the distance, then pressed her lips against the baby's damp hair. "It's alright, sweet Laura, it's alright. Mama loves you."

Vera stroked the baby's forehead, remembering how she'd looked at birth with the glistening white membrane stuck tight to her tiny head, covering her eyebrows, hair and ears. Poor little one. There should be a ceremony to guide your path and protect you, with all the clan members taking part. "What will it mean for you, my sweet Laura?" Vera whispered in her ear. She knew Laura's life path would be hard, no doubt of that, but she'd also have strength, luck, and special gifts of the spirit. "No tellin' what kinds of gifts they'll be."

Unable to resist their imploring looks, Vera raised her right arm and waved the other children, still waiting in the doorway, to come over to her bed. "Come on now, time to meet your new baby sister."

They rushed forward, jostled for the best positions as they gathered around the bed, stroking the baby's face and arms, holding her tiny hands, and assuring themselves that their ma was alright.

"That's enough for now," Vera said, after each child had a turn with the baby, "I'm awful tired. Ruth, will you fix something to eat for supper? And please close the curtain so the baby and I can sleep."

Ruth nodded, then herded the little ones away from the bed. She closed off the area by pulling together two blankets suspended from a rope stretched from wall to wall just below the muslin-covered ceiling. Something moving on top of the muslin above the bed caught her eye, a clear sign that some type of vermin had fallen through the sod and been caught by the cloth. Wooden pegs, pounded diagonally into the angle between ceiling and plaster-covered sod walls, kept the fabric taut. Ruth could see that Ma would need to replace the muslin soon since it had torn away from some of the pegs and sagged in many places from the weight of the dirt and small creatures it held.

Vera cuddled her daughter's soft, warm body against her breasts. She listened to the faint, whispery sounds of the baby's breathing, then drifted off to sleep, newborn in her arms, both exhausted from the rigors of birth.

Hours later, Vera woke to the sound of her husband stumbling to his side of the bed. She kept her eyes closed and her breathing regular, hoping he'd think she was still asleep. He stank of alcohol and sweat, cursing in the darkness as he pulled off his boots, overalls and shirt, then dropped on the bed and shoved his legs under the covers, still dressed in his dirty long-johns.

Vera heard the children stirring, disturbed by the sounds their father made, before they slipped back into sleep on their straw pallets just a few feet from her bed. Jon's heavy, rhythmic snores let her know when he was asleep, so she could climb out of bed with baby Laura in her arms.

Vera knew the baby needed to nurse but didn't want Laura to wake up enough to cry. Moving in slow motion to avoid making any noise, Vera sat down in an old wooden rocker near the foot of the bed and brought the baby to her breast. Little Laura rooted around for a moment before she latched on and suckled with greed, working her tiny, contented fingers against her mother's skin. As she rocked, soothed by the quiet perfection of the moment, Vera began to sing the Cherokee Morning Song, an ancient melody passed down from one generation to another, just as she remembered hearing it when she was little. She loved the words, but the meaning—I am of the

Great Spirit, Ho, It is so, It is so—was even more precious.

We N' De Ya Ho,
We N' De Ya Ho
We N' De Ya,
We N' De Ya
Ho, Ho Ho Ho
He Ya Ho,
He Ya Ho
Ya Ya Yaaa

She thought only Laura could hear the words, but she was wrong. All of a sudden, her body snapped forward propelled by a hard slap to the back of her head. "I tole you about talkin' Cherokee in my house. If'n I hear it again, I'll knock you clean out'a that chair."

Jon's voice was low, more like a menacing growl than speech. The threat was real as demonstrated by the force of the blow, the promise of more violence clear.

Vera didn't make a sound, nor did she turn to look at her husband. She could sense his presence as he stood behind the chair, looming over her. Squeezing her eyes closed against the pain radiating from the back of her head, she fought against the urge to react. She stayed still, her head bowed forward over her daughter's body, then resumed rocking and nursing after she felt Jon move away from behind her. Within minutes, Vera heard a liquid torrent as he used the thunder-jug from under their bed, then the noisy creaking when he lowered his body back onto the rope mattress. The pungent urine odor stung Vera's nose as she sat, waiting, until his snores once again filled the sod house. Only then did Vera let the tears run from her eyes while she changed Laura's diaper and rocked her back to sleep.

Vera stayed in the chair a long time, rocking and stroking Laura's warm little body, because she didn't want to climb back into bed next to her husband. How could I have thought he was a good man? If only I'd taken more time to get to know him. There's worse things than being alone.

Jon had first introduced himself at a church picnic. As Vera helped the other women set out bowls of food on long wooden tables, she noticed him watching her from where he stood with two other men. She felt his eyes on her throughout the afternoon, but he didn't speak to her until people started leaving.

"Hello miss, I'm Jon Cavanaugh," he'd said. "You're the schoolteacher, ain't you?"

"Yes, I'm Vera Miller." They talked a long time, seated on wooden benches in the churchyard. She told him about her students, and he told her about purchasing a homestead.

Vera enjoyed talking to Jon and considered him a handsome man. He was tall with dark brown, wavy hair, deep blue eyes, a dark complexion, big, strong looking hands, and a muscular, powerful build. He also had a scar running from just below his right eye to the base of his ear. The scar was pale, a wide, raised welt standing out against his dark skin. Vera tried not to stare, but couldn't help wondering what had happened to him. Jon was courteous but didn't smile as they talked.

One week after they met, Jon caught Vera at school after her students had all left. He wasted little time before getting to the point of his visit, a marriage proposal. He explained that he needed a wife to help him work his homestead, and she needed a husband. They were both strong, young, and living away from their families. They were also God-fearing, so should share the same ideals about the commandments to marry and raise children. Vera, after a day to think about it, accepted. It seemed like a reasonable decision based on sound ideals, a good match for them both.

Vera remembered her wedding day and wished she could go back and change things. No fancy clothes, flowers, or music, just standing in front of a preacher early in the morning. After saying "I do," she'd watched Jon nod to the parson, then lead the way outside to his wagon, piled high with their belongings. No kiss, no hugs, not even any soft words.

Reaching Jon's homestead had taken all day, and the condition of the place when they arrived was much more primitive than Vera had expected. No house at all, just a crude, three-sided lean-to built into the side of a small hill. She hadn't said a word, though, just followed her new husband's lead, helping him transfer the wagon contents inside and then trying to create some order. When the wagon was empty, Jon put the horse and wagon into the barn which was in much better condition than the lean-to, while Vera started a fire and began to prepare supper. Vera hadn't known what to expect when the sunlight faded, and the darkness drove them inside by the fire. She'd hung a blanket over a rope stretched across the length of the open side of the lean-to, providing them with shelter from the night. When she'd finished, Jon had reached for her without a single word, pulling her toward their bed against the wall. Vera sat down on the thin straw mattress next to him, then was shoved flat on her back and taken like an animal in the field. Vera hadn't fought or protested, understanding it was her duty as a wife to submit to her husband.

Jon wasn't a talkative man, but during long hours trapped together during their first winter, they'd talked about their family histories.

Vera's parents had died in a fire the year before she'd started teaching, only six months after her brother had gotten married and moved away to be with his wife's family. Vera couldn't rebuild the burned buildings or work her father's farm by herself. No clan members lived nearby, and the tribal reservation was miles away. Teaching in a nearby town was her only choice. The previous teacher had married and moved away, so the School Board was happy to accept her. Her education at a Christian off-reservation day school was sufficient for her to teach elementary school students.

Jon's mother had died giving birth to him, her fourth baby. His father had neither the time nor patience to deal with a baby, so he hired a newly freed slave, Millie, to take care of the home and the children, and to serve as a wet nurse. Jon's father had grown up with slaves in the family, so he treated Millie the same way. Jon had one sister, the second oldest child, whom Millie taught about women's work and about a woman's place. Jon's father was a firm believer in punishing youngsters who disobeyed him, using either a razor-strap or riding crop. The scar on Jon's face came from his father's whip, when Jon had tried to turn away once to escape punishment, a lesson he'd never forgotten. When Jon's pa died, the oldest son inherited everything, forcing Jon, his other brother, and their sister to leave and find their own way.

Vera's thoughts were interrupted when Laura started fussing against her shoulder. The motion of the rocker and comforting touch of Vera's hands on her back soothed the baby to sleep. Vera kissed the top of her head. If only they'd talked about family and raisin' young'uns earlier. Never would have married a man with no softness or love inside him. Wasting time looking back though, no way to change things now. Got to get some sleep.

Vera carried the sleeping baby back to the bed, tucked the warm little body tight against her side, and was soon dreaming, breathing in the sweet smell of her baby's breath.

Vera and baby Laura were together almost all the time for the first few weeks, a cloth sling holding the baby tight to Vera's body. Laura slept to the soothing sounds of her mother's breathing and heartbeat, comforted by the warmth of her mother's voice and body, and the familiar scent of her skin. When Vera needed a few moments without the sling, she would hand the baby to

Ruth, always reminding her to hold baby Laura with care.

"I know, Ma, I know how to hold her." Ruth would roll her eyes each time and reply. "I'm nine now, you don't need to remind me every time." The baby took only seconds to settle into Ruth's thin arms, so different from Vera's rounded body. "See, she likes me holdin' her."

"She sure does, Ruth." Vera smiled as she replied, enjoying the sweet picture of her daughters together. "She knows you and loves you already."

Of course, whenever Ruth helped Vera with baby Laura, both Lizbeth and Becca clamored for their turns.

"Ruth, you've had her long enough, it's my turn now." Lizbeth always whined. "I'm seven, nearly big as you. Let me have her."

"Me, too. If Lizbeth gets a turn, I do, too," five-year- old Becca would chime in.

Ruth knew it was up to her to handle the two girls' requests. "You can both have a turn, but you gotta sit down first," she'd say, positioning baby Laura into one small lap after another.

Vera never worried about the baby with Ruth in charge. She loved watching and listening to her daughters care for baby Laura, their love for her clear even while they squabbled with each other for their turns. Vera also loved seeing how content the baby was with her older sisters whether Laura was sleeping or watching them with wide open eyes.

"Ruth is quite a little mother," Vera said one day, as she sat rocking and sewing. It was much too hot to work inside, so she'd dragged the rocker and a basket of mending outside and placed them in the shade next to the front of the house. Ruth sat near her, caring for baby Laura. Lizbeth, Becca and Ben played hide and seek, running and giggling, in and out of the barn.

Ma and Pa would've loved them so much. Vera sighed as she watched her children. Near fourteen years and she still missed 'em every single day.

"Ma," Ruth asked, breaking into Vera's thoughts. "Laura is such a pretty baby. What was I like as a baby?"

"You were the happiest of all my babies. Didn't cry, just made little noises right after you were born. Miz Dobbs didn't even have to slap your bottom."

Happy with that answer, Ruth turned her attention back to Laura.

Vera's thoughts drifted back to the day Ruth was one week old. She'd never forget that day, never till the day she died. Vera sat in the same rocking chair where she sat now, bursting with happiness, holding her baby daughter. She'd been singing softly to the sleeping infant, the same song she liked to sing to Laura, when Jon walked over to her.

"What's that song? Didn't sound like no reg'lar words I ever heard," he'd said.

"Just a lullaby my uncle taught me when I was young. Men sing the lullabies in Cherokee culture," Vera answered.

"Cherokee? Your uncle's a Cherokee? You tellin' me you're a damned half-breed?"

Vera stood up and placed the baby into her basket.

"No, I'm not a half-breed, I'm full blood Cherokee."

Jon's slap split Vera's lip and knocked her down. His hands were fisted at his sides as he stood staring at her on the ground, his entire body stiff with rage.

"You tricked me into marryin' a dirty Indian? You lyin' whore."

Vera had tried explaining that she'd never hidden anything. It wasn't her fault he'd never seen an Indian teacher before, or an Indian woman who wore her hair up. It wasn't her fault that the Christian name she'd been given by parents educated off the reservation had confused him. He'd never asked, and she'd assumed he knew and didn't care. But her words had no effect.

"Iffen anybody in town ever finds out about you bein' a Indian, I'll never live it down. And now my own blood daughter isa stinkin' half-breed? So help me God if this gets out I'll beat you to death myself." Jon's words, spoken in cadence with his fists striking her face and body, left no doubt he meant what he said.

That day was the first time Vera had been beaten. She'd never been hit before, but from then on, she had to endure both her husband's contempt and his thoughtless violence.

Shaking her head, Vera brought her attention back to the present. The past was over. She couldn't change it. Just got to protect the young'uns best as she could.

Vera kept a smile pasted on her face, not wanting her facial expression to invite questions about her thoughts. She watched Ruth handle all three of her younger sisters, moving the baby from lap to lap without ever losing her patience.

Ben, her only son, showed little interest in the baby. It made Vera sad, but she understood. He was three years old and already trying to follow his father's instructions to "be a man." Although his face and body still had the soft contours of babyhood, he almost never let her hold him anymore. And on those rare occasions when he came to her for comfort, he'd pull away if his pa came near them.

Poor Ben. He'd do anything to get attention from his pa. But if he got hurt, all he'd hear was "Stop that cryin'. Men don't cry." If he got caught havin' fun playin' with his sisters, Jon would yell at him, "What's the matter with you, boy, playin' sissy games with girls." And the rare times his pa'd see him huggin' her, Jon'd tell him to "stop bein' a baby."

Sometimes Ben would poke at baby Laura as she rested on one of his sister's laps, but he seldom talked to her or asked to hold her.

And Jon's relationship with the baby? He demanded respect and obedience from his children, not considering affection of any value. Vera took care to keep baby Laura out of his way, knowing it was safer for both of them.

STRIVE AND PROTECT

CHAPTER ONE

Betrayal

November, 1923

Laura was excited throughout dinner, eager to see the highest rated movie of the year. She skipped rather than strolled at Bruce's side when they finished eating and headed toward the Argosy. Bruce had parked the car, a shiny black Buick Touring Car convertible, and his most prized possession, a block away from the cafe.

The theater's large marque announced The Covered Wagon, in huge letters. The names J. Warren Kerrigan and Lois Wilson, stars of the film, appeared right below the title in smaller letters. Bruce gave their tickets to the usher at the door, then led Laura into the opulent interior.

Laura's low-heeled shoes sank into thick maroon carpeting. Heavy tapestries hung on the walls between glass cases containing posters for upcoming feature films, and muffled the whispered conversations around her. Soon they settled in plush seats, waiting for the heavy curtains to rise. She was glad the interior was dim after being surrounded by pretty women that made her feel almost dowdy by comparison. They wore shimmering silk and satin, accented by fur wraps and feather bedecked hats. Her forest green wool frock with pale gold at the cuffs, collar, and narrow band accenting the dropped waist above narrow pleats seemed ordinary by comparison. Her patterned black stockings and cloche hat sporting a pale gold bow couldn't compare to sleek, silken hosiery and high fashion hats.

Laura took a shallow breath—all she could manage with the tight brassiere that compressed her chest—and gazed at the heavy velvet curtains. She resolved to think only of the movie and the handsome man next to her.

Laura's attention never wavered from the film, entranced from the movie title to the closing credits. She loved movies and the magnificent music and sound effects produced by the magnificent Wurlitzer theater organ. Her fingers danced over imaginary keys along with the organist seated at the gold and black console in the orchestra pit.

"That was the bees knees. No wonder it's the most popular movie around." Laura and Bruce maneuvered through the dense crowd.

"Thank you so much for bringing me. Tonight has been the best evening ever."

"You're welcome." Bruce placed his arm around Laura's slim waist, holding her close even though she stiffened at his touch. At last, they got out of the theater and headed for the car.

"Let's find a quiet place to talk. I've got something important to ask you."

Laura's mood changed from excitement to worry in an instant. She cared about Bruce very much—in fact, sometimes she thought she might be in love with him—but his tone sounded serious. She stayed quiet until they got back into the car, listening for any clues to what was on his mind. Bruce chattered about the movie, paying no attention to Laura's distracted responses. He parked the car near St. Thomas Catholic Church, then led Laura to a secluded bench under the trees on the park-like grounds.

"It's so peaceful here," Laura said, settling on a bench. She shivered a little, wondering what was coming.

"Yes, and perfect for us," Bruce said. "Hey, don't look so serious. I've got an exciting idea."

Laura tried to control her rapid breathing, waiting to hear what he had to say.

"What are you doing for Thanksgiving?" Bruce said.

"Uh, just having dinner in the dining hall, I guess," she said, a little surprised by the question. "Nothing special. The YWCA has a lot of rules, but we're not required to eat there. I could skip the Thanksgiving dinner if you want me to."

"Well, my family celebration should be over by three."

The family celebration? Is he inviting me to join them?

Bruce continued talking. "What would you say about us going to Oklahoma City for the weekend? If we left at three thirty, we could get there Thursday night, and then come back Sunday evening. I'll get us a room in the best hotel in town. We can do whatever you want for two whole, wonderful days." Bruce pulled her to him.

Laura shoved him away, not sure she understood what he'd said. "What? Are you asking me to join you for Thanksgiving dinner and then take a trip?"

"Wish I could, but my parents are old-fashioned. I've told them how much I care about you, but Mother's hung up on her society rules. She'd never be able to see past you being half Indian."

"How can you say you care about me? It sounds like your mother isn't the only one hung up on stupid society rules."

Bruce reached for her hand but Laura stayed out of range. "It's not just that. My father's most important goal is having me take over the bank when he's ready to retire, but he insists that I have to find a wife with the perfect pedigree or he won't pass it on to me."

Laura stood and stepped away from the bench, shaking her head in shocked disbelief.

"Don't be like that, doll. I'm in no hurry to settle down with some boring society debutante. I'd rather keep seeing you, and a weekend together would be so great, just the two of us." Bruce leaned forward and his voice thickened. "Say yes, baby, please. You know you want to."

Laura's emotions cycled from confusion and shame, to pain, then blinding anger. "You and your parents don't think I'm good enough to sit at your table, but you want to take me to a hotel in Oklahoma City? You can't even consider me for a wife, but I'd be okay as a girlfriend on the side?"

"Don't look like that," Bruce implored. "We've had fun together, and I just want to keep having fun. I never said anything about us being more than that."

Laura fought hard to keep from crying. "Going to a movie or having dinner is different from sharing a hotel room for the weekend. I can't imagine what I've done to make you think that would be okay." She trembled from head to toe, throat burning. "Take me home, right now."

"Oh, come on. Stop acting like some kind of innocent little school girl. You told me your history. What's the problem? It's not like you're a virgin—and with your own father yet."

Laura slapped Bruce as hard as she could, almost knocking him off the bench.

"He raped me," she screamed. Her hand stung like fire, but the flaming red mark on Bruce's face was worth it.

Without saying a word, Laura ran away, back the way they'd come.

Bruce yelled. "Come back here, you little bitch. No girl hits me and gets away with it. Where the hell do you think you're going?"

"Leave me alone. I never want to see you again." Laura spit the words back over her shoulder.

"You know you don't mean that. Come here and I'll take you home." Bruce's words were softer, but his tone couldn't make up for what he'd said.

Laura ran even faster, staring straight ahead as she passed the ivy-covered stone walls of the church. She angled toward the road, sliding on the damp grass as she passed dark trees, lit only by the moonlight.

No more words pursued her, but Laura heard Bruce's car starting. When he drew even with her, Bruce leaned out the window and said, "It's a long way to the YWCA. Get in the car. You know I'm right."

Laura didn't turn her head or acknowledge him at all. Bruce drove alongside her and kept talking. Then he gave up and sped away. Only then did she slow down to a snail's pace, struggling to see through the tears that coursed down her face.

How could she have been so stupid? A handsome, rich guy like Bruce with his college education and a Father who owned a bank? Why, oh why had she trusted him?

Hot tears still fell as Laura reached the YWCA front door. She was late and had to listen to a lecture before being allowed to go to her room. Once there, Laura paced back and forth, from wall to wall, raging inside.

She pressed her hands into her temples, unable to keep the words inside. "What's the matter with you? Miss Emma warned you and warned you not to tell anyone about your past. They will use whatever you tell them to hurt and manipulate you."

Over and over the same phrases reverberated inside Laura's mind, even after she stopped speaking them aloud. At long last she stopped circling the room and sat down. She had only one choice, and that was to get as far away as possible. Tulsa was a big city with plenty of room to start over. She'd be smart this time. She'd gotten along just fine without a boyfriend before.

Decision made, Laura pulled her suitcase from under the bed and started to pack her things. She left fresh clothes for the morning on the dresser, together with her comb and toothbrush, set the clock for an hour before dawn, then climbed into bed.

DESPERATE CHOICES

Chapter One

Is Papa Crying

July 1938, Aurora, Missouri

Three more days. Three more to find out if Glen
would be back to his old self. Laura watched her
husband sleep, his sandy brown hair curled
against his forehead. The drugs in his system
kept him from dreaming, a blessed relief from
the nightmares that had haunted him since his
mental breakdown. Dr. Farnsworth had
suggested weaning him off his medications,
skipping one of his three doses each day.

The next evening, Glen didn't seem any
different after taking two pills that day. She
wondered if his behavior would change after
being cut to one pill the following day.

When Laura woke in the morning, she was
shocked to find Glen sitting on the edge of the
bed, staring at the window.

"Good morning, honey." She padded
around the bed, knelt down and looked into his

blue eyes. "You're awake early. Are you hungry?" She kept her tone light, hoping he'd respond. His eyes were open and appeared focused, but he wasn't looking at her, he was looking through her.

"How about some coffee before the kids wake up?" Laura thought she saw a faint flicker of something in his eyes. She grabbed her old, green chenille robe and pulled it on. "Let's stop at the bathroom first, then you can keep me company while I put the coffee on and start breakfast."

Laura noticed that Glen held his head a little more erect at the table. There was a slight tremor in his hands. He didn't speak though, so she stopped trying to engage him in conversation.

"Here, Glen," Laura said, handing him his pill. She made sure he swallowed it, grateful that he didn't fuss about taking his medication. She'd better get the chores done fast, since there was no telling how long it would last.

Laura worked as fast as possible, caring for the animals and garden, keeping Glen close by. "Good thing we bought these folding chairs when we used to have people over," she said. "You can keep me company while I'm working." Glen sat, feet and knees together, back straight and eyes focused straight ahead, at the edge of the garden while Laura watered and pulled weeds.

"It was a lot easier when you helped with chores around here, honey. The kids try, but they're too young to accomplish a lot." Laura glanced at Glen, but his face remained blank.

She made many trips to the house and outbuildings to check on the children as they first did their chores, then played. She carried the chair with her when she moved from place to place, while Glen followed, sitting down when she unfolded the chair. "Here you go," she'd say each time. "Are you comfortable? Would you like a glass of water?"

At dinner, June sat on Glen's right at the table. She stared at him while Laura started filling the children's plates. She observed him following Laura's motions with his eyes. "Papa, do you feel better?" Her voice was high and full of hope. No answer, but Glen seemed to twitch as if he'd been touched.

Laura willed him to respond to his daughter, but saw no indication he was aware of her at all. If he could eat and drink at a normal pace, why wouldn't he answer his daughter? Or at least look at her. "I'm sorry, Junebug, I guess he needs more time."

June nodded, her blue eyes bright with unshed tears. "But how much time, Mama? When will Papa get well?"

Laura shrugged and shook her head. "I don't know, honey."

All four children looked glum as they finished their meal.

"I have an idea. You guys have been working so hard to help me and keep an eye on your papa this last week, I think you need some extra play time and a treat. No more chores for you this afternoon, and I'll bake a cake for supper." Laura leaned forward. "How about chocolate icing, too?"

The smiles were a little slow in coming, but then all four cheered and ran out the back door with June carrying David on her hip.

Laura spent the rest of the afternoon in the kitchen baking, first the promised cake and then oatmeal raisin cookies. The kids ran in and out, checking on the progress, while Glen sat on a chair next to the small table where she worked. "Smells good, doesn't it?" She dropped spoonfuls of dough on the cookie sheet, as the sweet aroma of the cake in the oven filled the room.

"Can we have some dough?" June begged from the washroom doorway, her brothers peeking around her. "A little bite for each of us?"

Laura started to say no, then laughed and relented. "Okay, then out you go until I'm done." She handed each child a small spoonful of dough, and waved them out the door. "Our kids are pretty special," she said to Glen.

He stayed in the room with her while she worked, but grew more and more agitated. The muscles in his face and arms twitched, his hands clenched, and his legs bounced up and down. Now and then he cocked his head as if listening to someone, and more than once Laura thought she heard him mumble under his breath. As she pulled the last batch out of the oven, Glen stood and stalked through the dining room and out the front door.

Laura left the cookie sheet on the stove top and followed, afraid to let him out of her sight. He stopped on the porch, one hand on an upright post in front of the steps leading to the yard. Laura stood about two feet behind him. "It's pretty out here, isn't it, honey? Feels good to stretch your legs."

Not a word in response, but Glen's head moved toward the right as if to hear her better. If only she could think of something to say. Then Laura noticed Dr. Farnsworth's car coming toward the house.

"Glen, Dr. Farnsworth is coming to visit. He'll be pleased to find you outside." Thank goodness. Maybe the doctor could do something to help him.

Glen didn't say anything, but Laura saw his hand clench tight on the post, his knuckles white, while he tucked his other hand into his front trouser pocket. Glen's breathing sped up

as they waited until the doctor parked his car
and approached the steps.

"Hello Dr. Farnsworth, you're early,"
Laura said. She stepped from behind Glen.
"Look who came outside by himself today." Her
voice sounded brittle and artificial.

Dr. Farnsworth looked as dapper as ever
in his dark suit as he approached the steps, his
gray hair, mustache, and goatee impeccable.

"Good afternoon, Mr. and Mrs. Webber. I
had a cancellation today and hoped you
wouldn't mind my coming out early." Dr.
Farnsworth's tone and facial expression were
neutral, devoid of sentiment as he approached
the porch, his gaze focused on Glen. "It's good
to see you outside, Mr. Webber, beautiful day
isn't it?"

Laura saw Glen's jaw clench and move
side to side, but he didn't speak. She placed her
hand on his back, surprised when his muscles
tightened and he pulled away at her touch.

Dr. Farnsworth climbed the first two
stairs, one slow, deliberate step at a time. "Mr.
Webber, you appear much better today. Would
you mind my giving you a quick checkup?"

Glen didn't look at him, but moved back
two steps toward the middle of the porch. He
stepped backwards again as the doctor climbed
the last two stairs, keeping the same distance
between them.

Laura opened her mouth to speak, but after a quick head shake by the doctor, remained quiet. Her hands were clasped so hard she could feel the nails biting into her palms.

Dr. Farnsworth paused at the top of the steps, then moved toward two chairs and a small table grouped together near the door. He placed his medical bag on the table and removed his stethoscope. "Mr. Webber, would you mind sitting down for a few minutes? I'd like to check your heart and lungs. Won't take long, I promise."

Glen turned his body and faced the doctor. Laura noticed his forearm muscles flexing and his hands tightened into fists.

"No, I'm not leaving him," Glen said, staring at the porch floor where there seemed to be something no one else could see. He focused on the doctor. "I know he's gone, I know that, but I'm not leaving him." Glen's body was a study in defiance and pain. He dropped to his knees, threw his head back and began to wail. His entire body shook with the force of the ungodly cries that ripped from his throat.

"Please, please do something." It was hard for Laura to breathe, much less talk. "I can't bear to see him hurt like this. Can't you do something?" She grabbed Dr. Farnsworth's arm with both of her hands.

"Mrs. Webber, all I can do is give him something to knock him out. This breakdown is far beyond my abilities. The only help available to him is the Springfield Mental Hospital. I've spoken to them about your husband, and they have room."

"How can I do that to him?" Laura clasped her hands together, kneeling near Glen.

He continued to rock on his knees, arms tucked around his torso, screaming and moaning. "What am I supposed to do?"

The screech of the screen door opening behind her startled Laura. "Mama, what's wrong? Is Papa crying?" Laura leaped to the door, pushing hard to keep a frightened June from coming outside. "Stay inside, sweetheart, you and your brothers need to stay inside."

"Dr. Farnsworth, do what you've got to do. Please, the kids can't see this."

The doctor, his own eyes glistening, nodded, pulled a syringe from his bag and filled it. Glen didn't react to the needle plunging into his arm, just continued rocking and yelling. In minutes he stopped making the awful noises and his body relaxed. The doctor pulled him to his feet and began walking him down the steps. At the foot of the stairs, he turned to Laura. "I'm taking him straight to the hospital before the shot wears off. I'm sorry there isn't more I can do for him."

Laura's entire body shook as she watched the men make their way toward the car. She realized June had stopped screaming and banging on the door, then heard footsteps pounding away from the door toward the hallway. Within minutes June and her brothers came running around the side of the house as Dr. Farnsworth was putting Glen into his car.

Laura ran down the steps and caught June in her arms, holding her tight until the doctor's car pulled away. "Honey, your papa is sick, and the doctor is taking him to get help."

"No, no, bring him back." June's fists beat into Laura's chest as soon as her arms were free. The boys clustered together next to Laura. June, crying and calling for their papa to come back, stared at the car as it disappeared from view.

Laura didn't even try to stop June's blows, absorbing them until June wore herself out. She dropped to her knees and wrapped her arms around all four children. "I want him here, too, I didn't want him to go away. But Papa's hurting and we can't help him. You don't want your papa to be in pain, do you?"

Their cries and tears hurt Laura much more than June's punches, and the worst pain was not being able to help them. "Dr. Farnsworth is taking Papa to a special kind of hospital. They have a room all ready for him, and know how to make him well again."

The tears and cries diminished, but all four children held tight to Laura. "Mama, when will Papa come back?" June's raspy voice was hard to recognize.

"I don't know, sweetheart. I wish I knew."

"But they will fix him, won't they?" Raymond's eyes were huge, and his voice was filled with longing.

"Of course they will, honey." Laura tightened her arms around her babies. "That's what doctors and hospitals do."

Laura almost added the words "I promise" but somehow held them back. Memories of sad endings when she worked in the hospital in Tulsa flashed through her mind. More memories came of doctors ready to "let nature take its course" and nurses who let patients die who'd been deemed hopeless.

"Papa will be fine, but it may take a while for the hospital to find the right medicine to make him well," Laura said, trying to soothe the children she held in a tight huddle, rocking until the sobs subsided.

At long last, Laura stood and lifted David into her arms. The other children stayed close to her sides as they walked back into the house. Please God, if you're listening, please help him.

"God always listens, honey, but sometimes his plans aren't easy to understand."

Laura's steps faltered as the words rang inside her head. Ma? Can't you help me? I can't stand this. It's too much. Laura hadn't heard her ma's voice or felt her presence in a long time.

"Yes, you can. You're a strong woman, and can do whatever you have to. Your children need you. I know you won't let them down."

Laura started to reply, but her ma was gone. She'd left right after she'd delivered her message.

www.ingramcontent.com/pod-product-compliance
Lightning Source LLC
Chambersburg PA
CBHW072019020726
47501CB00006B/1865